A desperate police detective hires private investigator Carlos "Chuck" McCrary to find out who framed him for murdering a mob boss.

Double Fake, Double Murder

Lots of People Want Garrison Franco Dead... but one of them is a cop

Gangster Garrison Franco is gunned down in the street, killed by a bullet from my buddy Jorge Castellano's gun. Jorge hires me, Carlos McCrary, to find out who framed him.

When my prime suspect is killed with a bullet from *my* gun, the cops slap the cuffs on me and haul me off to jail too. The case against me is tighter than a guitar string.

Even my own defense attorney wants me to take a plea deal.

It looks like my friend Jorge will spend his life in prison, and I'll be there next to him.

Yeah, I'm screwed.

Also by Dallas Gorham

I'm No Hero

Six Murders Too Many

Double Fake, Double Murder

Quarterback Trap

Dangerous Friends

Day of the Tiger

McCrary's Justice

Yesterday's Trouble

Four Years Gone

All Dallas Gorham works are available on Amazon.com.

Double Fake, Double Murder

A Carlos McCrary, Private Investigator, Mystery Thriller

By Dallas Gorham

19091602

ISBN-13: 978-1502511256

ISBN-10: 1502511258

Double Fake, Double Murder

A Carlos McCrary, Private Investigator, Mystery Thriller

Chapter 1

The gunman lifted his handgun, took a slow breath, and gripped the pistol tighter. *He'd better show up soon.* Standing in the shadowed entrance of the warehouse, he stared across the empty parking lot, willing his target to appear. Sweat dripped down the back of his neck.

A car crawled down the deserted street and coasted to a stop in the dark gap between two streetlights. The driver's door opened. Garrison Franco stepped from the car, his right arm held straight down.

That's got to be him.

The keys in the ignition set off the car's warning bell, *ding, ding, ding.* The driver pushed the door closed with his left hand, silencing the alarm.

In the distance, a siren shrieked. The sound echoed off the concrete block walls of the industrial neighborhood. The hidden man flinched. *If a black-and-white comes barreling down the street, I'm screwed.*

The siren faded. *False alarm. Sound must carry for blocks down these streets at night.* The gunman rolled his shoulders to ease the tightness. Sweat had plastered the black shirt to his back. The ski mask made his face itch. *God, this thing is hot.* He resisted the urge to scratch. *No unnecessary movement.*

The gun that the driver held close to his leg was barely visible in the streetlight. He rotated slowly in a circle.

The gunman clenched the pistol grip. *He suspects a trap. Smart man.*

The driver flexed his knees, rotating on the balls of his feet. His gaze passed like a searchlight across the darkened buildings that lined the street.

He'll never see me in the dark with this ski mask on. He had stood in the street and tested the line of sight earlier. The parking lot added forty yards to the distance from the warehouse to the street. The extra distance hid the gunman better, but it made the pistol shot more difficult. *I just have to hold my hands extra steady; that's all.*

The hit man shifted his weight from foot to foot. *Come on! Come on! You're turning the wrong way.* He needed a shot to the target's chest, not his back.

Franco continued to pivot, surveying the empty buildings. His gaze reached the near side of the street, the circle nearly complete.

The gunman raised his pistol in a two-hand grip. *Almost there... keep turning, you sorry SOB.* Leaning against the wall, he held his breath, sighted with one eye, and squeezed off four rounds. *Perfect!*

Franco's jacket jumped as three of the four bullets ripped through his body and shattered the car windows behind him. A scream of pain filled the night as his body bounced off the car door. His gun clunked to the asphalt. He grunted a curse as he collapsed and sprawled on the street.

The gunman jogged to the curb and peered both ways down the street. No one. He rolled up the ski mask. Cool night air made the itching feel better.

The shooter hurried to the fallen man, careful to avoid the spreading pool of blood. He rolled Franco onto his back and felt for a pulse. *God, the bastard is still alive.* He jammed the muzzle against Franco's forehead and fired again. The back of Franco's head splashed brains, blood, and hair in a macabre halo on the street.

The shooter found the shell casing and stuck it in a pocket. Searching the dead man's pockets, he transferred the contents to his own.

With gloved hands, he retrieved the fallen gun and wrapped Franco's fingers around it. He gripped the dead man's hand from the palm side, opposite where the gunshot residue would spray and aimed at the building next door to the one from which he had fired. A cantilevered roof overhung the entrance porch. *About four feet high, center of the left wall. Don't hit the window; that might set off a burglar alarm.* He fired. *A little high.* He aimed and fired a second time. *That's better.* He fired again. *That should look convincing.*

A light glimmered in a third-story window above the porch. Was it a candle? The window had been dark when he arrived. The light went out. *Shit. Is that a witness? These buildings are warehouses. No one's supposed to live here.*

Returning to his shooting position, he pulled a flashlight from his pocket and glanced at the window next door. Shielding the lens with two fingers before he switched it on, he aimed it at the pavement and spotted two spent shell casings. He glanced again at the window and bit his lip. He scooped up the casings and searched for the others, his breath coming faster. Six feet away, he found another one. *Only one more shell. Where is the damn thing?* His breath came thick and ragged now. *Don't panic, don't panic. It's gotta be here somewhere.* A glint of brass in the crack between the entrance landing and the asphalt parking lot gave him hope.

He shined the light into the crack and reached for the casing. *Too far down.* He snatched off his leather gloves and jammed his little finger farther into the crack. He felt the brass, but he couldn't hook it. The little finger of his other hand yielded no better result. He cast around for anything to dig out the casing. *A paper clip, a coat hanger, a piece of wire—practically anything.* Nothing.

Movement in the third-floor window next door caught his attention. A figure, dimly illuminated by the streetlight, moved back from the darkened window.

Christ! It is a witness.

He pulled the ski mask over his face and bolted down the street.

Chapter 2

I finished reading the first section of the *Port City Press-Journal* and flipped to the local news. *Break Expected in Franco Murder* splashed across the top of the page. Underneath was a picture of Detective Kelly Contreras at a news conference, acting authoritative and sexy. *Maybe I have a subconscious urge for a woman who can hold her own with me.*

My cellphone rang while I read the story. I didn't recognize the number. "Good morning, McCrary Investigations. This is Carlos McCrary. How can I help you?"

"*Amigo*, it's Jorge Castellano."

I always smile when I hear my old friend's voice. I leaned back in my office chair, pulled the bottom desk drawer open with a practiced toe, and propped my feet on the edge. I'm never too busy to catch up with old friends. The newspaper could wait.

I switched to Spanish. "Hey, it's the Cuban Supercop. Been a while, bro'. How is the detective business at the North Shore?" Jorge Castellano was a Port City Police detective working out of the North Shore Precinct.

"Not so good, *amigo*."

"What's up?"

"I need your help."

My office door was closed, so I put the phone on speaker. "Sure, bro', anything you want."

"I'm in trouble. I need a private investigator."

"I'm in my office. Can you come down here?"

"No, I'm at the precinct."

I peered at my watch. "So, come over after your shift."

"I'm not at work."

"Then why are you at the precinct?"

"I'm in jail. I've been arrested for murder."

Chapter 3

A fist closed around my stomach as a sergeant led Jorge into the precinct visitation room. He wore orange jail clothes, wrinkled and stained, and shuffled along like a seventy-year-old man, his ankles shackled.

The sergeant's face was familiar but I couldn't dredge his name from my memory. It would probably wake me in the middle of the night. I settled for exchanging nods with him. The cop shrugged as though telling me he didn't like watching over another cop. I waved at Jorge through the wire-reinforced glass partition.

"Thanks, Barry," Jorge said. "You know I don't take this personally, right? You're doing your job."

Barry Kleinschmidt. That's his name. Kleinschmidt clapped Jorge on the shoulder. "Don't let the bastards grind you down, Jorge. You did Port City a favor. That rat bastard Franco deserved it." He moved back and stood by the wall.

Jorge sat in a metal chair. I did the same on my side of the wire mesh.

Jorge's eyes were bloodshot, and he hadn't shaved. "Boy, am I glad to see you."

I studied my friend through the wire barrier and tried to smile. It wasn't easy. "You look like death warmed over, *amigo.*"

Jorge rubbed his stubbled cheek. "I feel worse than I look. I didn't sleep all night."

"You should've called me the instant they arrested you."

"I thought it was a misunderstanding. I figured that when I explained everything, they'd take me back home. Instead, they processed me into a cell and slammed the door. Next thing I know, it's 6:00 a.m. and they're serving breakfast. I decided to eat before I called you."

"Well, I'm here now."

Jorge's eyes widened. "I didn't do it. I've said that all night long to anybody who'd listen." His hands shook. "No one pays any attention. They won't listen to me. Nobody will *listen*."

Jorge's obvious frustration demonstrated the wisdom of Grandpa McCrary's advice: "Everyone has a story to tell. Sometimes the best thing you can do for them is to listen to it." Unfortunately, with Jorge facing a murder charge, this jail was the wrong place to tell his story—not until he had an attorney. Jorge had been trying all night to find a sympathetic ear. I hoped he hadn't done or said anything stupid. Then I realized that it was too late to hope; whatever he had said was already out there. Best to shut Jorge up before he hurt his cause even more.

"Kleinschmidt said 'that rat bastard Franco.' Is this about the Garrison Franco shooting?"

Jorge started to speak.

I raised both hands to stop him. "I know you're pissed, Jorge, but don't say anything more about the case. Just answer yes or no. Nothing you tell me is privileged. Don't talk about the case with anyone until your attorney retains me. And don't talk to any cops—even to deny you did it."

Jorge seemed about to protest.

"I mean it, *amigo*. Don't talk to anyone, friend or stranger. Right now, the cops aren't on your side." I leaned toward the partition and lowered my voice. "Nobody around here is on your side."

Jorge scowled. "I get so frustrated that they all think I did it."

"You heard Sergeant Kleinschmidt. Even if they think you whacked him, they consider it a public service. Who's your attorney?"

Jorge glanced at the sergeant. "I can't afford an attorney. I'll take my chances with a public defender."

"Okay. At your arraignment, the judge will allow you to ask for a PD. Who was the arresting officer?"

"Kelly Contreras and Bigs Bigelow."

"That's a break. I'll call Kelly and poke around a little. I'll come back tomorrow and find out who your attorney is. I'll get the public defender's office to retain me, so my work will be covered by their attorney-client privilege. Then you can tell me what happened."

Jorge frowned. "*Amigo*, you don't want to hear what happened?"

"I do, but not here, not now, and not until you have an attorney." I gestured at the institutional green walls. "We need to meet in an interview room without this partition and without an audience." I pointed to Sergeant Kleinschmidt at the wall. "You can tell me all about this mess. Just wait until tomorrow or the next day."

"Sure thing."

"Anything you need? Anybody you want me to call?"

"I've talked to Karen and my parents. Dan knows, of course. But how the hell can I pay you?"

"You and I go back a long way, bro'. You took a bullet for me."

Jorge smiled a little. "Just a flesh wound."

I had been a rookie patrol officer, and it was my first time to break up a fight between rival gangs. Police policy was to respond in force and arrest the leaders of both gangs. Young, foolish, and idealistic, I tried to be a peacemaker. I stepped between the two gang leaders. Jorge, standing on the sidelines where I should have been, saw one gangbanger aim a pistol at my back. He yelled a warning and tackled me to the ground as the gangbanger fired. The bullet hit Jorge instead of me.

"You knocked me to the ground like a linebacker on a blitz. If you had been a second later..." I shook my head. It still made my butt pucker when I thought about how close I came to being killed. "I'm not worried about money."

"Well, I am. You gotta make a living, and I don't have that kind of money. And don't give me your crap about *truth, justice, and the American way*." Jorge stared at his hands. "I wasn't thinking clearly when I called you."

"*Amigo*, you've had my back more than once. Now it's my turn. I collected a large check from another client—and I mean *large*—so I have enough money to last for the duration." The surviving client on the Simonetti case had paid me a million-dollar bonus, and I was feeling pretty damned rich. "I'll put your fee on the cuff. After we get you out of this mess, you'll find a way to pay me. Or not. I don't care much either way."

Jorge started to object and I raised a hand. "Don't say another word about money until this is over. You know what I always say about friendship."

"What's that?"

"What are friends for, if you can't use and abuse them once in a while?"

Chapter 4

When Kelly Contreras was promoted to detective, she tried wearing tailored jackets in various sizes so she could wear her new gold shield on the breast pocket like the male detectives did. Whatever jacket she tried, her ample bosom and service pistol combined to make it seem like either a straitjacket or a circus tent. She tried leaving off the jacket and wearing her shield on her shirt pocket, but it called more attention to her breasts. She'd settled on clipping the shield to her gun belt. Male detectives achieved formality by wearing a tie. She settled that by wearing a scarf around her neck. Today, she'd chosen a gold and black one to go with her white silk blouse.

When Chuck McCrary walked into the North Shore Precinct squad room, Kelly's heart did a stutter step. She was glad she had touched up her makeup on her last trip to the restroom. Now she patted her hair into place and straightened her scarf. She'd had a crush on Chuck when he'd been a detective there, but the guy had been oblivious to her hints. After he left the force, she had debated calling him to ask him on a date. She'd waited too long, and he'd taken up with Terry Kovacs, a patrol cop from the same precinct. *Oh well, it wasn't meant to be,* she thought. *Still, you never know...* She waved Chuck over. "I'm glad you called. I know how close you and Jorge are."

"Thanks for seeing me. Where's your partner?"

"Bigs went to pick up lunch. He'll be back soon. Make yourself at home." She gestured to the visitor's chair. *God, he looks good in that suit and tie.*

Chuck sat. "I saw your picture on the front page of the local section this morning. I guess the break in the case the *Pee-Jay* story referred to was the arrest of Jorge."

Kelly put her hand on Chuck's. "I can't tell you how bad Bigs and I both feel about arresting Jorge. But the lieutenant always says to follow the evidence, and that's where it led."

"I don't blame you and Bigs. You didn't have a choice." He smiled at her and she nearly melted inside. "On the plus side, you represented Port City's finest well in the picture."

She felt her cheeks flush. *Oh, God, when he smiles like that...* "You really think so?"

"Absolutely. You looked like a star in a cop movie."

"They got my best side."

"What can you tell me?"

"Bigs and I processed the case by the book from the get-go. We did this right."

"There's the right way, the wrong way, and the Army way."

Kelly scratched her head. "Jorge says that too. I don't get the joke."

"Just thinking out loud. Jorge and I were grunts in the Army—he was in Desert Storm and I was in Operation Enduring Freedom. Sometimes doing something the *right* way isn't the *best* way. To get results, sometimes you do things the *Army* way."

"Any cop knows that there is no such thing as a perfect investigation. If Bigs and I missed something, we want you to find it. We *need* you to find it—for Jorge's sake." She pulled two large binders off the credenza and handed one to Chuck. "We made you a copy of the murder book."

"What did I do to deserve this?"

"Barry Kleinschmidt called after you left the visitation room. He overheard you tell Jorge you'd poke around. Bigs and I don't like the way the Franco case worked out either. Maybe your Army way will find something we missed."

"How bad is it?"

She frowned. *As bad as it gets.* "The case is tight as a guitar string. What do you know about the victim?"

"Garrison Franco, street thug and mid-level drug dealer. Mafioso wannabe. A few weeks ago, the newspaper said he was killed in a drug deal gone bad."

"That's what Bigs and I thought at first, but we found evidence that linked Jorge Castellano to Franco's death."

"What evidence?"

She tapped the file. "Take your pick. Start with motive: Jorge and his partner, Dan Murphy, had tried for months to make a case against Franco for drug dealing. A couple of weeks after they began their investigation, Franco threatened Castellano for interfering with his business."

"That gives Franco a motive to kill Jorge, not the other way around."

"Actually, Franco told Castellano that his wife was very attractive and that her hours at the gym had paid off. Franco showed him a candid photo of Karen taken while she exited the gym. Jorge grabbed Franco by the throat, threw him across the sidewalk, and slammed him into a wall. Dan had to pull him off. Jorge shouted that if he ever saw Franco near his wife, he'd kill him."

"Any witnesses?"

"Dan Murphy. And Jorge admitted it to Bigs and me."

"People make threats all the time that they don't mean," said Chuck. "What else you got?"

"The most damning evidence is the ballistics test. One bullet that hit Franco was in good enough shape for a ballistics match. It came from Castellano's service pistol."

"How close was the match?"

Kelly opened Chuck's copy of the murder book and rotated it so he could read it. "See for yourself."

Chuck flipped to the color photograph of the ballistics test. One side featured the test bullet fired from Jorge's service pistol. The other side was the forensics photo of the bullet recovered at the crime scene. He studied the two photos. "That's a match. What else you got?"

"The night of the killing, Jorge received an anonymous tip that we traced to a burner phone. The tipster claimed he had a video of Franco doing a drug deal. The guy promised to deliver the video to Jorge and to testify at Franco's trial if the DA could get him into the witness protection program."

"How do we know that?"

"Jorge's statement. Dan Murphy confirmed that Jorge called him at home and told him about the call. This happened a little after ten o'clock the night of the murder. Bigs and I confirmed the call with phone records. Jorge told me the caller had been frightened and insisted on meeting him in secret and that he come alone."

"Sounds like a setup."

"Jorge and Dan thought the same thing," Kelly said. "Dan followed Jorge to the meet and parked around the corner in case Jorge needed backup."

"And what happened?"

The Latina detective shrugged. "The caller never showed. Jorge hung around the meeting place for an hour, then they gave up and went home." She closed the binder. "While they waited for the no-show witness, Franco was gunned down four blocks away."

"Did either Jorge or Dan hear the shots?"

"No such luck. Industrial area with three-story, concrete block and stucco buildings. Great soundproofing."

"Yeah," Chuck agreed, "they make freeway sound barriers out of concrete. Dan Murphy should be Jorge's alibi for the time of the shooting."

"Nope. Murphy waited a block away around a corner. He listened to Jorge's open cellphone line, but he couldn't see Jorge."

"I know Jorge, but I don't know Murphy well. Could Murphy have sneaked off and killed Franco himself?"

"Bigs and I examined the GPS recorders in both unmarked cars. Neither one left the spots the guys stated in their incident reports."

"But if Jorge did it, he left his car and traveled to the crime scene on foot. The same logic says that Murphy could also have gone there on foot. Any security cameras in the neighborhood?"

"There were two logical streets that either Jorge or Dan could use to get to the site: 85th and 86th streets plus the alleys. We canvassed every business on both streets. We found three security cameras at two businesses. None of the alleys had cameras. No sign of anyone walking on the street, but that doesn't mean squat because of the alleys. We figure Jorge snuck down an alley."

The elevator dinged. Kelly's partner got off carrying two brown paper bags in his massive hands. He maneuvered his six-and-half-feet of bulk skillfully between the desks.

Arnie "Bigs" Bigelow had retired as a defensive lineman for the Port City Pelicans when he was in his early thirties. He had been such a dominating force for the Pelican defense that sportswriters dubbed the entire defensive line *The Bigs Brigade*. Kelly met Bigs when he trained at the police academy between football seasons. He became a ride-along, unpaid volunteer in the off-season.

When the Pelicans retired his jersey, he decided to do something meaningful with the rest of his life, so he joined the Port City Police Department. He worked his way up to detective and Kelly grabbed him for a partner.

"Got your lunch, Kelly. Hey, Chuck. You had lunch?" He set the bags on Kelly's desk and shook hands. His giant hand swallowed the young PI's.

"I'm good. Y'all go ahead." Chuck picked up his binder. "I'll take this binder to that empty desk and read it while you eat. I'll come back in a bit."

Kelly and Bigs stuffed their Chinese take-out dishes into the bags Bigs had brought them in. Kelly dropped the trash into a waste can beside her desk and waved Chuck over. "Okay, back to work. How can we help?"

"Walk me through this."

"Lieutenant Weiner told us to treat this like the victim was a solid citizen instead of a drug dealer. 'By the book,' she said."

Chuck smiled. "Mother Weiner always says that scumbags deserve justice too."

All the cops who worked for Lieutenant Joyce Weiner called her "Mother" because she was a Jewish mother to them as well as in real life. Kelly knew that Chuck was one of the lucky ones who had worked for her back in the day.

"We examined Franco's car and gun for prints," said Kelly. "Dug out one spent shell from the wall behind the car. We reviewed the autopsy. The kill shot was right to the forehead after Franco had already fallen from the first bullets. Franco got off three rounds before he fell. We found bullet holes in a building that overlooked the crime scene. After that, we didn't have much to go on. We put the case on hold until the ballistics came back."

She tapped the murder book. "That's when we learned that Jorge's gun was the murder weapon."

Chuck frowned. "It must've been pretty cut and dried from there."

"What did we miss?" Bigs asked.

"I'll study the book again tonight. So far, it's solid work, guys."

"Don't bullshit a bullshitter. Bigs and I both wear pants, so don't try to blow smoke up my skirt. What'd you find?"

"You're right: No case is perfect. Something's tickling the back of my mind. I haven't figured it out yet."

"What are you gonna do now?"

"You two did the investigation the right way. I'm going to do it the Army way—outside the box."

Chapter 5

The gray plastic plaque on the door announced *Darcy V. Yankton, JD, Assistant Public Defender*. Industrial, machine-cut letters, government-issue austerity. At least they were saving our tax dollars. I knocked twice and walked in.

Inside, a thirty-something woman in a dark blue pantsuit with a patterned silk scarf worked at a metal desk with a chipped plastic laminate top. Blonde, blue-eyed. She would have looked pretty if she'd worn makeup. I thought of a young Hillary Clinton portrait I had seen during her presidential campaign. Behind Yankton, a matching credenza overflowed with three stacks of file folders that reached slightly above the windowsills. She took off her reading glasses.

"Ms. Yankton?" I asked.

She closed the file she was working on, raised her eyes, and smiled. "What can I do for you?"

"I'm Chuck McCrary." I handed her a business card. "I'm here to help you defend Jorge Castellano."

She peeked at the card and dropped it on her desk without reading it. "What's your interest in Mr. Castellano?"

"Jorge and I worked together for three years out of the North Shore Precinct. I'm now a private investigator. Didn't he tell you I'd call?"

She put her reading glasses back on and read the card this time. Maybe I should have added a scale of justice logo on the card, or maybe a giant magnifying glass. Oh, well, too late. Her smile disappeared. "I recognize your name. The newspaper and TV reporters called you Carlos, not Chuck."

"Carlos is the name on my birth certificate. I guess Carlos is more politically correct for a Mexican-American. My friends call me Chuck." She didn't act like she wanted to be my friend.

"You were involved in that Simonetti thing, weren't you, McCrary? Those murdered heiresses I read about in the newspaper. You killed a half dozen people yourself, didn't you?" She slid the card back across the desk toward me, rejecting my card and me.

"It was five, and they shot at me first."

She frowned. "I don't approve of vigilantes, McCrary."

"Me neither. If you'd read the rest of the newspaper stories, you'd know that the Port City DA called all five shootings self-defense. Or didn't you read that part?"

"You took the law into your own hands."

"You ever been shot at, counselor?"

She scoffed. "Of course not."

"When someone shoots at me, what would you have me do? Turn the other cheek? Reason with them? I didn't come here to argue with you, Ms. Yankton; I came here to help you defend Jorge. You and I are on the same side. I'll be your investigator for his defense."

"We have our own investigators. We don't hire outsiders."

"But you can hire them when necessary. Jorge thinks it's necessary."

"I don't, and it's my case and my call. The police have motive, method, and opportunity. The investigation is completed, McCrary." She leaned back and crossed her arms. I'd always heard that crossed arms meant a closed mind. I hoped this was an exception.

"May I sit down?"

"You're not staying."

Her mind was closed, so I had to open it again. But how?

"The motive and the method are wrong," I said.

"I've read the file. It all fits."

I couldn't believe what I was hearing. "My God, you think he's guilty, don't you? How can you defend him if you don't believe him?"

She stood and leaned over her desk, waving a finger in my face. "Don't be so naïve, McCrary. I don't have to believe him to represent him. Guilty or not guilty, he still gets a fair trial. Even if he is a cop."

"What's that supposed to mean?"

She plopped into her desk chair. "Cops often take the law into their own hands when they can get away with it. Everyone knows that. That's why we make them wear body-cams now." She shrugged. "May I speak frankly?"

It sounded to me like she was already speaking frankly, but maybe not.

"By all means."

"This is my workload." She gestured at the credenza behind her. "Catch-up is our *modus operandi*. We're always four to six weeks behind. The Castellano case—" She grabbed a file off the stack and dropped it on her desk with a thud. "It's not complicated. It's a textbook example of a rogue cop being caught. He's better off to take whatever plea deal I can get him."

"One problem counselor... Jorge is not a rogue cop. He didn't do it."

"Every defendant says that."

"I believe him."

"You and Castellano have a history, I believe."

I took a slow breath while I struggled to keep my voice calm. "You say that like it's a bad thing."

"You're a former cop. I prefer my investigators to be unbiased and objective."

I tried to smile. I might even have succeeded, but it was an effort. "When it comes to Jorge Castellano, I'm neither unbiased nor objective. I've known him for years. He saved my life when I was a police detective."

"I admire your loyalty, McCrary, but that doesn't mean he didn't do it."

"You're right, of course. Nevertheless, he is innocent. I'll help you prove it when I find out who really killed Garrison Franco. Didn't Jorge tell you I'd call?"

"I don't need outside help, especially yours, and especially for a rogue cop."

It was time to wave the flag in her face. "Counselor, whether or not you believe Jorge is guilty, your professional ethics require that you give him the best defense possible."

She squinted one eye. "So?"

"The best defense includes a quality investigation by competent experts." I spread my arms and bowed. "And here I am."

"And you're modest too."

"It's a curse."

She didn't smile. My humor often goes unappreciated—or, worse yet, unrecognized.

She shook her head. "The public defender's office doesn't have a budget to hire outside investigators."

"Not a problem. I made separate arrangements with Jorge."

"What arrangements?"

"As I said, he saved my life. I can never repay that debt."

"I won't use a vigilante... a... a... *cowboy* as my investigator."

"Then it's good that I'm neither a vigilante nor a cowboy, although I was raised on a farm. If your in-house investigators are swamped like you, they can't do the job that Jorge deserves. That's why you need me. Besides," I smiled my best and friendliest smile, "I'm free."

She sighed. "McCrary, I don't like you, and I don't like the shoot-first attitude that people like you have. That said, you are correct about my obligation to provide any client, guilty or innocent, the best defense I can. Therefore, I will engage you as my investigator on one condition."

"And that is...?"

"You operate by the book. You don't take the law into your own hands. You run everything by me."

"Agreed."

"Okay. Sit down. The PD's office will pay you a dollar to make it legal."

"Shall I send you an invoice?" I smiled; she ignored it.

"Let's keep it simple." She pulled a dollar from her purse and handed it across the desk. "I'll put this on my expense report, in case anyone asks." She waited for me to stuff the bill in my pocket. "Have you seen the case against him?"

"Yes. Kelly Contreras gave me a copy of the murder book."

"Where will you begin?"

"Where else? At the beginning."

Chapter 6

I parked my white Dodge Caravan in the used furniture store parking lot on 84th Street. Kelly said that 85th and 86th were the logical routes for Jorge or Dan to take if either of them were the shooter. Maybe the shooter wasn't logical. Or maybe he knew about the security cameras on 85th and 86th.

An electronic door dinged when I walked into the Second Time Around store.

An old man stood behind the counter, talking on the phone. He had long white hair and a face so wrinkled that he resembled a Chinese Shar Pei. "Just a sec', somebody's come in." He put his hand over the mouthpiece. "Can I help you?"

I pointed at the phone. "Go ahead. I can wait." Good ol' considerate Chuck.

"Let me call you back." Shar Pei man hung up. "How can I help you?"

"Are those security cameras out front?"

The shopkeeper narrowed his eyes. "Why do you ask?"

"I'm a private investigator. I'm trying to find security footage from a night about three weeks ago."

The old man nodded. "Yeah, they're real, but the hard drive stores only seven days' worth of footage."

"Any offsite backups with video from three weeks ago?"

"Sorry."

Two hours and two blocks farther east on 84th street, I spotted an ATM outside a convenience store. Banks always use offsite storage for their security footage and so do convenience stores.

I photographed the ATM and the storefront to remind me to follow up on them later and moved on to the next business. Two more blocks to go, then I'd start on the south side.

An hour later, I'd canvassed all the way to Second Avenue. I crossed the street and worked my way back along the south side. I'd covered two blocks when I reached the Day and Night Diner. My stomach growled and I peered at my cellphone: 6.30. No wonder I was hungry. Some of the stores would close soon. I would finish the canvass the next day.

I pushed open the door to the diner, and a brass bell tinkled. A middle-aged black woman in a generic server's uniform stood behind the counter stacking cups. I slid onto a stool and grabbed a menu from a metal rack fastened to the back of the counter.

The server smiled. "Be right with you, hon'." She finished stacking the cups, grabbed an order pad, and walked over. "What can I get you?"

"Is that pecan pie over there?" I asked, pointing to the glass case at the end of the counter.

"Sure is. Baked fresh daily in our own kitchen. It's my favorite. If there's any left over at the end of my shift, I always eat a piece." She patted her stomach. "As you can see."

I stuck the menu back in its stainless-steel rack. "I'll have the meatloaf special and pecan pie for dessert—" I read the name sewn on her uniform. "Veraleesa."

"What would you like to drink?"

"Unsweetened iced tea."

"Coming up." Five minutes later, she set the meatloaf plate and a glass of iced tea on the table. "You new around here?"

"How did you know?"

"Worked here thirteen years. I know all the regulars. You haven't eaten here before—at least not during my shift."

"You have the evening shift?"

"Six p.m. to two a.m. Been working it the whole thirteen years."

"You like the late hours?"

"I never was a morning person. This way I can sleep 'til noon every day, not just on weekends. You're not asking what time I get off, are you? I'm old enough to be your mother. Not to mention you being white and all."

I laughed with her. "No, no. Although if I were a couple of years older…" I winked.

"You scamp." A woman in a booth raised her coffee cup and Veraleesa waved at her. "Be right there."

I had finished half the meatloaf when she returned. It was delicious. "You're not here for the food, are you?"

"You're very perceptive."

"You a cop?"

"What makes you say that?"

"You look like a detective. Not too many people wear suits in here. Lots of my regulars are cops, both uniformed and plainclothes."

"I used to be a detective."

"Also, I saw the lump from your gun beneath the jacket when I walked behind you to refill those customers."

"Good eye. You would've made a good detective. I'm a private investigator. My name is Chuck McCrary."

I handed her a business card. She stuck it in her apron pocket. At least she didn't shove it back across the counter at me.

"I'm Veraleesa Kotanay. What you investigating?"

"A murder in the neighborhood three weeks ago."

"The Garrison Franco thing?"

"How'd you know?"

"Cops eat here all the time; they talk to me. They love our banana cream and lemon meringue pies. Next time, try one of those. Cops usually investigate street crimes. Muggings, car thefts, burglaries, and such. Murder is pretty rare."

"Do you remember a pretty Latina detective named Kelly Contreras?"

"No, can't say I do."

"Her partner is a big black man, six-foot-six and maybe three hundred pounds. Name of Arnold Bigelow."

"Didn't there used to be a football player by that name? Bigs Bigelow?"

"Yeah, that's Arnie. He played defensive lineman for the Port City Pelicans."

"I remember him now. All-Pro. *Bigs Brigade* they called it. I've never seen either of them in here—I would remember Bigs Bigelow. Are they investigating the murder too?"

"They finished their investigation. They arrested a friend of mine. but I know he didn't do it. I'm going to find the real killer."

"Good for you."

"You have security cameras here?"

"In this neighborhood? With us open all hours? We have no choice."

"How would I go about seeing your footage from three weeks ago?"

Chapter 7

I paused the playback and ran it backwards. Then I played it again. "Right there, Snoop," I said while I paused the video. "Watch this."

Raymond "Snoop" Snopolski sat next to me at the computer monitor in my office. Snoop was a detective for the Port City PD for over thirty years. After he retired, he got a PI license. He said it was more for something to do than for the money, but he and his wife Janet had two teenaged daughters that would need college money soon. Mostly, he did trial preparation work for lawyers. I used him for trial prep and also for surveillance and backup.

Snoop raised his reading glasses a fraction of an inch and leaned closer to the monitor. "Play it again." He watched for a moment. "It's hard to see because of the reflections from inside the diner."

"You sure it's not because your eyes are getting old?"

"*Humph.* One of these days, you'll find your arms are too short to read the newspaper, bud, and you'll need reading glasses too. Then I'm gonna laugh my ass off and make jokes about you getting old. At least I can still outshoot you."

I laughed. "Look beyond the reflections. What do you see across the street?"

"Somebody's jogging on the sidewalk."

"Notice how he's dressed?"

"Dark shirt, long-sleeved. Dark pants. Dark shoes. Maybe a dark watch cap, but I can't tell. Makes it real hard to see him."

"Maybe that was the idea. Why would anyone wear a long-sleeved shirt in Port City in the summertime, and at night? He's sneaking around, that's why. A guy might wear a dress shirt, maybe, but not a dark sport shirt." I played the clip again.

"Observe his stride, Chuck."

"That's right. His left arm is bent the whole time like he's holding a cellphone to his ear. Who jogs with their cellphone to their ear? No one. If you talk on the phone while you jog, you use a Bluetooth."

I fast-forwarded the clip while we watched the time index in the corner. "Okay, now compare it to this one." A similar figure jogged across the screen back the way he had come forty-five minutes earlier.

"I see it, Chuck. Dressed the same way. Still holding that phone. It's a long way across the street, but I think it's the same guy."

"Okay. Now let's study the tapes from the ATM and the convenience store."

Chapter 8

I knocked lightly on the open door, then stepped inside. "I found a lead for another credible suspect, Ms. Yankton."

"We don't have to be best buddies to be on a first name basis, McCrary. Call me Darcy."

That was progress. Any minute now, we'd sing Kumbaya. "Only if you call me Chuck."

"Sit down, Chuck, and tell me about your credible suspect." She sounded bored. Or tired. Maybe both.

"I canvassed all the businesses on 84th Street between Sixth and Second Avenue. I found three surveillance cameras with footage from the night of the shooting. Would you like to see what I found?" I reached for my briefcase.

She raised a hand like a traffic cop. "I won't spend the next hour watching grainy images on a computer screen. Just tell me—briefly."

"Right after midnight, a man jogged east down 84th Street with a cellphone to his ear. He was dressed in black from head to toe, including long sleeves to cover his arms. He ran back the same way forty-five minutes later, still carrying a phone."

"So?"

"Don't you get it, counselor? This could be huge. Tell me: Who jogs after midnight? No one. Who has a cellphone screwed to their ear when they jog? No one. Who wears long sleeves in the summer in South Florida? No one. Who jogs in long pants in the summer? No one."

The lawyer leaned back and crossed her arms. Her mind was closing like a vault door. "A mysterious jogger a few blocks away from the shooting? That's your credible suspect?"

I leaned forward. Maybe she would catch my brainwaves. "This guy even wore dark shoes. Jogging at night is dangerous. Most people wear reflective clothing or reflective tape so an idiot driver who doesn't see them won't run them down. This guy didn't want anyone to notice him."

She waved a finger in my face. She'd done that before. I didn't like it any better this time. I resisted the urge to grab her finger and break it off.

"Let me tell you about the real world, *cowboy*. Unless you find the guy, it doesn't mean squat. The prosecutor would tear me up if I presented this. It's the old SODDI defense."

"Some other dude did it?"

"It would make us sound desperate."

"In case you hadn't noticed, Darcy, Jorge *is* desperate."

Chapter 9

"Hit me again." Teresa Kovacs held out her glass for me to fill. "How's it going with Jorge's case?"

Terry Kovacs and I had been dating for several months. We had progressed to the point of an exclusive relationship. The exclusive part was my idea.

Three weeks before, Mother Weiner had said to me, "So you and Terry are going steady."

I had replied, "Only teenagers go steady, Mother. Adults have exclusive relationships."

"What's the difference, *boychik*?"

I tried to explain.

"Going steady," she'd said, and that was that.

However Lieutenant Weiner described the relationship, I wanted to find the right woman, fall in love, get married, and raise a family. Terry said she wanted to have fun for a while before settling down. We did have lots of fun. I had to admit that. Some weekends we barely left the bedroom.

We sat on my balcony with a pitcher of Sangria and a platter of cheese and crackers and watched the sun drop toward the horizon. Terry had removed her bikini top to catch the last of the sun's rays while the first reflections of the setting sun danced across the surface of Seeti Bay. A dozen boats swung at anchor. Terry and I had spent many an evening on *The Gator Raider Too*, while she swung at anchor near the same spot. After the sunset, we would go in the cabin, turn on the air conditioner, and rock the boat.

I refilled her glass and squeezed more lime in it.

"Ooh!" She jumped when a stray drop of lime juice hit her breast.

"Sorry. Would you like me to lick that off?"

She smirked. "Later, lover. I don't want to miss the sunset, but hold that thought." She dabbed the drop of lime juice with a napkin. "About Jorge's case?"

"His public defender is a tight-ass Yale attorney named Darcy Yankton. I researched her past cases. She defends poor, downtrodden tenants who are about to be evicted for non-payment of rent by what she would describe as a dirty, money-grubbing, bastard landlord."

"She have any murder experience?"

"Two murder cases in ten years in the PD's office. She plea-bargained both of them, so she's never run a murder trial."

"That's not good."

"Tell me about it. When I met her, she called Jorge a rogue cop. She thinks that all cops—and former cops—are bad guys. She sneers when she sees me. She called me a killer, a cowboy, and a vigilante."

"Jeez. How can you work with a lawyer like that?"

I wondered the same thing. "I don't have a choice. When a defendant chooses the PD's office, it's practically impossible to pick which attorney they get. You've got to have a strong reason to ask for a different attorney, like a conflict of interest, not a political conflict. But the worst thing is that Yankton thinks Jorge is guilty. She's going through the motions, pretending to defend him. I have to do this on my own."

Chapter 10

I peered at my watch for the umpteenth time while I paced the institutional green interview room. I was nervous and bored at the same time. Four steps, turn, repeat. My rubber-soled Rockport dress shoes squeaked a faint echo off the concrete-block walls of the hard room. Opposite the single door, a wire-reinforced exterior window showed a view of the courtyard from the eighth floor. I stopped pacing long enough to rearrange the murder book and my notepad for the third time where they lay on the metal table that was bolted to the concrete floor. I heard the doorknob turn.

Jorge entered the Spartan room and waited for the guard to close the door behind him. Jorge shook my hand and grabbed me in a bear hug. "God, I'm glad to see you."

I patted him on the back and squeezed his shoulders. "It'll be okay, *amigo*."

Jorge blinked back tears. "I hope so."

I slid into a metal chair and opened my notepad. "Tell me everything."

Jorge wiped his eyes with the back of his hand and sat across from me. "Where do I start?"

"Any enemies?"

"I've been a detective for ten years. We all have enemies."

"That kind of enemy backshoots you from ambush. They don't frame you for murder. Or, if they did try a frame, they'd screw it up. This was sophisticated. The killer knew what he was doing. Which enemy has the smarts to frame you?"

Jorge shrugged. "I've thought about that for the last three days. I come up blank."

"Any cops mad enough at you to frame you for murder?"

"Of course not."

"How about former cops? Any crooked cops who hold a grudge?"

"Nope. I never crossed paths with Internal Affairs, either as a target or a witness." Jorge rapped his knuckles on the table. "God willing, I never will."

"How about a jealous husband?"

"Never. Karen and I've been married eight years, and I've never strayed."

"I hate to ask, but has Karen ever…"

"No. She's never even flirted with another man. Never any trouble like that."

"You gamble?"

"Karen and I go to the dog track two or three times a year with Dan and Jessica. We have hot dogs, drink a couple of beers, and lose maybe twenty or thirty dollars."

"Any other gambling?"

"An occasional poker game at someone's home. But it's dollar limit. On a big night, I win or lose a hundred bucks."

"There's got to be something."

Both of us sat silent for a time.

"Tell me about the phone call," I said.

Chapter 11

Jorge closed his eyes, remembering. "I was watching TV with Karen when my phone rang. Our favorite cop show, *True Blue*, had started, so I know it was right at ten o'clock…"

…The opening credits for *True Blue* rolled across the television screen. Jorge paused it when his cellphone rang. It wasn't a regular contact because no name or picture showed on the screen. "Castellano."

An electronically altered voice said, "I understand you want to nail Garrison Franco."

He knew better than to ask who the caller was. "Yeah. You got something?"

"Two videos of Franco selling mollies."

Jorge sat straighter. He and Murphy had tried for the last six months to nail Franco for dealing heroin. This was the first he'd heard about Franco selling mollies. "Do they have sound?"

"One does, but the other one, the sound ain't so good."

"How'd you get the videos?"

"Cellphone. I held it like I was talking and pointed it at Franco. He was standing maybe ten feet away in the one with the good sound."

"What about the other one?" Jorge asked.

"We was in an auto garage and there's lots of banging and clanging. But the picture is good. I copied both videos to a stick drive."

"Can you bring it to the precinct?"

"Don't be stupid. My life wouldn't be worth a slice of month-old pizza if some wise guy saw me walk into the precinct. No, I'll hand you the drive in person."

"Where?"

"Eighty-sixth and Sixth, Northwest."

"When?"

"Midnight. Come alone. You bring anyone else and I won't show. Just you."

"Okay."

The caller disconnected.

Jorge handed the TV remote to his wife. "Work."

"Again? Can't it wait until tomorrow?"

"Karen, you know the drill; we've been through this a million times."

He hit a speed dial number. "Dan, we got a lead on a video of Garrison Franco dealing mollies."

Karen pointed the remote at the TV. "Be careful out there." *True Blue* began to play again.

An hour and a half later, Jorge parked near the corner of Northwest 84th Street and Fifth Avenue. He called Dan. "Okay, partner, I'm putting my phone in a pocket for a test." He dropped the phone into a jacket pocket and spoke in a conversational tone. "Mary had a little lamb… testing, testing." He pulled the phone from his pocket. "How'd that do?"

"Good. Let's move into position."

Jorge drove to Northwest 86th Street and Sixth Avenue. The commercial district was deserted. He parked at the curb and called Murphy again. "You in position?"

"Yeah. I'm parked on 85th between Fourth and Fifth."

"Good. Now we wait." Jorge tried in vain to make his heart beat slower.

"Stay quiet. Your guy may have hidden where he can see you. Just stick the phone in your pocket and be patient."

"Okay. These guys are never on time."

"Enough talk, Jorge. Zip it."

Jorge drummed his fingertips on the steering wheel. He took his own pulse. *Got to calm down.* He slowed his breathing. *In… out…*

The humid air cooled and golden halos appeared around the streetlights. The sole movement was a traffic light in the distance, clicking through its lonely circuit from green to yellow to red. Twice he stepped from the car and stretched when his butt fell asleep.

He consulted his watch for the fiftieth time when he heard a noise from his pocket. He put the phone to his ear. "Yeah?"

Murphy's voice came from the phone. "No joy?"

"*Nah.* The guy's a no-show. Shall we call it a night?"

"I'm tired." Jorge heard Murphy's car start. "Let's call it a day."

Chapter 12

I wrote Jorge's last sentence on my pad. "That's all?"

Jorge waved vaguely. "I didn't think any more about it until I heard the next day that Franco had been murdered."

"How long did you wait for the guy?"

"Dan logged his arrival at the backup site at 12:03 a.m. I parked at 12:05. Dan logged that he left at 1:17 a.m. and I logged out at 1:17 also."

"You and Dan didn't talk at all while you waited?" I asked.

"Not after we got into position."

"Too bad. A little conversation at the time Franco was shot and Dan could have given you an alibi."

"We all have 20/20 hindsight, right?"

"And you never heard the shots from Franco's shooting."

"Dan and I remember that an ambulance came by a few blocks from where I was staked out. It was about the time Franco was shot. Even so, I don't think we would've heard the shots. It's too far."

"What did you wear to the meet?"

"Slacks, a golf shirt, and a sports coat to hide the Kevlar vest. That's what I usually wear after work."

I wrote that down. "What color?"

"What difference does it make?"

"What color?"

Jorge closed his eyes. "Shirt was red, I think. Most of my golf shirts are pretty colorful. Jacket was silver."

"What about the slacks?"

"Khaki."

"Short-sleeve shirt?"

"Of course. What's this about, Chuck?"

"What kind of shoes?"

"That I remember. White Reeboks. My favorite shoes; I've had them since I graduated from the police academy. What's this about?"

I set the pen on the desk. "I found three surveillance tapes from two stores and an ATM on 84th street that show a man in dark long pants, dark long-sleeved shirt, and dark shoes, jogging east on the sidewalk on the north side at 12:12 a.m. He jogged back the way he came at one o'clock. He held a cellphone to his ear both times while he jogged."

"That makes no sense. Who jogs after midnight?"

"That's what Snoop and I thought. What clothes did Dan wear that night?"

"Dan? Now wait a minute. Dan's my partner—"

"What did he wear?"

"I never saw Dan that night. We set up the whole thing on the phone and took separate cars to the site. It couldn't have been Dan. His car never moved. I saw the GPS report."

"Your car never moved either, but Kelly arrested you for the murder."

"You show this video to Kelly yet?"

"No. But when I do, they'll say the jogger could be you. I can't tell from the video if he's wearing a vest under that shirt. It's too dark."

"I wasn't wearing black."

"But we can't prove that. *Amigo*, I didn't say that Dan is the jogger. I'd like to eliminate him as a suspect. If I knew what he wore that night, it would help."

I referred to the folder. "Homicide says one bullet that hit Franco definitely came from your Glock. The other slugs were damaged but were consistent with your weapon."

Jorge frowned. "That can't be. I had my gun with me the whole time."

"Could someone have switched guns?"

"I don't see how, Chuck. When my gun isn't on me, it's in my nightstand."

"Who else knows your gun is in your nightstand?"

"Karen, of course. She knows it's there in case she ever needs it."

"Anyone else?"

"My folks know. Dan, of course. Hell, I'd bet that most cops keep their guns in their nightstands unless they have kids. Where do you keep yours?"

I grinned. "On my nightstand or Terry's nightstand when I'm over there. What about the shell casings?"

"Kelly and Bigs didn't find any. Shooter must have policed his brass."

"How do they know they searched in the right place?"

Jorge grabbed the binder, flipped to a page, and spun it to show me. "Homicide found three slugs plugged into the front of the building and matched one to Franco's revolver. The shooter must have fired from there and policed his brass.

"Who fired first?" I asked. "If it was Franco, it could've been self-defense."

"No way to know. The autopsy says Franco could've taken a while to die from the chest shot, so he could have returned fire even if the shooter fired first."

"*Hmm.* Unless we figure out how someone switched guns with you, it doesn't look good, my friend."

"Don't forget they had to switch them back."

"Yeah, that's even worse. When did homicide take your weapon?" I asked.

"Two weeks later, when they made the ballistics match."

"Why the delay on the ballistics?"

"I asked around. The autopsy was delayed four days because of a backup in the ME's office. They had two people on vacation and two more at a medical convention."

That was true as far as it went. "Still, it was ten more days before they made the ballistics match. Why the delay?"

"Remember who the victim was, Chuck. Everyone thought it was a thug-on-thug killing, probably with a stolen gun. The crime lab is always behind and they didn't see a need to put a rush on it."

I pushed the folder away. "And then they made the match, and the shit hit the fan."

Chapter 13

I rolled into the parking lot at 8530 Northwest Second Avenue. Two cars remained in the warehouse lot. The area lay in deep shadow even though it was not yet sunset. I locked the Caravan and carried the murder book to the middle of the street.

Checking the diagrams and photos in the murder book, I located the area where Franco had stopped his car. I laid a rubber glove on the approximate spot where Franco had collapsed.

I studied the asphalt while I vectored back and forth over a ten-yard circle. The pavement was shadowed now, so I pulled a Maglite. A bloodstain would be long gone. It was the rainy season after all. Still, you never know. I combed the area in the circle but found nothing. I wasn't disappointed; I didn't expect to find anything, but I had to search. No stone unturned and all that.

I stared at the warehouse where I had parked. I sighted down my index finger at the building and imagined Franco shooting in the dark. The company offices occupied the front of the building and the front wall was mostly windows. The walls between the windows and the entrance were two concrete blocks wide—about three feet.

Returning to the warehouse, I didn't see the three bullet holes where Franco's shots had struck. I consulted the file photo of the bullet-riddled wall twice before I found the telltale smooth spots where the bullets had hit. The warehouse front had been repaired and repainted. There they were, a nice tight grouping of three shots. Funny that at least one bullet hadn't hit a window.

That was the thought that had tickled my mind when I first read the murder book: The tight grouping didn't make sense. Setting the book on the ground, I pulled out my notepad and wrote: *If Franco was wounded, he couldn't make a tight grouping. If Franco shot first, how did he know where the shooter was standing in the dark? Did GF see the shooter or hear him?* It made no sense.

I stepped onto the entrance porch and peered at the ceiling. Two recessed lights were mounted flush. Surveying the street, I imagined what the shooter would see if he stood on the porch. I needed to come back and test this at midnight, recreating the actual conditions.

Taking a shooter's stance, I triangulated the path the bullets would have taken by shining the Maglite at shoulder height above the spot where Franco's body had been found. The center of the Maglite beam marked the spot sixty yards from me where the bullet that missed Franco should have hit the wall behind him. There was a faded letter from a painted-over sign a foot to the left of the spot. I kept the letter in sight while I crossed the street and laid another glove on the sidewalk below the spot.

Returning to the porch where Franco's bullets had hit, I studied the other buildings on both sides of Second Avenue. Why did the shooter pick this particular spot? Was it the best? Were any of the other buildings better?

A murder book photo showed the location where the shooter's bullet had lodged in the wall behind Franco. Crossing to the east side of the street, I found the gouge in the concrete-block wall. It was twenty yards from where my second glove marked the other spot. This was getting curiouser and curiouser.

Standing before the gouged wall, I recalculated the line the shooter's bullet had taken. Extending the Maglite, I shined it above the glove I used to mark where Franco's body had lain. The line did not point where I expected. The shots came from the building next door to the building Franco had shot at. Maybe I had the wrong spot where the body was found. I pointed at the building where the three bullet holes had been found. The line didn't cross where they found Franco's body. I drew a new diagram in my notepad.

I returned to the van. While I hadn't made a breakthrough in the case, I had uncovered two anomalies: the grouping of Franco's shots and the line the shooter's bullets had taken. I pulled out of the lot and turned toward home.

In the rearview mirror, the porch lights flicked on in the deepening shadows. I pulled over and wrote myself a note: Porch lights on either a timer or light-sensing device.

Chapter 14

I already had a table at Java Jenny's when Dan Murphy paused in the doorway to scan the interior. I stood and waved.

We shook hands.

"Thanks for coming."

"It's the least I could do. Jorge's my partner, no matter what he's accused of."

A server approached as we sat down. "What can I get you?"

Murphy pointed at the display case. "One giant chocolate chip cookie and a large half-caf."

I tapped my cup. "Just a refill."

I waited for the server to leave. "Will you help me with the investigation?"

Murphy seemed uncomfortable. "Like I said, he's my partner, no matter what he's done."

"You think he did it?"

Murphy shrugged. "Kelly and Bigs are good cops. I'm sure they considered every possibility. Every cop in the department knew that Franco was a Grade A scumbag. No one wants to pin this on Jorge, but the evidence points to him. That's the logical conclusion."

"But what does your gut tell you? Did he do it? *Could* he do it?"

The server arrived. Murphy accepted his coffee and cookie. He took a bite and a sip before he answered. "You think you know a guy... I mean, we've been partners for three years."

"Will you help me?"

"Yeah, I'll help."

"Great. First question: When you went to backup Jorge that night, what were you wearing?"

"What was I wearing?" Murphy repeated. "Who remembers crap like that?"

"Humor me. What were you wearing?"

Murphy frowned. His lower lip stiffened. *Hmm.* There was something he didn't want to tell me.

"Blue jeans and a tee-shirt. That's what I wear after work and I don't remember changing clothes before the stakeout."

"What color was the tee-shirt?"

"Hell, I don't remember. I think it was one I bought at a rock concert I went to with Jessica. Yeah, now I remember. It was red with white lettering. We each bought one."

"Thanks." I wrote it on the notepad. "Who else would want Franco dead?"

Murphy laughed mirthlessly. "Half the hoods and all the cops in Port City."

"Give me three names to start."

He stared at the ceiling. "Toots Pollaio."

"Spell it."

He did. "Marcello Dominguez." Murphy waited while I wrote it down. "And Gus Guzman."

Murphy gave me as many details on the three men as he could remember.

Chapter 15

I followed Toots Pollaio and a friend to a cheap hotel and waited outside until Pollaio emerged alone and stumbled to his car.

Three o'clock in the afternoon and Toots was already drunk. Or high. This was a guy that Dan Murphy thought could plan a murder and frame a cop for it?

I watched through the tinted windows of my invisible minivan while Toots fumbled his car door open and fell into the driver seat. I thought of my white Dodge Caravan as invisible because there were eight gazillion white minivans in Port City. Mine attracted as much notice as one bee in a beehive.

Blue-black smoke spewed from the exhaust of the rusted 1999 Maxima while Toots screeched into oncoming traffic. A pickup truck swerved and slammed on its brakes. The truck driver gave Toots the finger from his open window. Toots drove on, oblivious.

I waited, then followed, hoping the sozzled fool didn't kill somebody before he led me wherever he was going.

Toots overshot the driveway and bumped over the curb into the lumpy parking lot of the Crooked Cue. His car bounced off the parking bumper and stopped at an angle across a faded stripe, blocking two spaces.

I drove fifty yards farther and parked at a pizza parlor across the street. I watched from my side mirror while Toots struggled to open the door before he entered the bar. I locked the van and followed.

Three neon-lit beer signs flashed in the picture windows that flanked the double glass doors. Green vinyl booths lined one wall and a half-dozen Formica tables filled the front. Four pool tables crowded the middle.

I grabbed an end stool at the bar and swiveled where I could view the whole room.

Toots stood in the back, talking to the bartender. The bartender pointed, and Toots pivoted to scan the sparse crowd. A thin, black man with an Afro stuffed under a knitted Rasta hat watched from a booth in the back corner. A black, red, green, and yellow dashiki draped his bony frame like a tent.

I noticed the bulges from Rasta Man's merchandise, or maybe his gun, even from that distance.

Toots walked over and slid into the booth across from Rasta Man.

The bartender noticed me. "What'll it be?"

"Port City Amber draft."

The bartender left.

I slouched at the bar and watched Rasta Man conduct business across the room. Customers passed folded bills as they shook hands with Rasta Man. Rasta Man stuffed the bills inside his dashiki and pulled out plastic baggies, which he slipped to the customers under the table.

The bartender returned with the beer, and I laid my Port City Pilots baseball hat on the bar. I pretended to make a call on my cellphone, and walked toward the restrooms in the back. When I passed the booth, I snapped a picture of Rasta Man. When I came out of the restroom, Toots was gone.

I returned to the stool and nursed my beer while I pretended to send and receive occasional text messages.

An hour later, Rasta Man had passed envelopes from underneath his dashiki to three different customers without leaving the booth.

Chapter 16

Kelly Contreras took the pictures from Chuck, using the opportunity to brush his hand with her fingertips. *Maybe someday Chuck will figure out that I have the hots for him,* she thought. *It hasn't worked for the last three years, but you never know. I may as well keep trying.* She flipped through the photos and handed them to Bigs. "I don't recognize him. How about you, Bigs?"

Bigs tapped the first picture with a finger. "I've seen the guy. Where did you take these?"

"That one was at the Crooked Cue. Toots went there to buy drugs from that guy. I followed him and took this one at a laundromat on Northwest 80th between Eighth and Ninth Avenue. The last one is at an apartment in the El Segundo Estates housing project. It was pretty late. Maybe he lives there. Here's the address." Chuck handed Kelly a sheet of paper. She got to touch his fingers again.

Kelly consulted the paper. "What's the connection to the Castellano case?"

He shrugged. "Maybe none. Dan Murphy told me that Toots Pollaio wanted to bring down Jorge. I followed Toots and he led me to this guy. I'll call him Rasta Man until you get me a name. Maybe Rasta Man took over Franco's territory. That makes him a suspect in my book."

Kelly pulled the keyboard toward her. "Let me verify something." She entered the address Chuck had given her and scanned the screen. "Rasta Man's name is Ashante Derringer. That's his apartment." She read off the screen. "Long list of arrests for possession with intent to distribute, DWI, assault, all against women. He'll hit a woman, but won't attack anyone he thinks might fight back. Derringer's a pussy."

"Kelly, do you ever listen to yourself talk?" Chuck said.

"What do you mean?"

"You called Derringer a 'pussy,' as if that's a synonym for a coward. You being a woman and all…"

She laughed. "I'm among friends. Would you rather I used a euphemism like 'wuss'? Or maybe I should call him a wimp. How about that?" She patted Chuck on the arm and grinned. *Maybe I come across as too masculine. Ohmigod, you don't suppose Chuck thinks I'm a lesbian?*

"Regardless of whether he's a pussy or a wimp, it sounds like Derringer wouldn't start a gunfight with a hood as tough as Franco."

Kelly touched the PI's arm again. "Yeah. On the other hand, Toots is pretty tough, even if he is gay. Like a boy named Sue, he had to be tough to survive. He has the balls to hit Franco."

"He has the balls but not the smarts," Bigs said. "He's dumb as a box of rocks. Toots isn't smart enough to frame a picture, let alone frame a cop for murder,"

Chapter 17

Dan Murphy handed me a printout. I scanned it while I nibbled on a chocolate chip cookie. "Marcello Dominguez's rap sheet reads like a *Who's Who* for drug dealers," I said.

"Two terms in Gentryville prison fighting mosquitos in the middle of the Everglades," Murphy replied.

I flipped another page. "That's like a graduate degree in drug dealing. He's forty-seven—in the prime of life. A scumbag ready to leap into the big time as head of *Los Barones Españoles,* The Spanish Barons."

"His gang members call him *El Duque*, The Duke."

"Maybe he thinks it gives him a certain cachet."

Murphy surveyed the nearby tables at Java Jenny's like he was making sure no one could overhear us. "*El Duque* made a connection with a drug cartel in Central America. The cartel corrupted a drug manufacturer down there and they make mollies for export to South Florida."

I knew *mollies* was slang for MDMA, Methylenedioxymeth-amphetamine—incredibly dangerous pills that sometimes killed the users instead of making them high.

"*El Duque* is setting up distributors for his new product line. I heard that Garrison Franco sold mollies from a source in Colorado. Franco was a competitor, so Dominguez had motive to kill him."

We called an undercover cop. He didn't know where Dominguez lived, but told us that *El Duque* hung out at a storefront on the outskirts of downtown Port City.

I drove past the storefront. The two-story, concrete block building wore peeling blue paint like worn-out old clothes. Busted windows on the second floor had darkened spaces behind the openings. *Probably don't use the second floor.* Local gangs had tagged the front in years past, but the first-floor windows were intact beneath the spray paint. A small parking lot adjoined the building. Layer after layer of overlapping graffiti covered the wall. The Spanish Barons used it as a clubhouse.

The vacant lot next door held three motorcycles, two old sedans, a pickup truck, a cargo van, and a shiny Lexus. The Lexus license plate was registered to Dominguez.

Three young hoods sat in folding chairs on the front porch, smoking cigarettes and drinking beer.

I parked a hundred fifty yards down the street near a convenience store busy with in-and-out traffic. I watched the building and parking lot with binoculars. Murphy had given me Dominguez's mug shot and the undercover cop had emailed me video, so I knew what Dominguez looked like.

I watched for three hours, taking one break to use the men's room in the convenience store. The three-man crew on the front porch rotated regularly. One man went inside and another took his place every half hour.

Two Spanish Barons came out of the clubhouse and strutted up the sidewalk on the other side from where I was parked. I set the binoculars on the seat and tapped the steering wheel in time to the music from my ear buds. If they noticed me at all, I hoped I appeared to be killing time waiting for someone.

The two hoods passed by and crossed the street behind the van. I watched them in my mirrors while they entered the convenience store. Two minutes later they came out, each carrying a case of beer.

I watched them all the way to the clubhouse.

Later a man Dominguez's height came out the front door without another man going in. I couldn't see his face because of the sun's angle, but the body language of the three gangsters on the front porch told me it was Dominguez. They sprang to attention when he stopped on the porch. It was *El Duque* all right.

He disappeared around the corner toward the vacant lot. A minute later, the Lexus exited the lot and made a right turn, bumping over the curb. I had figured that Dominguez would head west and I'd guessed right. I followed a block behind.

El Duque turned north into a narrow side street. I followed at what I hoped was a safe distance. I figured Dominguez was at least two hundred yards ahead before I rounded the same corner.

A half-block into the side street, I eyed my rearview mirror. Two ancient sedans rolled into the street behind me and blocked both lanes. A jolt of adrenaline pulsed through my veins.

Ahead, the street dead-ended at one of Port City's numerous canals. *El Duque* had parked his Lexus and was standing beside it with three other men watching my minivan approach.

Parked cars lined the curbs on both sides and made the traffic lanes too narrow for a three-point turn.

I accelerated another forty yards to a driveway on the right and careened into it, pulling all the way to the steel garage door. Slamming the van into reverse, I squealed backwards across the street. I banged my rear bumper into a parked car, jerked the van into drive, floored it, and spun the steering wheel hard right. I bounced off another parked car and headed straight for the two sedans blocking the street.

Two men jumped out of each sedan and took cover behind the four open car doors, guns aimed at me. I hoped to God those were pistols. If they were automatics, I was a dead man.

The only escape was a small gap between the facing doors of the two sedans, maybe a foot wide.

Tally-ho!

I jammed the accelerator to the firewall and aimed the Caravan like a javelin flying down the yellow stripe in the center of the street. Bullets smashed into the front of the van. Spider-web cracks marbled the windshield, obscuring my vision, but I smelled the smoke and felt the steam streaming from under the hood. Sticking my head out the side window, I tried to stay equidistant between the cars parked on either side while the van gained speed.

Momentum is mass times velocity. Four thousand pounds of Dodge speeding fifty-five miles per hour toward two gangsters made of flesh and blood. Thirty yards before impact, the gangsters jumped and ran.

My bumper sheared off the passenger door on one car and the driver's door on the other while the Caravan scraped between the sedans and barreled down the street toward freedom. In the mirror, the two doors sailed like Frisbees and bounced down the street after me.

Skidding into the oncoming traffic, I searched the rearview mirror for signs of pursuit. There were none; the wrecked doors and wrecked sedans must have blocked the street.

The engine temperature light shined an angry red; so did the warning light for the oil pressure. The check engine light and a bunch of other lights warned me the Dodge was on its last legs. The power steering was already *kaput* and I fought the wheel to stay in one lane. I breathed a silent prayer of thanks for the Chrysler engineers while the sweat poured down my face and ribs, soaking my shirt. Six blocks later, the shot-up engine of the valiant Dodge surrendered to its mortal wounds and clattered to a halt. I never thought the engine would last that long. In the sudden quiet, I could almost hear my heart pounding in my chest. I coasted to the curb and sat with both hands still on the wheel. Forcing my breathing to slow, I wondered if my pulse would ever return to normal.

After a couple of minutes, I unwrapped my fingers from the sweaty steering wheel, leaned out the door, and threw up on the pavement. I grabbed a tissue to wipe my lips, rinsed my mouth from a bottle of water, and called AAA.

Back to the drawing board. At least I was alive.

Chapter 18

I bought another used Dodge Caravan, a silver one, also ubiquitous and unremarkable.

Three days later, I figured the heat had died down. I set up a leapfrog tail on Dominguez. Snoop and I used two vehicles and swapped off every mile or so. I didn't want to be spotted again. Next time I might not be so lucky.

Dominguez left the clubhouse and drove in the direction of Little Havana. No surprise there. The surprise was that he kept traveling west until he was near the Everglades. He pulled up to the pink-stucco entrance to an upscale, gated community and waited while the wrought-iron gate rolled open.

I hung back and watched the best I could to see where the Lexus went, but it pulled out of sight within seconds of passing the gate. I was about to leave when another resident pulled to the gate. Tagging onto their bumper, I followed their car through. I drove around for a while, but never spotted the Lexus.

"Tell me again why you followed this guy?" Kelly studied the picture I'd given her.

"It's the front gate of Dominguez's neighborhood with his Lexus passing through," I said. "Dominguez was a big competitor of Garrison Franco in the market for mollies and had motive to kill him. This is where I lost him—this community west of Little Havana. Got any idea how to find out which house he lives in?"

Kelly's eyebrows rose. "Who told you that he competed with Franco?"

"Dan Murphy."

She appeared skeptical. "You'd think that Dan would know. He and Jorge were on Franco like stink on a skunk for dealing heroin before Franco got himself murdered." She picked up the picture. "Still... mollies, you said?"

"Yeah."

She turned to Bigs. "You hear any rumors about Franco dealing mollies?"

"Dominguez deals mollies; Franco deals heroin. I never heard any different on the street."

"Maybe Franco was trying to expand his product line." She reviewed the photo. "How many houses in the development, Chuck?"

"Almost two hundred."

Kelly shook her head. "You search the ownership records?"

"Of course," I replied. "There's nothing owned in his name, and there are too many land trusts, LLCs, and other intermediaries to chase down in less than a month. Could you get authorization to follow him with a drone?"

"*Nah*. Budget's too tight. The department has only four drones. We have no evidence against Dominguez; he's not a person of interest. Bigs and I have guys with hard evidence against them that we can't get a drone on."

"Are you *sure* he and Franco were competitors?" asked Bigs.

Chapter 19

"Why do we keep following Dominguez?" Snoop asked. "If you want to waste your money, you could send Janet and me to Paris. It would do the case as much good."

"It's right there in Rule Two: *When in doubt, follow somebody.* And I'm sure as hell in doubt."

"If you gotta follow somebody, let's follow a UPS truck. We'll learn as much about who shot Franco, and the UPS driver probably won't try to kill us."

"Dominguez is a drug dealer; Franco was a drug dealer."

"Big deal," Snoop said. "We gonna follow every drug dealer in Port City until one of us gets killed? Janet would love that."

"Dan Murphy said that Dominguez and Franco were competitors and that *El Duque* had a motive to kill Franco."

"Yeah, but Kelly and Bigs said they'd never heard that. Who you gonna believe, Kelly and Bigs or Murphy?"

"That's why I'm in doubt."

Snoop sighed. "Maybe Murphy's jerking your chain, sending you the wrong direction."

"Could be. He's 0-for-2 on the suspects I've investigated so far."

"Like I said: Maybe he's jerking your chain."

I met Murphy in the parking lot of a Cuban coffee shop near the North Shore Precinct. "Hey, Chuck. How's Jorge's case coming?"

"Snoop and I found a guy in surveillance videos from two businesses on 84th that might have been our shooter."

"That's good. What do they show?"

"Not enough for Jorge's lawyer, although she won't bother to look at them. She doesn't think it's useful unless I can find the guy in the video."

"Who's the lawyer?" Murphy asked.

"Some hard-nosed Yale graduate from the Public Defender's office who's never taken a murder case to trial. Her name's Darcy Yankton."

"Oh, Christ. I've heard of her. She the one who hates cops?"

"Oh, great. You mean she has a reputation for that?"

"She never met a cop she didn't hate. Anything I can do to help?"

"Yeah. I followed up on those names you gave me. Toots Pollaio is a dope-smoking mook who couldn't find his way out of a one-car garage with the door open. He's not smart enough to frame Jorge. Hell, he can't even drive a car without hitting the curb. And Marcello Dominguez sells mollies, not heroin. He and Franco were not competitors. Where did you hear that they were?"

"From one of my CI scumbags on the street. I guess he was misinformed. Sorry."

I watched him drive away. He didn't act sorry.

Chapter 20

I called on Sergeant Wilma Leonard at Organized Crime. I carried in two cappuccinos and handed her one.

"How'd you know about the cappuccinos?" she asked.

I gave her my best grin. "Snoop Snopolski sees all and knows all."

She laughed. A big, warm laugh from a big, warm woman. "Snoop and I go back a long way. He working for you now?"

"He's helping me out on the Jorge Castellano case."

She set the cappuccino on her desk. "I don't care what the evidence shows: Jorge did not gun down Garrison Franco. It is not in his nature."

"I agree. That's why I'm here. Dan Murphy said that Gus Guzman may have had a beef with Franco. What do you know about Guzman?"

She leaned back in her chair and sipped her cappuccino. "What do I know about Gus Guzman?" she repeated. "Gus runs a racing book—track odds minus ten percent. Or plus ten percent, depending on your viewpoint."

"How does his operation work?"

"Gus hires kids to pick up bets. If they get busted, they're juveniles and we can't do much to them."

"Pretty smart to use mules."

"Yeah," Wilma said. "He uses older, armed hoods to pay off winning bets, which can run into the thousands of dollars. Guzman doesn't want kids to carry around large amounts of money for the winners. It's too tempting, and it might make them targets for robbers."

"What is this guy, the bookie everybody elects as neighbor of the year?"

She smiled. "Let's put it this way: Gus was in business when I got here, over twenty years ago. He pays off his winners without a hassle and doesn't break any of his losers' bones. He simply won't take their bets until they pay him back. His operation is clean and tidy."

"Sounds like a model citizen as far as criminals go."

Wilma lowered her voice. "Let's be realistic. It's a victimless crime, and Gus doesn't get violent with anyone. We OC cops, we concentrate our resources on the bad actors. If we ever clean up the rest of the city, then we'll go after Gus."

"That should be right after the Second Coming. You think there's any way he could have had a beef with Garrison Franco?"

Wilma sipped her cappuccino. "I doubt Gus knew who Garrison Franco was."

Why would Dan Murphy send me after Gus Guzman? His suspect list was now 0-for-3.

Chapter 21

After much prodding from me and the police union, Darcy Yankton obtained bail for Jorge. I had an appointment with him at ten o'clock to report my progress. That would be a really short meeting, because I had nothing good to report. When I woke, my mind swirled with unorganized facts. I needed a long run to put my body on autopilot while my mind processed the data.

I parked the Silver Ghost crosswise on the far side of the parking lot. I didn't want anyone dinging the antique Avanti's doors. The golfers wouldn't arrive at the course for another hour, but I didn't take any chances.

The eastern sky hinted of the coming sunrise with a soft luminescence behind the scattered clouds. A three-quarter moon hung low in the west. In the stillness, I paused a moment to absorb the view over the driving range.

The pre-dawn morning was as quiet and cool as it gets in Port City this time of year. Humidity hung like a damp curtain and bathed the grass with a dewy carpet that shimmered in the moonlight.

I stretched for a few minutes before taking off down the nearest cart path, leaving a wake of foggy mist when I ran through the low spots on the undulating fairways. My feet fell into a rhythmic pattern and so did my mind.

Motive: Franco threatened Jorge's wife. Okay, but if Jorge didn't do it... If? what's this if? Think positive: Jorge didn't do it, so who else had a motive to murder Franco? None of the names Dan gave me had a good enough motive, or any motive at all.

I passed the fourth green and ran up the cart path toward the fifth tee box.

Method: It keeps coming back to Jorge's gun. All Glock 17s look alike, except for minor wear marks on the grips or maybe a scratch or two on the casing. At first glance, even a cop wouldn't notice if someone had switched his gun. Jorge says he never lets his pistol out of his sight, but it must be out of his sight sometime.

I ran past the ninth green and headed out over the back nine.

Opportunity: Nothing I can do about that. Jorge could have walked or run over to the crime scene and shot Franco. So could Murphy. So could the jogging man or a thousand other people on the streets I didn't check.

By the time I finished the four miles around all eighteen holes, I'd formed some conclusions. I didn't like the result.

I headed for Jerry's Gym to work out and shower.

Chapter 22

"Jorge Castellano to see you, Chuck."

I gave the receptionist a smile. "Thanks."

Jorge jumped to his feet. "Boy am I glad to see you."

We shook hands, slapping each other on the back.

"Come on, *amigo*. Bring your coffee." I led him down the hall to my office.

"How're you feeling, Jorge?"

"Nervous as hell. I tossed and turned all night, wondering what you'd found. Karen kicked me out of bed at four a.m. so she could sleep. Where do I stand?"

"The shooter may have fired from a different hiding place than the murder book shows. You remember there was a bullet that missed Franco and imbedded in a wall across the street?"

"Yeah, I remember."

"I stood at that bullet mark and triangulated where the bullet was fired. It wasn't fired from the building with the three bullet holes."

"What does that mean? The shooter was standing someplace else?"

"Maybe. Or else the murder book has the wrong spot where Franco's body was found. That's a possibility, but they would have had to be off by more than ten yards." I waved a hand. "I'll come back to that later. I examined every piece of evidence, every procedure that Bigs and Kelly followed. It's the same stuff you or I would have done. It's solid everywhere else except that they didn't canvass 84th Street. I told you about the mysterious jogger Snoop and I found on the surveillance tape, didn't I?"

"That's a lead, isn't it?"

"I took it to Darcy Yankton. She said, and I quote, '*Hmm...* unless you find the guy, it doesn't mean anything.'"

Jorge slumped.

I lifted a finger in a wait-a-minute gesture. "I said the murder book is solid. I did not say it was complete. Remember the right way, the wrong way, and the Army way. I evaluated the shots from a sniper's perspective. The killer fired from over forty yards away and at night. Three out of four rounds hit Franco, and the fourth came close. Could a street punk make a shot grouping that close? In the dark? Could you?"

"No, I couldn't. I never thought of that. The shooter must be a crack shot."

"Could Dan Murphy make that shot?"

Jorge frowned. "Dan and I go to the firing range all the time. He's an expert marksman. Dan could group shots that close together, but why would he kill Franco? He has no motive." He paused. "No, no, no. I can't believe it's Dan."

"I noticed another thing that doesn't make sense, *amigo*. It's like Sherlock Holmes's dog that didn't bark. The killer lured you to the warehouse district with a fake phone call."

"Yeah, so?"

"So, how did he lure Franco to the murder site? He must have had something Franco wanted. What would make Franco come out at midnight to a deserted street in the warehouse district?"

"Beats me. You got any ideas?"

"Maybe the shooter was someone Franco was afraid of—like a cop. A cop could make a credible threat that would draw him out at midnight."

"A cop? What cop? It couldn't be Dan. It couldn't be."

"Another thing, *amigo,* Franco's shots at that building were in a tight group of three bullets. What are the odds he could make those shots when he was mortally wounded? They would have sprayed all over the place, maybe broken a window or two."

"What if Franco shot first?" asked Jorge.

"Then how did Franco know where the killer was hiding? It was after midnight, and the guy was standing on a dark porch, probably dressed in black. How did Franco even know it was an ambush? He had to think he was meeting someone."

Jorge frowned. "What do you make of that?"

"The killer surprised Franco and shot first. Then after Franco was down, he made those three shots at the wrong building with Franco's own gun."

Chapter 23

I put my cellphone on speaker. "Snoop, you in position?"

"The GPS says I'm parked right where Murphy parked that night."

"Good." The time on the cellphone screen said 12:29 a.m. Just right. "Open the windows and kill the engine. I'll fire a few rounds sometime in the next few minutes when you're not expecting it."

"Will do. G'bye." Snoop's picture disappeared from the screen.

I parked the Silver Ghost in the street where Franco's car had been found and switched on the flashers. I slung ear protectors around my neck and walked to the building entrance where the shooter had supposedly waited in ambush.

I climbed the steps to the entrance porch and tried the front door. Force of habit from years as a patrol cop. Locked, of course. I carried a Glock 17, the same model the killer used. Franco had stopped his car in the same darkened area between two streetlights where I had parked the Avanti. The porch where I stood was not the closest to the killing field.

I jogged onto the parking lot and studied the surrounding buildings. Where would I lurk if I wanted to ambush someone? I walked south. I stopped and surveyed the position of the Avanti, studied the next building where I now stood. The shooter would pick the building I was now in front of.

Returning to the first porch, I ejected the Glock magazine and replaced it with a magazine filled with blanks. I pulled the ear protectors over my head, racked the slide, and fired four blank rounds at the ground. I removed the ear protectors and the gunshots echoed eerily down the deserted street while I picked up the four brass cartridges.

I walked to the middle of the street, donned the ear protectors, and fired three more rounds at the pavement.

After collecting the cartridges again, I called Snoop. "You hear anything?"

"You fire yet?"

My heart fell. "Yeah, Snoop, I fired seven rounds."

"Sorry, buddy. Silent as a tomb over here."

"Thanks, Snoop. I'll see you tomorrow."

To my left, a light flicked on in a third-floor window of the building from which I'd fired the first four rounds.

I replaced the blank magazine with the real one and held the Glock beside my right thigh. I studied the lit window on the third floor. A shadow passed across the ceiling as someone approached to have a gander. I pulled out a Maglite and aimed at the window to signal the unknown person.

A figure appeared, silhouetted by the light behind him or her. Maybe someone had witnessed the murder.

I walked closer and stopped below the window. I shouted upwards. "Hello."

The figure vanished and the light went out.

I wasn't about to let this guy get away. The front door was locked; I'd checked. He must have come in from the alley. Sprinting to the building's north side, I found a narrow walkway to the alley. I ran down the walk, wheeled into the alley, and skidded to a stop.

The streetlights at either end of the block cast a dim glow on the scene.

I stuck the Maglite in a pocket and raised the Glock. A truck entrance with a pedestrian door in one side dominated the center of the alley wall. A piece of plastic was taped over the window in the pedestrian door. The alley windows were dark.

I ducked below the windows and crept sideways along the wall to the truck entrance. I pulled the ear protectors from around my neck and dropped them to the pavement. Pressing my ear to the heavy-gauge steel, I listened. Nothing.

The plastic that covered the window in the door had been torn loose at one corner. Lifting it, I found the broken window. Someone had removed the glass shards in the corner nearest to the door handle. Perhaps the person I'd seen was a squatter. That's how the guy gained access to the third floor.

Holstering the pistol, I reached through the broken window with my left hand. The heavy steel door would protect everything except my arm if the guy inside began shooting.

I felt the door handle and twisted. The door latch disengaged and I pulled the door open an inch. I crouched below the window, keeping the steel door between me and whoever waited inside. Drawing the Glock, I pulled the pedestrian door wide open, stood with my back against the wall, and listened again. Nothing.

I wedged the ear protectors under the door to hold it open. Diving into the darkness inside the warehouse, I rolled twice to get away from the doorway where the faint light from the alley could silhouette me.

A faint thump in the distance. Could have been a door; could have been something else—or someone else. I sniffed. French fries? Well, why not? Smiling in the darkness, I moved further away from the door.

I waited while my eyes adjusted to the faint light that seeped through the door and the dirty windows. Then I discerned the outline of a stairway against the wall on the left.

I crept to the bottom step and started up. The French fry smell grew stronger, joined by something else... something burning. Marijuana?

Reaching the landing on the second floor, I smelled a third smell, familiar, but I couldn't place it.

The hallway on the third floor was not quite as dark as the inside of a coffin. Not quite. The doorway at the front of the building on the left stood open.

I tiptoed past several doors until I reached the last doorway and peeked inside. A faint light from the street trickled through the window. The light-colored linoleum floor showed no furniture in the visible part of the room.

I listened for two minutes. Nothing. I tucked and rolled into the room as quietly as I could. Scooting my back against the wall, I extended the Maglite as far as I could reach to the left. If somebody shot at the light, I hoped he would aim at my left hand, not my stomach. I clicked the Maglite on.

From across the room, a faint wisp of smoke rose from a candle melted onto a TV tray. That was the other burning smell. He used a candle when he didn't want the electric light. Crumpled McDonald's sacks lay heaped in a corner. A torn sleeping bag sprawled open on the floor. A table lamp with no shade sat on the floor near the window. One stained, upholstered chair with stuffing oozing from the back and a metal folding chair made up the rest of the room's décor.

I heard a door open in the hallway behind me, followed by running feet. After I saw him in the window, the guy had moved to a room at the rear of the building and hidden behind me until I passed. Smart.

I bolted into the hallway. The Maglite beam caught a man sprinting toward the stairway. I ran down the hallway, crossed the stairway landing in two strides, and chased the fleeing man down the stairs three at a time. I'd run halfway down the last flight when the running man hit the bottom and wheeled around the railing toward the open door.

I vaulted the railing, reached my left arm as far as I could, and swung the Maglite at the runner. The three-cell flashlight measured over a foot long and weighed a smidge less than two pounds. The heft made it a good club. I'd used a similar one when I'd worn a uniform—in Special Forces and as a Port City Police patrolman.

The flashlight grazed the runner's head and knocked him off his feet. He sprawled across the concrete floor.

I rammed a knee into the small of his back and jammed my Glock into his ear. "Don't move. That's a pistol in your ear. It will blow a hole in your skull the size of a baseball. Do you want that?"

The man stopped struggling. "Don't shoot, man. I'm cool."

Chapter 24

I positioned the Maglite on the floor so the light bounced off the wall and lit the room. Frisking the guy with my left hand, I felt a lump and slipped a switchblade into my jacket pocket. The baggie of marijuana went into another pocket. A plastic bag with cigarette papers and a Bic lighter completed the collection. I picked up the Maglite. "You can get up now."

The guy climbed to his feet, hands in the air. He was as tall as I was, but skinny.

I stepped back a few feet. "Turn around."

He wasn't a man—just a teenager. Underfed, dirty, and smelly. A wispy soul patch and a ghost of a mustache. This kid didn't shave every day, and he appeared maybe sixteen. I didn't lower my guard. In three years as a police detective, I'd taken my share of guns and knives from kids younger than this one. The fact that I'd disarmed the kid didn't mean he wasn't dangerous. "How old are you, kid?"

"Eighteen."

"Sure you are." I holstered my pistol, and he relaxed a little. "What's your name?"

The boy stared with lidded eyes, almost apathetic.

"They let you live here?"

The kid shrugged.

I showed him my cellphone. "Maybe I should call the cops and tell them there's a squatter camped out in this building. A squatter with an illegal weapon and illegal drugs in his possession."

The boy raised a hand for me to stop. "Whaddya mean, 'call the cops'? Ain't you a cop?"

"No, I'm a private investigator."

"Then turn off the damned light. The cops might see it. I's not supposed to be here."

"Where are you supposed to be?"

The boy crossed his arms and stared at the ceiling. "If you not a cop, I don't got to talk to you."

"I was a cop until a year ago, and I know guys who would bust you for possession and trespass if I say the word. You want me to do that?"

The boy's shoulders slumped, and I pressed my advantage. "They let you live here?"

"The company don't know. They use the first floor and part of the second. They don't never go up there." He waved towards the stairway. "I comes in at night after they gone, and I's gone in the morning before they gets here. They don't know I exist, and that's the way I like it."

"You here every night?" I figured the kid had witnessed Franco's murder, but with an attitude like a cornered animal, he sure as hell wouldn't tell me about it.

The boy shrugged again.

"Son, it's not a hard question: Are you here every night?"

"I ain't yo' son."

"Figure of speech. What's your name?"

"Sneakers."

"What's it say on your driver's license?"

"Don't got no driver's license."

"Okay, what about your birth certificate? You've got one of those. What's it say on that?"

The boy studied the floor between us. "Bill Clinton Watkins. But don't nobody call me by that name."

I grinned. Good old friendly Chuck. "Okay. Sneakers then. Are you here every night?"

"Got no place else to be. You got a name, man?"

"Chuck McCrary." I didn't offer to shake hands—too dangerous. "If you're not supposed to be here, where are you supposed to be?"

"Ain't supposed to be nowhere."

"Where are your parents?"

Sneakers shrugged.

"Kid, I'm getting annoyed with you shrugging when I ask a question. Where are your parents?"

"My mama, she stays here and there. She don't have no regular place."

"Is she homeless?"

"Mostly." His eyes flared. "She likes to get high and shit like that more than she likes me."

"What about your father?"

Sneakers started to shrug, then thought better of it. "I ain't seen him since I can remember."

I reflected on my own, more Norman Rockwell childhood. Father and mother happily married. Grandparents shooting video and taking pictures at birthdays and holidays. High school graduation. Army Special Forces. College education. I had met kids like Sneakers when I was a cop, but I didn't understand the world they lived in. It was another planet inhabited by aliens whose language I didn't speak. I didn't know what to say, so I nodded. "Did I smell French fries up there?"

Sneakers shrugged.

"I told you not to shrug when I ask you a question."

The boy's eyes flared. "How the hell I know what you smelled, man?"

"You're right—stupid question. Look, I'm a little hungry. I'm going to get something to eat. How about I buy you dinner? I know an all-night diner with a cool waitress and bodacious pie. It's a few blocks away."

"What are you, queer or somethin'?"

"No, I'm straight. I figured you could use a good meal, and I need a favor. I figure a meal would pay you for the favor."

"What's the favor?"

We crossed the parking lot.

When he saw the Silver Ghost, Sneakers jerked to a stop like a dog reaching the end of his chain.

"Those your wheels, man?"

"Yes."

"That's an Avanti, ain't it? Early 60's?"

"It's a 1963 Studebaker Avanti. My grandfather gave it to me as a graduation present."

"High school or college?"

"University of Florida."

"That's a slick ride, dude."

"Thanks. I think so too. My grandfather called it the Silver Ghost. In the 1970s, he put a CB radio in it; Silver Ghost was his handle."

"What's a CB radio?"

Kids nowadays—no sense of history.

Chapter 25

Sneakers slurped the last of the chocolate shake and chased
the final drop around the bottom of the cup with a plastic straw.
He had packed away two double-meat burgers, a large order of
fries, and two slices of pecan pie. He stretched against the back
of the booth.

Veraleesa Kotenay strolled over and patted my shoulder.
Apparently, I was a regular now. "You two get enough to eat?"

I returned her smile. "I'm good, but I could use more
coffee." I regarded the boy. "How about you?"

"I'm good."

Veraleesa went to get the coffee.

Sneakers and I were the only customers in the diner.

"How about that favor now?" I asked.

His eyes narrowed. "I already told you I don't do no blow
jobs."

"And I already told you I'm not gay."

"What you want?"

"A few weeks ago, there was a shooting in front of your
building about 12:30 at night. What did you see?"

"I heard the shots, man. They woke me up, but I didn't see
nothing."

"Okay, I got that, but tonight, when I fired those shots, you
gawked out the window. Did you peek out the window the night
Garrison Franco was shot?"

"That the guy that he killed?"

He clamped a hand over his mouth. Too late.

Sneakers cut his eyes around the room as if seeking an escape.

I held my gaze on the youngster and waited.

Sneakers contemplated the tabletop. "Yeah, man, I looked out the window." He stared at me and narrowed his eyes. "But I didn't see nothing."

I touched his forearm. "Think about it, Sneakers. Any little thing you remember might help. Did you see a car parked in the middle of the street?"

Sneakers pulled his arm away. "Didn't see nothing." He paused a moment. "If you not a cop, why you care?"

"I'm a private investigator. The cops arrested the wrong guy. He hired me to find the real killer." I realized I had leaned forward while I questioned Sneakers. I leaned back, adopted a more relaxed posture, reducing the tension.

"So, this is only a job to you?"

"No, the guy is also a close friend. He can't even afford to pay me."

"Then why you doing it?"

"I told you: The guy they arrested is my friend. I owe him."

"You don't owe nobody nothing."

Veraleesa refilled my cup. "Scoot over, big guy. I gotta hear this." She sat down beside me and set the coffee carafe on the table. "Good ahead, home boy. Tell us how nobody owes nobody nothin'."

That surprised me, but I kept watching Sneakers. "You think I don't owe anybody?"

"Everybody out for theyselves. Everybody know that. Don't nobody look out for nobody else."

"You don't know much about real life, kid," Veraleesa said.

The kid scowled at her. "You don't know nothin' about nothin', bitch."

I raised a hand. "Sneakers, you can't speak that way to my friend."

"What's it to you, man?"

"It's not done. It's rude, crude, and socially unacceptable."

"You think I care about that shit?"

"Someday, if you're lucky, you'll care about that."

The boy laughed. It was not a happy sound. "What planet are you from, dude?"

"Also… if you insult one of my friends, I'll beat the crap out of you." I never raised my voice. Somehow that made it more menacing. The kid stopped laughing.

"Sneakers, I owe lots of people who helped me along the way. People who help me to this day. People like Veraleesa."

The boy seemed a little surprised. "What you owe the bit—her for?"

"Veraleesa helped me find a clue that may help solve the murder case I'm working on." I smiled at her. "And she serves the best pie in Port City."

While I spoke, I had the depressing thought that Sneakers may not have had anyone help him in his entire young life. And where was he now? Living a dead-end life, squatting in a semi-abandoned building. He had barely begun life's adventure and, if he ended up like most kids with his background, he'd be dead or in prison before his thirtieth birthday. "Kid, I know life seems depressing to you, but it doesn't have to stay that way."

Sneakers sneered. "Yeah, ri-i-ight. Tomorrow is another day. The sun will come out tomorrow and all that shit. You sound like one of them stupid people in that stupid play about that stupid orphan."

"You mean *Annie*?"

"Yeah, that the one."

"Where did you see *Annie*?"

Sneakers mumbled, "When I was in school."

"They took you to see *Annie*?"

He smirked. "Yeah, we was being 'culturally enriched.'"

"Sneakers, we both know that no billionaire Daddy Warbucks is going to adopt you. Or me. That doesn't happen in real life."

"You got that right."

"Nevertheless, your life can improve. You can make your life better."

Sneakers half-stood at the table. "Yeah, Whitey. And how would that shit work, huh? I go back to school? How would I get to school? I get a job? Who would hire me? And if they did, how would I get to work?" He grabbed his worn-out shirt with both hands. "These be the only clothes I got, Whitey. Maybe I go back to foster care? They got seven hundred fifty dollars a month from the state to take care of me. They fed me shit like rice and beans once a day, and I had to beg for that. I ran away from them turkeys six months ago."

He pushed his empty dishes aside and crossed his arms on the table. He dropped his face into his arms and his shoulders began to shake.

Veraleesa refilled my cup and stood. She removed the empty dishes. She patted Sneakers on the shoulder and walked to the rear of the diner.

I remembered an Afghan boy, even younger than Sneakers, whose family the Taliban had murdered. That boy had an entire village of friends and extended family to fill the gap. He was never alone.

Sneakers had no one.

"You sure you want to go to the warehouse?"

"Got no place else to go."

I cranked the Avanti. "Buckle your seat belt." I pulled out of the parking lot. "I could take you to the Department of Children and Families. They'd put you up someplace tonight with a real bed."

The boy sneered. "Been there, done that. Don't want no more DCF. You try that shit again, I run away again. You hear me, man?"

"Okay. It's your decision."

"I'm okay with my sleeping bag."

I had slept rough in Afghanistan plenty of times when we were on a mission. I'd never liked it.

"Where'd you get that sleeping bag anyway?"

"I found it in a pile of stuff on the curb outside one of the projects. They was throwing it away."

"That where you got the chairs?"

"Yeah."

"How'd you carry that big chair up two flights of stairs?"

"The guy who give me the grass. He helped me one night."

"Is he a friend?"

"Don't got no friends."

My insides twisted again at the matter-of-fact way the boy announced his aloneness.

"Then why did he help carry it?"

"I run errands for him. He pay me from time to time."

"You carry drugs for him? You his mule?"

Sneakers gawked at me. "What you know about mules?"

"People that drug dealers hire to carry their drugs. If they're juveniles and they're arrested, they get off easy. Is that what you do?"

"Maybe."

"You have any brothers or sisters?"

"Used to have a little sister."

"Used to?"

He spread his hands.

"What happened to her?"

"She dead." He showed no emotion.

I remembered my brother and sisters, all happy and healthy. It took a moment before I could speak. "I'm sorry to hear that. How'd that happen?"

"A shooting on the street. A stray bullet went through the window into our bedroom. Hit her in the chest." The boy spoke matter-of-factly.

I felt terrible for him, not solely for the loss of his sister, but for the boy's lack of emotion while he told the story of his sister's death.

"When did that happen?"

"She was six and I was eight."

"Were you there?"

"I was sleeping on the top bunk. She was on the bottom."

"God, that's horrible."

The boy stared out the window in silence.

I didn't say anything for a while. I drove another couple of blocks before I spoke. "Any other brothers or sisters?"

"Not that I know of."

"Aunts or uncles?"

"My Aunt Desiree, she in prison. Got another aunt. Momma told me she live in Atlanta. Don't remember ever meeting her. My Uncle Detonio, he got shot five years ago. He belong to the wrong gang."

"Any cousins?"

"All dead, in jail, or else gangbangers."

"Why aren't you in a gang?"

For once, Sneakers showed animation. "Those dudes are crazy, man. Everybody know that."

I angled down the alley behind the warehouse and stopped at the pedestrian door. "We're here. Here's my card. If you think of anything else about that shooting, give me a call. Try to stay away from drug dealers. They'll get you killed."

"Can I have my knife back?"

I handed him the switchblade.

Sneakers opened the door.

"Wait." I reached in my pocket and gave him a fifty-dollar bill.

"How I gonna spend a fifty-dollar bill?"

"You're right." I pulled out two twenties and a ten. "Let me change that for you."

He raised his eyebrows. "You sure you ain't queer? Dudes who offer me that much money want me to drop my pants."

I laughed with him. "Tell you what, Sneakers. I'll give you another twenty dollars if you'll do me one more small favor."

He slapped his thighs. "*Haw, haw, haw.* I knew it. Here come the small favor."

"Seriously, Sneakers, I'll give you another twenty dollars if you'll promise me to call them 'gay' from now on."

His eyes widened. "You serious, man?"

"As serious as a drug bust."

"For twenty bucks, I can do that, man. But what's it to you? You ain't quee—gay."

"Most gays find the word insulting and offensive."

"So what? Why you care about them? You ain't one of them."

"How would you feel if someone called Veraleesa a nigger?"

He gazed out the windshield without expression. "That be Veraleesa's problem."

"How about if they called *you* a nigger?"

He frowned. "That's different."

"Maybe you'd feel the same way I feel when someone calls me a spic or a wetback."

"Spic? You ain't no spic. You a white man." He studied me more closely. "A white man with a good tan."

In Spanish I said, "Just because I speak proper English doesn't mean that I'm not a Mexican-American."

"What did you say, man?"

I translated.

"Here's a small life lesson, Sneakers: It's okay to care about people, even people you don't know. It doesn't hurt, and it might help you in the future."

Sneakers walked toward the access door shaking his head and laughing. "You somethin' else, dude."

Chapter 26

I stared out my office window at Bayfront Boulevard, but I didn't see the sunshiny day or the flowers planted on the median or the palm trees that lined the sidewalks. All I saw was Sneakers, a kid on a dead-end street living a dead-end life. A kid without hope. A boy who had never known a "normal" family life. But what was "normal" nowadays? I came from generations of intact families filled with love. Families where marriage came before children. Families where divorce was rare. Families where every child finished high school and most went to college.

Sneakers didn't have a clue how to accomplish anything more than bare physical survival. For him, "long range" meant tomorrow morning.

Who was going to teach this kid? Who even cared about Sneakers?

I called Renate Crowell, a reporter with the *Port City Press-Journal*. I studied her picture on the screen while I waited for the call to go through. When she interviewed me in the hospital for the Simonetti story, she'd insisted that we take each other's pictures for our phone contacts. I figured that my picture on Renate's phone still showed the background of the hospital room.

The phone rang twice and she answered. "Hello, handsome. Did you call to ask me out? My offer to cook dinner at my place still stands."

My heart froze in my chest, and my stomach tied in knots. Ever since middle school, I'd been shy around girls. The last time I spoke to Renate, she'd flirted with me, but she knew I was in a relationship with Terry. Panic-stricken, I stared at the phone and wondered what to say.

"You there, big guy?"

I ignored her question and pretended she had said hello.

"I may have a story for you, Renate."

"Well, that's the next best thing to a dinner invitation. You sure know how to sweet talk a girl. What do you have?"

"Foster care fraud at the Department of Children and Families."

"Old news, hotshot. Everybody knows that DCF is rife with fraud. They have to kill a kid to rate a story in the *Pee-Jay*."

"I found a kid who ran away from his foster home six months ago. The foster parents fed him one meal a day of rice and beans. They collected seven hundred fifty dollars a month to care for the kid. They were collecting money for caring for six other foster kids in a three-bedroom house."

"Maybe," she said. "You have anything else?"

"The kid says the DCF inspector never came to the house the whole time he lived there. You might find that the foster parents still collect their money even though the kid ran away. Just a thought."

"For an amateur, you've found a pretty good angle. What else do you have?"

"The foster parents don't live with the foster children. The foster parents live in the house next door and leave the kids alone every night. The youngest is five. My contact appears about sixteen."

"Oh, jeez. Maybe I can do something. Where can I interview your kid?" she asked.

"You can't; he doesn't want to be found. Maybe you could research him in the public records and trace his so-called foster parents. His name is Bill Clinton Watkins."

"You're kidding."

"Hey," I replied, "my grandparents have neighbors named after Franklin Roosevelt and my parents' next-door neighbor is named after John Kennedy. Why not Bill Clinton?"

"Why not, indeed? Okay, is that all you have? These allegations and the kid's name?"

"They're pretty serious allegations."

Renate waved a hand. "Allegations are a dime a dozen, handsome. They don't make the news unless they involve someone who's rich, famous, or a politician—preferably all three. Then we plaster them all over the front page and rehash them for weeks."

"So young, but yet so cynical. What did you study in college—sarcasm?"

"I majored in skepticism. Don't worry, hot shot. Good thing for you I specialize in making mountains out of molehills. I'm not working anything else hot right now. I'll check it out and get back to you."

Chapter 27

I poured Terry more Chianti and tasted my lasagna.

Terry twirled her spaghetti on a fork and used it to sop up meat sauce. She took a bite and licked her lips as she winked at me. "Lover, you're quiet tonight."

It was time to bite the bullet. I put down my fork. "I found this kid a couple of nights ago. He squats in a warehouse building near the site where Franco was hit."

"What about him?"

"I can't get him out of my mind."

"What's so special about this kid?"

"He's sixteen, he's run away from several years' worth of bad foster homes, and he's been squatting in a partially-occupied warehouse, living hand-to-mouth for the last six months. He has nothing going for him."

Terry sipped her wine. "I don't mean to sound callous, but so what? There are thousands of kids like him in Port City and millions around the world. I'm a cop and you were one. We've seen kids like this before. Why does this one grab you?"

"I feel bad for him. He's not had much schooling, so I don't know how smart he is, except maybe street smart. He's in bad shape physically. He's callous without being tough. He's emotionally stunted—"

"You wouldn't recognize 'emotionally stunted' if it bit you on the ass."

"Hey, I have emotions. I'm a sensitive person, for a barbarian." I sipped Chianti.

She snickered. "Tell me more, Mr. Sensitive."

"Kid's got no friends. His family consists of a junkie mother and other relatives who are dead or in prison. His possessions are a torn sleeping bag, junk furniture, and the clothes on his back—which are ancient, by the way."

My lasagna had passed the taste test. I forked into it.

"And?" Terry prodded.

"The odds are that in five to ten years this kid will be dead or, if he's lucky, in prison. He doesn't know anything about…" I struggled for the right word. "Civilization, maybe? Whatever behaviors or conditions that so-called 'normal' people consider as the real world. He's never even gone to church, other than getting occasional meals at a rescue mission."

"You don't go to church."

"Not true; I attend church regularly."

"I spend nearly every weekend with you. You don't go to church."

"I attend services every Easter, and on Christmas when I visit Mom and Dad in Texas, and every Sunday when I visit my grandparents, either in Texas or Mexico."

Terry smiled. "Easter and Christmas don't qualify as 'regular,' but I'll go with you this Christmas, assuming you take me to meet your folks."

That was a shocker. Of course, Christmas was several months away. A lot could happen between then and Christmas. Was Terry getting as serious about me as I was about her? "I look forward to it. Anyway, Sneakers doesn't know how to hold a fork. He doesn't know the first thing about common courtesy, good manners, or being sociable. No one taught him anything about how life works for the majority of people. He's like one of those urban coyotes—a wild animal that lives in the city but hides from humans. He's… feral? Yeah. You've heard of feral cats? Cats that escaped domestication or were abandoned and returned to a wild state?"

"There's one near my apartment. He hides in the bushes and runs if anyone tries to pet him. One of my neighbors feeds him from time to time. That's why he hangs around."

"That's what Sneakers is like: He's a feral human."

"Are you considering doing anything about him?"

"Don't know yet, but every time I see him, it's like watching a train wreck happening in slow-motion."

Chapter 28

The next time I called Mom and Dad, I told Dad about Sneakers.

"You think he witnessed this hoodlum's murder?"

"He probably did, but he doesn't trust anybody."

"Son, I think your interest in this boy is more than professional. Why does this kid upset you?"

I thought about that for a moment. "The kid's a seed that fell in a crack in the rocks. There was no soil, and it wasn't a good place to grow, but that seed sprouted in spite of the environment. It struggled to survive, but it grew. It grew stunted and twisted, but it grew. I think about his potential and the absolute waste of a human life. That's what galls me."

"*Hmm.* Anything else?"

"Yeah, Dad. Sneakers is the total opposite of me. I had every advantage; he's had no advantages. I have two parents who love me; he doesn't even know his father, and he hasn't seen his mother in forever. I have a good education; he dropped out after eighth grade. Yet he hangs in there and tries."

"And you admire him."

"Yeah. In spite of everything, I admire this kid. I wonder how well I'd survive if I had been born into his conditions."

"Son, I remember you reading one of my detective novels in high school. A character in that book described the hero as a 'knight errant,' and you asked me what that meant. We looked it up together in the dictionary. You remember what it said?"

I smiled at the memory. "It's a knight who travels in search of adventure, to champion the underdog, to right wrongs, and to defend justice. Reading that book inspired me to be a knight errant like that detective in the book."

Dad laughed. "Once you came home from middle school with a black eye and a cut lip. I asked what you fought about. The fight wasn't even about you. You'd fought a school bully to protect a younger kid."

"That's when you signed me up for boxing lessons."

"Ever since you were a boy, I've known that you're an anachronism, a throwback to another time, the age of the knight errant. Whatever your interest in this Sneakers kid, it's not because he might be a witness. You see this kid as an opportunity to make one small piece of the world a better place."

Dad was right, of course. He was always right.

Chapter 29

"Ted Rayburn," I repeated. "Where do I know that name from?"

Dan Murphy squinted at me from across the table. "He was a dirty cop—maybe. But a dirty private eye definitely. It was before your time."

"What's his story?"

Murphy took a huge bite of cookie and chewed. "Rayburn was a narc. He and his partner Benny Benton used to arrest drug dealers. You ever been on a drug bust?"

I set down my Diet Dr. Pepper. "Just once. I was in uniform. I covered the rear in case anyone tried to escape out the back door. It wasn't very exciting. I never even saw the bad guys."

Murphy waved that away. "That's not what I mean. You see, drug dealers don't take credit cards. It's not unusual to find twenty, thirty thousand dollars or more on the site, along with the contraband."

"Sure, everyone knows that."

"Ted and Benny handled dirty, unrecorded cash. I mean, thousands and thousands in unmarked bills." Murphy raised one eyebrow.

I motioned him to go on.

"Some of the dealers that Ted and Benny collared said that the cops confiscated more money than ever found its way into evidence."

"How so?"

"Like the perp says he had forty thousand dollars in his apartment, and Ted and Benny turn thirty thousand into evidence."

"Don't all the perps say that?"

Murphy shook his head. "No, they don't. I mean, it happens sometimes. Cop's word against a drug dealer's. Who's gonna believe a drug dealer? But with Ted and Benny it happened a lot. The thing is, there's no record of how much cash should be there when they're busted. Someone has to count it first. So, who knows what happens before it's counted?"

I made a note. "How much we talking about?"

"They weren't greedy. Five or ten thousand at a time, and only every few months." He paused. "At first. Then it happened more frequently."

"What happened?"

"Ted and Benny busted a dealer who'd done a deal with a Fed undercover narc. The Fed paid the dealer fifty thousand in marked bills. The Feds expected the dealer to split the marked money with his distributor. They were waiting to catch a bigger fish." Murphy ate the last of the cookie and licked his fingers.

"The dealer still had fifty thousand in marked bills when Ted and Benny busted him?"

"Yeah. Half the bills made it into evidence."

"What happened to the other half?"

Murphy laughed. "Some of it was laundered through a casino in Nassau."

"How did the bills wind up in the Bahamas?"

"Ted Rayburn and his wife took a cruise to the Bahamas two weeks after the drug bust. Internal Affairs asked Ted about it and he said it was a coincidence, yada, yada, benefit of the doubt, yada, yada." He shrugged. "Internal Affairs had no provable case, but morally, Ted Rayburn and Benny Benton were toast in the Department."

"What happened to them?"

Murphy smirked. "They were both requested to resign 'for the good of the Department.'"

"Where's Benny now?"

"Last I heard, he landed a job as head of security for a casino on an Indian reservation in Connecticut. A casino. Ain't that ironic?" Murphy laughed. "You see, the rest of the marked bills didn't turn up right away. My guess is that the other half of the missing bills was Benny's share of the cut, and Benny was smart enough to lie low for a while. He launders the bills at various stores around New England. Some bills still turn up at the Federal Reserve Bank in New York."

"Was Jorge the guy who investigated them?"

"Oh, no. Nothing like that."

"Then what's the connection to Jorge? Why is Rayburn on your list of people who want Jorge dead?"

Murphy laughed. "After he resigned from the job, Ted became a private eye, like you."

"So?"

"So, this rich banker's wife hires Ted to catch her husband with his girlfriend. Ted gets the goods on the guy, but Ted has a bright idea. The banker is a lot richer than the wife, so Ted rousts the banker. He shows the guy the evidence, but he offers to keep quiet if the banker pays him more money than the wife is paying. The banker knows a good thing when he sees it, so he pays Ted and Ted tells the wife that the banker is clean."

"When was this?" I asked.

"It was ten or twelve years ago, before you moved to Port City."

"What's that got to do with Jorge?"

"You should ask him."

Chapter 30

Jorge plopped down on a concrete bench shaded by a handful of sabal palms. "Let's sit here, Chuck."

North Beach stretched from the edge of the boardwalk to the ocean.

Jorge crossed his legs. "*Mmm, mmm, mmm.* Take a gander at that one."

"The girl in the red bikini?" I asked.

"No, the one on the blanket to her left. Yellow bikini. Just took her top off. Must be double-D cups."

"Now I see why you wanted to meet here, *amigo.*"

"It's got the best view in the city. Dan and I always have our confabs here."

I slipped on sunglasses against the glare. I could still see well enough to admire Miss Yellow Bikini. "Yeah, well, we still need to take care of business. Tell me about you and Ted Rayburn."

"Why? He's in prison."

"He's out now."

Jorge pulled his gaze away from the beach. "He was sentenced to ten to fifteen years. It hasn't been ten years."

"Prison overcrowding, plus good behavior," I said. "He got out nine months ago."

"I'd forgotten about Ted Rayburn."

"That's why I want to know about him. Dan Murphy said he was fired for stealing drug money, became a private eye, and blackmailed a customer who cheated on his wife."

"All true, as far as it goes." Jorge's eyes drifted back to Miss Yellow Bikini. "Sort of makes life worth living, doesn't it? You think her boyfriend appreciates what he's got? Or should I say, what *she's* got?"

"Business, *amigo*, business."

Jorge twisted toward me—reluctantly, I thought. "Rayburn didn't stop with the banker. He did so well milking that poor schlub that he decided to expand."

"How so?"

"Next time a woman client comes to him with a cheating husband, he tries it again."

My eyes wandered of their own accord to Miss Yellow Bikini. "You think she knows we're watching her?"

Jorge smirked. "I'm not watching *her*; I'm watching *them*."

I *harrumphed*. "That remark displays a sexist, chauvinistic, piggish attitude that is demeaning to women and beneath the dignity of every enlightened twenty-first century man. You ought to be ashamed of yourself."

"And I am indeed truly ashamed, chagrinned, and embarrassed." Jorge grinned. "Of course, she knows we're watching her." He clapped me on the shoulder. "That's why she does it, bro'. That's why she does it. Now who's forgetting about business?"

"Okay, so I'm a red-blooded American boy. Anyway, what happened with the new cheating husband?"

"The guy was an Atlantic County Commissioner with his eyes on the Florida Senate."

"Sounds like a perfect candidate for blackmail."

"He was. Rayburn approaches the Commish with pictures of him and his PR manager walking into a motel room in Orlando. Ted asks the guy for a payoff to keep quiet about the affair."

Jorge leaned toward me. "Here's where it gets good. What Rayburn didn't know was that the PR manager was pregnant and she'd already told the not-too-happy boyfriend. The girlfriend was Catholic and wouldn't have an abortion. The Commish knew that the pregnancy would be obvious in four months regardless. He figured that when the affair came out—and it was bound to come out—his career would be toast regardless of what he did."

"So, the commissioner was immune to blackmail because exposure was inevitable."

"Right, so the daddy-to-be does something smart." Jorge leaned back.

"What did he do?"

"He comes to us to run a sting on Rayburn. The captain assigns it to me. I put a wire on the Commissioner, hand him ten thousand in marked bills, and video him giving the cash to Rayburn. We sent Teddy Rayburn to prison for ten to fifteen years." He laughed.

"What happened to the commissioner?"

Jorge waggled his hand. "So-so. The poor schlub is a hero for helping catch a crooked former cop, and a jerk for knocking up his girlfriend, y'know? Divorce, child support to the girlfriend, and alimony to the ex-wife. He lost his house and his political career and went back to practicing law. Last I heard, he was scrambling to make his alimony payments."

"Who was the commissioner?"

"Armando Acevedo."

I did a quick internet search on my phone. "This is not good, *amigo*." I showed the screen to Jorge. "Acevedo died in a hit-and-run accident last month. The driver hasn't been found."

Chapter 31

Kelly Contreras gazed up from her lunch when Chuck McCrary entered the squad room. Somehow, Chuck brightened her day, no matter why he appeared. She sat up straighter, thrusting her chest out. *For a man who's a top-notch detective, why doesn't he notice me as something more than a cop?*

She set her sandwich aside, and smiled. "Nice to see you, Chuck. Have a seat." She waved him into a chair.

"What do you know about the hit-and-run on Armando Acevedo?"

"Not our case."

Bigs kept eating Chinese takeout at the next desk.

"Maybe it ought to be," Chuck said.

Bigs waved with his chopsticks. "How come?"

Chuck filled them in on Ted Rayburn's history with Jorge Castellano and Armando Acevedo. "Rayburn could have nailed Acevedo with that hit-and-run, and he has the skills to frame Jorge for the Franco hit."

She picked up the rest of her sandwich. "Whaddya think, Bigs?"

Kelly led Bigs and me into Lieutenant Joyce Weiner's office.

The LT nodded at Kelly and Bigs. "Hey, Chuck. Somehow, I don't think this is a social call. Sit down, all of you."

We did.

"This about the Castellano case?"

Kelly briefed the lieutenant on the relationship between Rayburn, Castellano, and Acevedo. "Chuck thinks maybe Ted Rayburn is behind both murders."

Weiner tapped her right index finger on the desk. "Okay. Kelly, you and Bigs find out who's got the Acevedo hit-and-run. Take the case over. You know the drill. Find out Rayburn's whereabouts at the time of the Franco hit and the Acevedo hit-and-run. If he doesn't have two iron-clad witnesses, turn him inside out."

Chapter 32

I had promised Darcy Yankton to run everything by her, and so far, her contribution to Jorge's defense had been to shoot down every idea I had. Nevertheless, I went to her office.

"Darcy, I may have a witness to the murder."

She opened a notepad. "Now we're getting somewhere. Who is it?"

"His name is Bill Clinton Watkins. He was squatting in the top floor of a warehouse that overlooks the crime scene."

"Squatting? What does that mean?"

"He's a sixteen-year-old kid who ran away from his foster home six months ago. The company that rents the warehouse uses the bottom two floors. The kid found a way into the third floor and that's where he was living when I found him. He's like a stowaway in the building; the owners don't even know he's there."

"Where is he now?"

"Still squatting in the warehouse."

"You didn't turn him over to DCF?"

"I promised I wouldn't. It's a long story."

"The law is clear on that. He's a minor. Call DCF."

"If I do that, he'll never trust me," I said. "And he'll never tell what he knows."

She dropped her pen on the desk. "Damn it, I warned you about taking the law into your own hands. This is exactly the kind of cowboy behavior that makes me regret engaging you as my investigator. You're breaking about a dozen laws, you know."

Shooting me down again. "Darcy, the kid sleeps on the floor, begs in the streets, and works as a drug mule, all while he fends off sexual predators who want to take advantage of him."

"You see? That's no way to live. Call DCF."

"Despite all that, he told me that if I reported him to DCF, he'd run away again. Cut me some slack, will you? I'm the good guy here. Cracking a murder case is more important than ratting out a teenager."

She scowled but picked up her pen again. "Okay, okay. What did he see?"

"So far, he hasn't confided in me. The shots woke him up, and he looked out the window. But, so far, he claims he didn't see anything."

Before she could shoot me down again, I plowed ahead. "Counselor, the kid doesn't trust anybody. He hates the cops, he hates the system, he has no friends, no family, and no future. He'll come around once he gets to know me."

"You're Mr. Charming all right."

"It's a gift."

"What do you *think* he saw?"

"Based on a remark he let slip, I'm convinced he saw the killer."

"And when do you think he'll tell you what he saw?"

I shrugged. "How long is a piece of string?"

"What the hell does that mean?"

"It means that it takes as long as it takes."

"Look, cowboy, our case is weak to non-existent so far. A teenage runaway who hates the system will not make a credible witness. And I recently learned that the prosecuting attorney is Mabel the Marauder."

"The DA took this case personally? I thought she delegates everything."

"This is an election year. She could use a high-profile scalp to wear on her belt for her reelection campaign. This case grabs headlines: *Cop Turned Cop-Killer* headlines."

Chapter 33

Terry and I had good seats behind the third base dugout. A former cop buddy who ran security for the Port City Pilots scored the tickets for me. The rain had stopped an hour before the first pitch, but the humidity still drooped oppressively in the summer evening. By the second inning, my shirt would be plastered to my back.

"God, the humidity must be a hundred and ten percent," Terry said.

"That's why God gave mankind beer."

Terry laughed. She pointed to the players on the field. "Tell me again: Who is that other team, the ones with that ridiculous cartoon on their sleeves?"

"Those are the Cleveland Indians."

"Indians. Don't the real Indians find that cartoon image offensive?"

"Probably some do."

"Why doesn't someone make the team change its name?"

"I think it has something to do with the First Amendment. This is America, with a capital A, and we have the right to offend anybody we want."

"You joke about everything."

"Baseball is not supposed to be serious. Until the playoffs." I sipped a draft beer, my second.

"Don't they sell Pinot Grigio?"

"Such outrageous thoughts." I gave her a wide-eyed expression. "Wash your mouth out with soap, woman. This is baseball. You're *supposed* to drink beer."

"I don't like beer. How can you drink that stuff?"

"Practice. Years and years of dedicated practice." I took a drink to demonstrate my dedication.

Terry gestured with her beer cup. "That woman over there has white wine. They must sell it here."

"She's a revolutionary. We won't speak of her; it would encourage the decline and fall of civilization."

"Well, I'm bored and you owe me big time for this."

"I'll give you a full-body massage later."

"Will you start with my feet?" She batted her eyes.

"If that's part of your body."

"I like the game better already."

The designated hitter for the Port City Pilots smashed a double into left center. He drove in three runs, putting the Pilots up seven to six. Everyone in the stands stood and cheered.

Terry stood with the rest of the crowd, but she didn't cheer. "Why did we stand up?"

"It's like a standing ovation at a concert. Ozzy Richmond hit a double and drove in three runs."

"Oh, I know what a double is. It's when the hitter gets to second base."

I patted her on the shoulder. "You're catching on."

"Would you like to get to second base? Maybe a home run?" She rubbed my back as we sat down.

"Later, absolutely. Right now, let's enjoy the game." I sipped my beer.

"Earlier you said you wanted to talk about the boy you found in the warehouse the other night. The kid with the funny name."

"Sneakers. Let's talk about him after the game."

"What kind of name is Sneakers?"

"Nickname, street name, I don't know what you'd call it, but we can discuss it at great length… after the game."

Juice Ball Cordoba hit a long fly to the warning track in deep left field for the third out. The Pilots grabbed their gear and took to the field, hanging on to a one-run lead. The top of the Indians' batting order was coming up.

"What's his real name?" Terry asked.

"Juice Ball? It's Gerald Cordoba."

"No, I mean your kid, Sneakers."

"Bill Clinton Watkins."

"What's wrong with that name? Not cool enough?"

"Beats me. He says 'don't nobody call me that name.'" I figured out Terry's game, and it wasn't baseball. "You're not going to let this wait until after the game, are you?"

"Can't you talk to me and watch the game at the same time?"

"Sweetheart, when I talk to you, you deserve my full attention. I don't want to be distracted by other things… like watching a baseball game."

"You're pretty good at this, you know."

"Good at what?"

"Telling me to shut up about the kid, but saying it diplomatically." She patted my thigh. She left her hand on my leg and stroked it gently. She knew exactly the reaction she would get.

I surrendered, gracefully I hoped, and squeezed her hand. "Okay. Let's talk about Sneakers."

"What about him?"

"The kid has no one. It's like he was raised in the woods by bears. He begs on the street and scrounges food from dumpsters behind restaurants when he doesn't have enough money for a Big Mac. And he hides from the world every night on the top floor of a partially-occupied warehouse."

"That's sad."

"Statistically, Sneaker has no chance of living a life that you or I would consider normal."

The crowd cheered and I jumped up to see an Indian hit a pop fly. One down.

I sat down. "He'll be dead or in prison by the time he's thirty, unless somebody takes an interest in him."

"And that somebody would be you?"

"Maybe." I stared at my beer cup, twirled it in my hands. "I won't feel right if I stand by and watch this kid get flushed down the toilet because no one ever cared about him. He doesn't deserve that."

Terry sipped her beer, made a face. "No one deserves that, but it happens all the time."

"I know. It's just…"

Another cheer after the second Indian batter grounded out to first.

"Chuck, what do you intend to do about this kid?"

"I'm not sure what I *can* do. I'm not a guidance counselor. I'm not his family. I'm not a foster parent. I'm not qualified to rescue a child."

"Not true, baby. You have no *training* to rescue a child, but you've made it your life's work to rescue people, even when you make it up as you go along."

"True enough."

"If you rescue this kid, how would that affect us?"

Uh-oh, here it was: the question I had been dreading. "Uncertain. Whatever I do, it would take a few nights and weekends away from our time together."

She leaned against my arm. "I'm pretty possessive, you know."

"And I am delighted about that."

"Seriously, what good could you do for Sneakers?"

"I've thought about that. I could buy him good books to read. Maybe enroll him in a private tutoring program. I'm not sure, Queens."

"And where and how would he meet the tutor. That plan is not doable, and we both know it. Keep thinking."

Dipsy Donohue fanned the last Indian. It was bottom of the eighth and the Pilots' turn at bat.

She sipped her beer. She was on her first beer, and it was the eighth inning. Terry obviously knew nothing about the game's hallowed traditions.

I decided to get a third beer and asked Terry to be the designated driver.

She agreed and the Pilots threw the Indians out on a double play in the top of the ninth. The Pilots won seven to six.

Terry merged the Avanti into the line of cars exiting the garage. "I feel bad about this kid too, lover, but there are thousands of boys and girls—maybe millions—just like him. Don't you feel bad about those kids too?"

"Yeah, but I don't *know* them. I ate a meal with this kid."

"You bought the meal too," she said.

"That's beside the point. We had a real conversation that meant something."

"So, have you decided what you're going to do for him?"

I fell silent while I thought about Terry's question. "Well, I can't adopt him."

"What about the Department of Children and Families?"

"He's been there, done that. Won't go through it again."

We drove on in silence. Terry merged onto the causeway over Seeti Bay toward Port City Beach and my condo. "It's not like you to let things hang, lover. You have this passion to do something, *anything*, even if it's wrong."

"Yeah. Rule Sixteen: *Sometimes you have to do something, even if it's wrong. At least you'll know you tried.* This thing has me stumped."

"Okay. So, what *are* you going to do?"

I sighed. "I don't see any alternative but to give you a full-body massage."

I finished Terry's massage, but my heart wasn't in it. Neither was another important part of my body. "I'm sorry, babe. Maybe in the morning."

"That's okay, lover. I can tell this thing with Sneakers bothers you."

"I'm used to being bothered. It goes with the territory. There will always be people I can't save. I got used to that when I was a cop. I'm sure you did too."

"We get used to it because it eats us up if we don't. Mother Weiner always says, 'You can't save them all. Your job is to serve and protect the ones in front of you. You're not a missionary.'"

Terry put her hand on my forearm.

I kissed it lightly. "On the other hand, this kid may have witnessed the Franco murder."

Chapter 34

After sunset, I parked at the warehouse where Sneakers squatted. I flashed the Maglite across the third-floor window. He came to the window. I pointed toward the rear of the building and walked around to the pedestrian door.

Sneakers came out. "What you want, man?"

"A piece of pecan pie from the Day and Night Diner. How about I buy you dinner again?"

"You don't have to ask me twice." He pronounced "ask" as "ax."

Veraleesa waved at us when we walked in. "Hello, gentlemen. Sit anywhere. I'll be with you in a second."

This time when Sneakers read the menu, I watched his eyes. He seemed to be a good reader, but I needed to know for sure.

After Veraleesa took our order, I pulled a newspaper clipping from my pocket. "This is from the Sports Section of the *Pee-Jay.*"

"What's the *Pee-Jay?*"

"The *Port City Press-Journal.*" I realized the boy had never read a newspaper. I handed him the clipping. "Here, read this."

The boy shrugged and smoothed out the clipping on the tabletop.

I put my hand on the paper. "Would you read it aloud, please?"

"Why for?"

"Because I asked you to and because I bought dinner again. Is that a good enough reason? Humor me."

"Okay, man. That ain't much to ask." He began to read the article aloud. He read it well and didn't stumble over any of the words.

He finished and handed the clipping back.

"Keep it if you like."

He shrugged and stuffed it in his shirt pocket. "What's this shit about?"

"My girlfriend Terry and I went to that game last night."

Sneakers sat a little straighter. "No shit, man?" This was the first time in our acquaintance that he had shown the slightest interest in anything. Maybe baseball could be the key to open his eyes.

"Would you like to go to a game sometime?"

"With you?"

"With me."

Sneakers smirked. "You sure you ain't *gay*?"

"I have a hot girlfriend to prove it."

"Would she come with us?"

"No. She suffers from a bad upbringing that left her with no interest in baseball."

"What's that 'bad upbringing' shit?"

"It was a joke. 'Upbringing' means the way a person is raised. The joke implies that a good upbringing includes instilling in your children a love for baseball. It implies that anyone who doesn't share my interest in baseball is... misguided." I smiled. "In fact, my girlfriend's parents raised her very well. I hate to admit it, but it's okay not to love baseball. She and I have lots of other things in common."

"So, what's the joke, dude?"

"You don't think it's funny even after I explained it?"

"Nope."

"I get that a lot."

"Can I still go to a game?"

The Pilots had left town for a week of away games, but I promised Sneakers I would buy tickets for the next home series. I confirmed their schedule on my phone and picked a game for the next Sunday. That would give me a chance to spend Saturday and Saturday night with Terry.

I gave him fifty dollars in small bills when I let him off at the warehouse. I wished I could do more. This boy needed more than money.

"I sure am glad you ain't gay, man."

Chapter 35

I waved at a chair and Bigs sat down. He looked tired. That wasn't like him.

Kelly had called from their car to make sure I was in the office. Said she and Bigs had news about Ted Rayburn. She hadn't said whether it was good news or bad news, but she sounded unhappy.

Kelly remained standing.

Maybe she wanted to gaze out the window, or maybe she wanted to be far away when her partner told me why they had come.

Bigs started. "The good news, Chuck, is that Rayburn doesn't have an alibi for the night of the Franco murder or the Acevedo hit-and-run."

"And the bad news?"

"Neither do ninety percent of the people in South Florida. Hell, the ME placed the time of Franco's death at between 11:00 p.m. and 3:00 a.m. Nobody has an alibi for that time of night. Samey-samey for the Acevedo hit."

I said, "Unless they're guilty and arrange a fake alibi."

Bigs almost smiled. "Unless that."

"Bigs, the LT told you and Kelly to turn him inside out if he didn't have two iron-clad witnesses."

Kelly spoke up. "We did, Chuck. We grilled the SOB for three hours. He laughed at us. Remember, he was a cop. He knows his rights, he knows the law, and he knows police procedure. He said if we had any evidence, we would have asked him about it specifically."

"What about the Acevedo hit-and-run?"

"Same thing. He admitted he hated Acevedo's guts. Admitted he was glad the guy was dead. He said Acevedo's ex-wife feels the same way and asked why we weren't investigating her for the hit."

"You try the phantom witness?"

"Rayburn *invented* the phantom witness trick. If we claimed to have a witness who placed him near the crime scene, he would demand to know who it was. He would lawyer up, and the lawyer would demand to see the video of the witness interview." Kelly shook her head. "Couldn't use the phantom witness."

"Bottom line," said Bigs, "is that Kelly and I are out of options." His shoulders slumped. "We wanted to tell you in person. I feel bad about this, but we have to put the Rayburn investigation on the shelf."

I had expected that. I already had a Plan B.

Chapter 36

It was 3:30 on a partly cloudy afternoon by the time Sneakers and I made our way to the Port City Pilots Stadium parking garage. The Detroit Tigers had beaten the Pilots seven to two.

"Let this be a lesson, Sneakers: Life is full of disappointments. One must learn to take them in stride."

"You joke about everything, man?"

"Pretty much."

"But you don't always laugh or smile when you joke."

"That's right; people call it deadpan humor or dry humor."

"How can I tell when you're joking?"

"Sometimes you can't tell when someone is joking. There's an old saying: 'There's many a true word spoken in jest.' Sometimes a person appears to be joking but they mean exactly what they say."

"But what about you?"

"Put what I say—what anyone says for that matter—in context. Ask yourself how it fits with other stuff they've said and other stuff you already know. If you still can't decide, ask me."

"Does that mean you're going to keep coming around?"

There it was. "Let's talk about that later."

Sneakers' eyes narrowed as he considered my answer. "Okay. Where we going now?"

I was encouraged by his questions. Until now, he had been passive in our interactions, allowing me to take the lead, and seldom questioning anything.

"I'm hungry. Those two hot dogs wore off. You hungry?"

"I'm always hungry."

I nearly laughed, then realized that he meant it literally. "Let's try someplace you haven't eaten. You ever eaten Cuban food?"

"Don't think so. How do I know if I'll like it?"

"You might not. But, if you don't, you can order something else. Fair enough?"

I jumped onto the westbound toll road and drove Sneakers toward the newer part of Port City out near the Everglades.

We discussed the finer points of baseball like any two fans would. Whether it made sense to steal second with one out. Was it better to bunt down the third base line or the first base line? What were the merits of the designated hitter rule, if any?

I didn't know where Sneakers learned about baseball, but he knew a lot.

When we headed west, late afternoon thunderclouds built up ahead of us.

The toll road fed onto a boulevard lined with palm trees and flowers planted in the green strip in the center.

I asked, "You ever been to this part of the city?"

"I never been nowhere." He paused, then added, "except to see that musical *Annie.*"

I laughed.

"Was that dry humor?" Sneakers asked.

"Exactly. Keep it up and you'll be a real comedian like me."

"If that's more dry humor, it ain't funny."

I hung a left onto a residential street while thunder growled in the distance. Lightning bolts smacked the horizon out in the Everglades.

The next block had an "Open House" sign stuck in the yard. I parked the Avanti at the curb. "Let's take a tour."

"I thought we was gonna eat."

"We will, but let's take a side trip first."

"Why, man? It look like rain."

"You afraid you'll melt if you get wet? Come on, you'll have fun."

I had researched the new neighborhood the previous afternoon. The young man I spoke to the previous day stood in the door. He wore shiny loafers with no socks, pressed khakis, and a neat golf shirt with a real estate broker's logo embroidered on it. He wore a neatly trimmed beard and had close-cropped hair. He was the same height as Sneakers and me and in his late twenties. I was secretly pleased to see that he was black. Maybe Sneakers could relate to him.

"How do you do, gentlemen? Welcome to our open house. I'm Tarvius Russell." He shook hands. "Here's an information sheet." He handed out a sheet with color pictures on one side and information about the house on the other. "Would you follow me, please?"

Russell led us on a brief but thorough tour. He covered all three bedrooms, both bathrooms, the fenced backyard, and the two-car garage.

Sneakers didn't say a word, but his head gyrated like it was on a swivel while he walked into every closet, every room. He stepped into the backyard and took in the cedar fence and the back patio.

Scattered raindrops fell and Sneakers scurried under the aluminum roof over the back patio where Tarvius and I were standing. The rain made a peaceful drumming sound.

When the real estate agent finished the tour, he returned us to the living room, "Any questions?"

"Tarvius," I asked, "what kind of people can afford to live in a house like this?"

"See that house across the street with the blue Camry in front?"

Sneakers and I both rotated in that direction.

"It's pretty much the same floor plan as this house and the same price. I sold that to a young couple last month. She's a hospital orderly. He's an auto mechanic. They have two children."

"Do either of them have a college degree?"

"No, they don't. I remember helping them with their loan application."

"Did they finish high school?"

"Yes, they both went to Wekita Springs High School. In fact, I believe that's where they met."

"Thanks, Tarvius, I owe you one." I handed him a business card.

When we were back in the Avanti, Sneakers stared ahead in silence until we arrived at the Cuban restaurant.

We scurried through the rain and took a table inside.

Sneakers stared at the menu. "I don't know what any of this stuff is."

I pointed at a picture on the menu. "I'm having the *boliche mechado*. It's a Cuban *carne asada*."

"Don't know what that is neither."

"Sorry. Pot roast. I think you'll like it. It comes with three side orders. I'm for sure ordering *maduros*, which are sweet plantains. Do you know what those are?"

Sneakers made no sign.

"A plantain tastes like a cooked banana. Real sweet. I'm also having *yuca*, like a stringy potato, but with garlic, and yellow rice. Try those too."

Sneakers eyeballed the menu, but he didn't see it. He remained unexpressive, but I sensed a strong emotion bubbling beneath the surface. I just didn't know which one.

"My friend, I try to make life an adventure. I'm always learning new things, trying new things, meeting new people, and going new places." I waited until Sneakers raised his gaze to me.

"You have nothing to lose. If you don't like a dish, we'll order something else, or we'll go to the diner."

Sneakers shrugged.

The *boliche mechado* came and I noticed that Sneakers didn't know how to hold a knife properly. He managed to cut the meat, but it was hard to watch. I made another mental note for Sneakers's education on how the world works.

Sneakers liked the plantains and the yellow rice. He took one sniff of the yuca and pushed it aside. I can always eat more yuca.

For dessert, I ordered *flan* and let Sneakers try a bite.

Sneakers ordered the key lime pie instead.

The server cleared the empty dishes and I ordered two Cuban coffees.

Sneakers had been quiet ever since we left the open house, speaking no more than he had to.

I let the silence stretch while we sipped the strong black coffee. I knew Sneakers wanted to say something but had not yet found the words.

He sighed. "Why you doin' all this, man?"

"Doing what?"

His eyes flashed. "Being so goddamn nice to me, man. Buying me food, giving me money, taking me to a baseball game, for crissakes. Why you doin' all that?" He pounded a fist on the table. "What's in it for you?"

I counted to five before answering. "Why do you think I'm doing it?"

"Shit, I don't know, man. That's why I asked."

"To tell you the truth, I do it because I can—because it's the right thing to do. This afternoon I wanted to show you what's possible. For you."

Tears streaked the kid's cheeks. He hid his face. His shoulders shook.

Chapter 37

While I waited for Sneakers's tears to subside, I thought about life and hope and opportunity. Why *was* I doing these things for Sneakers? It was more than him being a potential witness.

Right then, I made a potentially life-changing decision. Life-changing for three lives. Terry wouldn't like it, but that's life.

Sneakers raised his head, his cheeks traced with tear tracks. "I'm okay."

"Sneakers, I'm going to ask you a stupid question, but I want you to think carefully before you answer. Okay?"

"Okay, I guess."

"How do you like your life so far?"

The youngster scowled. "How you think I like it, man?"

"A wise man once said, 'If you keep doing what you've been doing, you'll keep getting the same results.' Do you take my meaning?"

"I think so. If you want to get anywhere, you have to get movin'. You can't stay in the same old place, doing the same old shit."

"Right. This afternoon I showed you what an average guy, with average luck, and an average education can accomplish. You are far above average. You could accomplish even more. If you do something different with your life, you'll see better results."

He regarded me with narrowed eyes. "What you got in mind?"

"You remember that discussion when we first met about whether anybody owes anything to anybody?"

"What about it?"

"Those people I owe, a lot of them taught me how to live, how to do what I do, and how to get what I want. I'd like to teach you what they taught me. Would you like to learn how to get what you want?"

"I don't want nothin'."

"Then you're already a big success, because that's what you've got—nothing. You've achieved all your life goals, then?"

"Why you wanna do that, man?"

"Do what?"

"Ask me all these questions about life and goals and shit."

"Everyone needs goals. You need to want something bad enough to do something different to get it. As far as I can tell, you're not living. You exist from one day to the next, waiting for the ax to fall."

"Why should you care, man?"

"My friend, I can never pay back the people I owe, but I can pay it forward if I teach someone else what they taught me. And here you are. For the first time in your life, you caught a break. You're in the right place at the right time." I smiled. "You want to change your life? Make it an adventure?"

Sneakers thought for a moment. He shrugged. "Like you say, man, I ain't going nowhere now. What do I do?"

"You're coming to stay with me for a while. I'll be your mentor."

"What's that?"

"I'll give you a dictionary when we get home. You can look it up."

Sneakers grinned. "You sure you ain't gay?"

As we drove across the causeway, the rain stopped and the high-rise buildings along Port City Beach came into view, sharp-edged in the crisp afternoon sunlight. The clouds over the Everglades parted, and a rainbow painted the eastern horizon. I hoped it was an omen.

"You live over there, man?"

"Yeah. See the building with the red and blue stripes? The one with all the balconies?" I pointed.

"Yeah."

"I live on the fourteenth floor."

When I unlocked the door, Sneakers ran to the glass sliding doors. I showed him how to unlock the sliders, and we stepped onto the balcony. The rainbow was slowly fading.

Sneakers pointed out to sea. "How far you see from here?"

"About twenty-five miles. Those ships you see are six miles out, in the Gulf Stream."

The boy rotated to the west. "Is that my neighborhood over there?"

"Yeah."

"Cool."

"C'mon. I'll show you around. Then you can pick your room."

"My room?"

"I'm giving you one of my guest rooms."

"You got more than one?"

"I have two—and an office. Take your pick which one you want."

"I never had my own room before."

When we finished, we sat on the balcony and watched the sun dip toward the Everglades.

"Man, I didn't know you was rich."

"I expect to be rich one day, but I'm not there yet. Okay, enough about me. Let's have your first lesson. How to speak proper English."

"I speak English."

"I said proper English. Did you notice the way Tarvius Russell spoke?"

"Whaddya mean?"

"Did he speak like the people in the neighborhood where you grew up?"

"No, he talk white."

"He doesn't talk white. He speaks standard English."

"You understand me okay."

I leaned my backside to the rail. "What does a dog do when it meets another dog?"

Sneakers laughed. "It smells the other dog's butt."

"Why do you suppose it does that?"

He shrugged. "That's what dogs do."

"What about when a dog meets another animal, say a cat or a horse? Even a human?"

"It smells them too."

"That's right. Why?"

"Beats me, man."

"Animals rely on their sense of smell to decide whether another animal is their kind. They recognize their own kind by the way they smell." I waited to see if he understood.

"Yeah, is this dog from the neighborhood? Is this cat a friend? Shit like that."

"Right," I said. "Animals rely on smell. Humans rely on language to tell if another person is like them. We decide whether other people are like us by the way they talk. What did you know about Tarvius Russell the minute he opened his mouth?"

Sneakers beamed. "He not from my 'hood."

"There you go. You knew something important about Tarvius instantly. Did he talk like you? Was his accent the same or different? Did he use the same vocabulary?"

"I got it. Tarvius don't talk white. He talk regular English, like Barrack Obama."

"Bingo. To join the middle class, it helps to talk like the middle class."

"Ain't that phony?"

"It's common courtesy. When I'm in Mexico, I speak Spanish. When I was in Afghanistan, I spoke Pashto. If I were in France, I would speak French if I could. It's the same thing."

"You was in Afghanistan?"

"Yeah. Special Forces."

"Is that the Green Berets?"

"Yeah, people call us either name."

Sneakers stared at me. "Those Green Berets are tough mothers."

"Yeah, we are."

Sneakers thought about that. "You gonna teach me how to talk good and shit like that?"

"Yep. And the first thing is: Don't say 'shit' anymore."

"Why not?"

"Most people find it offensive and will think less of you."

"I think those people full of... crap."

I laughed. Sneakers was developing a sense of humor.

I made Chicken Marsala for a late dinner. The meal at the Cuban restaurant was two hours before. Besides, Sneakers was underweight. Sneakers observed from the other side of the kitchen island while I cut the chicken breasts into small strips.

"Where you learn to do shit like that?"

"Please say that again in proper English."

He chose each word carefully. "Where did you learn to cook?"

"My parents taught me most of it when I was a boy."

"I don't never remember my mother cooking."

We would take up double negatives another time. I didn't want to push too much, too soon.

Chapter 38

Monday morning, I took Sneakers to a men's clothing store where I had always wanted to shop but could never afford to until I hit it big with the Simonetti case.

Bobby Trafalgar saw us walk in. He wore a dark gray, pin-striped suit with a striped tie and matching handkerchief. His light blue dress shirt had a white collar and French cuffs.

"Hey, Chuck. Who's your friend?"

"Bobby Trafalgar, I'd like you to meet Bill Watkins."

Sneaker jerked his head toward me. His eyes widened.

Bobby stuck out his hand. "Nice to meet you, Bill."

Sneakers stared at it a moment before slowly extending his own.

Bobby shook the boy's hand. "What can I do for you, Bill?" he said, but he glanced at me for the answer.

"Bill needs everything. From underwear on out. This is your lucky day, Bobby."

Sneakers wore a new outfit. I gestured at his old clothes on the counter. "What would you like to do with these? Throw them away? Burn them? Give them to the poor?"

"The poor wouldn't want 'em, man. Let's let Bobby toss 'em."

We stacked boxes and packages on the counter. The stack got taller and we began a second stack, then a third.

Bobby totaled the bill, and Sneakers stared at the cash register. His eyes grew wide again. He stared at me like I was the Wizard of Oz. "You sure you not Daddy Warbucks?"

I smiled and gave Bobby a credit card. "I'll help you with the packages, *Bill*." I smiled at Bobby. "Maybe you could help us carry this?"

Sneakers scowled but grabbed a stack of boxes.

"What the fuck is this 'Bill' shit, man?" he said when we arrived at the van.

"My bad. I forgot to discuss your name with you. But before we do, there's another word you need to stop using. Guess what it is."

He smiled. "Yeah, yeah, yeah. Don't say 'fuck' no more."

"Right. You might have said, 'What the heck is this Bill stuff, man?' Got it?'

"Big fuckin' deal," the kid said. He laughed. "Couldn't resist. That was the last time, I promise."

"Okay." I started the van.

"I thought we was gonna talk about this Bill stuff."

"We will." I punched the A.C. onto *max*.

"Sports stars often have unusual nicknames," I said. "Some of them are a lot more unusual than Sneakers."

"Like Juice Ball Cordoba on the Pilots?" Sneakers asked.

"Right, but we ordinary people need a real name or conventional nickname for us to be respected. You're named after a president of the United States. By the way, his name isn't Bill Clinton. It's William Jefferson Clinton. Bill is an example of an acceptable conventional nickname. So is Chuck for Charles or Carlos. Barack Obama's nickname before he ran for president was Barry, also a good nickname."

"I don't like Bill. And I sure as hell don't like Clinton."

"Since President Clinton's real name was William Jefferson Clinton, it would be an easy matter to change your name to that. Do you like Will or Jeff?"

"What about Clint?" Sneakers said.

"I like it. That's a good masculine name."

"Clint. Clint. Clint Watkins." He tried the name out. "Hello, my name is Clint Watkins. That sound pretty good." He grinned and stuck out his hand. "How do you do? My name is Clint Watkins."

"Hello, Clint. My name is Chuck McCrary. I'm pleased to meet you."

We shook hands, acknowledging that our new adventure had begun.

It took two trips to carry Clint's new gear to the condo.

Clint set the boxes on his bed and lifted the tops off one or two. He dumped the contents of the sacks on his bed and stared at his new clothes, hands on his hips.

I gathered that he didn't have a clue how to hang clothes in a closet, how to put things in a chest of drawers, or even what went in the closet and what belonged in a drawer. This feral human had never been exposed to the concept of having a wardrobe.

I showed him that pants and sports shirts went in the closet; socks and underwear and pajamas went in a drawer. I demonstrated how to hang pants to keep the creases sharp, how to separate pants, jackets, and shirts. I taught him how to sort underwear and socks in a drawer and where to put shoes in a closet.

I had learned this basic stuff so early in childhood that I didn't remember learning it. I had to rethink how to teach it to someone else. It opened my eyes about how far Clint and I needed to travel.

I snapped my fingers. "Damn. I forgot about sports coats, dress shirts, ties, and suits. And dress shoes. We'll think about those tomorrow. Right now, let's have lunch. I'll grill burgers."

I showed Clint how to light the grill.

Clint watched me prepare the meat patties and sprinkle the salt, pepper, and garlic powder on them. I made eight patties and stuck four of them in the fridge for another time. "I'm going to grill the burgers. Want to come?"

"No, man. I'll make the salad while you gone." He grinned. "I watched you do it the last time."

When I came back, lettuce scraps and tomato juice were scattered across the kitchen island and the floor, but Clint had a serviceable salad ready. And iced tea.

After lunch, we cleaned up both the dishes and the mess Clint had made. We had a good laugh about it.

"Okay, Clint. I have to meet a guy who may have a lead on a case I'm working on. Put on your workout clothes and I'll take you to our gym on my way to work."

"What I gonna do there?"

"You're going to work out. Kennedy Carlson, the owner, will show you how. Ken is gay, and he's one of my best friends. Don't screw this up and piss him off."

Chapter 39

Dan Murphy was waiting at a table in Java Jenny's, munching a giant chocolate chip cookie when I walked in. He waved me over.

"Did Jorge tell you about Ted Rayburn?"

I pried off the lid to my coffee and added half-and-half. "Jorge and I had a *revealing* discussion sitting on a bench on the North Beach boardwalk. Pun intended."

"Revealing?" Murphy laughed. "I get it. The topless beach, right? He always meets me there too. He must not get enough at home. Must be why he tomcats around."

"Jorge does that?"

"Yeah, sure. Everybody likes a little strange once in a while. Why should Jorge be any different? What did he tell you about Rayburn?" He popped another bite of cookie in his mouth and wiped his chin.

"Jorge didn't know that Rayburn had been released from prison." I sipped my coffee.

"I didn't know myself until a month ago. Another cop told me he'd seen Rayburn on the street." He bit off more cookie. "Man, this is good."

"I have to get one of those. Be right back."

I thought about Murphy and Rayburn and Jorge while I walked to the counter. I bought two cookies and returned to the table.

"Here, Dan. I wouldn't want you to suffer."

Murphy grinned when I handed him the cookie. "There's always room for one more."

I unwrapped mine. "When I was with Jorge, I Googled Armando Acevedo. Less than a week after Rayburn was released from prison, someone killed Acevedo in a hit-and-run."

Murphy bit into the cookie. When he spoke, crumbs flew from his mouth. "Acevedo. That's the politician who helped Jorge with the sting. I'd forgotten his name. He's dead?"

"Yeah. Mother Weiner reassigned the hit-and-run case to Kelly Contreras and Bigs Bigelow, since they're in charge of Jorge's case."

"You think Rayburn murdered Acevedo?"

"Who knows?" I shrugged. "Anyway, Kelly and Bigs interrogated him. They got nothing and they had to let it drop."

"I didn't know about Acevedo." Murphy's eyes narrowed. "Maybe I can help you with that."

"How?"

"Let me think about it. I might have a surprise for you."

Chapter 40

Snoop eyed me from the table at Fat Tummy's, a local greasy spoon. "You're late, Chuck. I already ordered. I was afraid I would have to buy my own lunch." He had eaten half of a double-decker hamburger.

I dragged out a chair. "That'll be the day when you buy your own lunch. Besides this is the cheapest place in town. Why do you want to eat here when there are better, healthier places?"

"Nobody else has the Heart-Stopper hamburger."

A server handed me a menu, but I didn't need it. "I'll have a medium Sweep-the-Floor Vegetarian Pizza on whole wheat crust and unsweetened iced tea with a lemon wedge. Thanks." I handed the menu back and the server left.

Snoop took a long drink of his beer. "What's going on?"

I told Snoop what I'd learned about Ted Rayburn. "I need you to find out where Rayburn lives now. What does he do for a living? Does he have an office? Does he work alone or with somebody? What vehicles does he own? License plate numbers, etc. You know the drill."

"Sure. But why not ask Kelly or Bigs?"

"Acevedo is their case, and Rayburn is a person of interest. They are sworn Law Enforcement Officers; I'm not a LEO anymore. If they help me on this case, and I turn up something useful, it might be inadmissible because of chain of evidence considerations, due process, or unreasonable searches. Whatever nit-picky crap that a good defense attorney might claim. I don't want to complicate their investigation. You sound like you don't want the work."

Snoop blotted his mouth with a napkin. "I'm always in the market for easy work. Especially work where I'm not likely to be shot at. Janet doesn't like it when people shoot at me. She's funny that way."

Chapter 41

"How's it going with Sneakers?" Terry stabbed a bite of salad on her fork and sopped up dressing before she popped it in her mouth. *"Mmm*, that's good."

Terry and I had taken a waterfront table at The Crazy Lobster. I had sensed clouds on the horizon in our relationship. I hoped to chase them away with a romantic dinner at her favorite restaurant.

"He's not Sneakers any more. He picked a new name: Clint Watkins."

She raised an eyebrow. "All on his own? Just like that?"

"I explained that he needed a name that would command respect. We discussed a couple and he selected Clint." I munched a slice of garlic toast.

"It's a good name." She sipped her Pinot Grigio. "Has Clint moved in with you?"

"Yeah. Queens, I know I've neglected you while I'm getting Clint settled into his new routine. I'm sort of homeschooling him. I bought a dozen age-appropriate books, which he's reading. I taught him how to use a printed dictionary. I taught him how to research stuff on the internet."

"You'd better install a porn filter."

"Already did. I remember what it's like to be sixteen years old. And I'm teaching him social skills."

"King, your own social skills could use a little polishing. You've been neglecting your main squeeze."

"I know, babe, and I'll make it up to you. Clint won't take this much time forever, despite his background. He's a lot smarter than I expected and he reads well." I sipped my Merlot.

She frowned. "He took the guest room overlooking the beach?"

"I let him pick. He told me he'd never had his own room before."

"Wow," Terry said softly.

"My sentiments exactly. Anyway, I thought it would make him feel better about the move into a new environment."

Terry twirled her wine glass stem between her thumb and forefinger. "You might not have known that when I stare into a glass of wine, I can see the future. I see that Clint's living in your condo will put a major crimp in my sitting on your lap on the balcony while we watch the sunset."

"Is that what you call it? 'Sitting on my lap?'" I smiled. "We can still watch the sunset, but without the lap-sitting part."

Terry didn't smile back. "And Clint will surely enjoy the sunset with us."

"We could move the chaise to the master bedroom balcony. You could 'sit on my lap' there and ride me like a racehorse." I made air quotes.

"I know you; you wouldn't feel right shutting Clint out. Neither would I. We'd both feel guilty." She set her wine glass down, dabbed her lips with a napkin.

She was right, so I said nothing. I reached across the table and rubbed the back of her hand.

She took a bite of crab cake. "Also, I can't lay my head on your lap on the couch in front of the TV anymore."

"If I remember correctly—and I have vivid memories of us on that couch—you do more than lay your head on my lap." I smiled again, hoping to lighten the moment.

It didn't work.

She pulled her hand away. "Whatever I do, or you do, or we do, we couldn't do it in the living room anymore."

"Also true." Terry was on a roll. I waited for the rest.

"We can't wash clothes in the nude anymore, and I can't sit on the washing machine while it runs."

This was worse than I thought.

"Queens, we'll make adjustments. We can always use the bedroom. Couples have had to adjust to having kids for thousands of years."

She set her fork down with a *clank*. "Sneakers—excuse me—*Clint* is not a kid; he's a *project*." She placed her hands flat on either side of her place setting.

For a second, I was afraid she was going to stand up and stalk out.

"And Clint is not *our* kid. Even if he were, he's *your* project, not mine."

She was right again: I had thrust this whole Clint thing right in the middle of our love affair. My potentially life-changing decision was causing the first ripples on all three lives: Terry's, Clint's, and mine. Would our relationship survive the strain?

"Chuck, when people have kids, they do it by choice. This wasn't my choice; it was yours." She picked up her fork again and shoved her food around on the plate. "Even then, the couple's children start out as babies, then the couple adjusts gradually to the new relationships." She shook her head. "This is like straightening teeth with a hammer."

I held her hand. "I can't throw him back on the street."

"No, of course not." She pulled her hand away. "I don't know what I want, but I know it's not this. I have to think about it."

Chapter 42

When I answered the door, Dan Murphy stood there with a briefcase. I hadn't expected company, but when the building receptionist called, I remembered Murphy had said he might help with the Rayburn investigation. Maybe this was the surprise he had mentioned.

"Come in, Dan." We moved to the living room. "Want a beer?"

"I never say 'no.'"

"Tell you what, it's such a nice day, I'll bring the beers out to the balcony." I gestured the way. "The door's open. Port City Amber all right?"

"Sounds great."

I went to the kitchen and brought two beers.

Murphy took a long pull on his bottle.

I sat in a deck chair. "You brought something for me?"

The detective laid his hand on the briefcase sitting beside his chair. "I copied the entire Rayburn file."

I expected him to open the briefcase and hand me the file, but he didn't. Of course, he hadn't said he would give me the file. Maybe he expected me to read it and give it back. I didn't know him well enough to be pushy. After all, he was the one doing the favor.

Murphy set down his beer. "I heard you've taken in a street kid."

"Yeah, he's in school right now."

"I thought school was out for the summer."

"It is. I send Clint to remedial tutoring at Port City Prep every day."

"You drive him?"

"Sometimes. Usually I use Uber."

We talked for a while about kids. Murphy didn't have any but wanted some. He and Jessica had been married twelve years and it didn't look like it was going to happen. We talked about life and sports and women. All the regular guy stuff.

Two beers later, Murphy gazed back inside the apartment. "I need to make a pit stop, buddy."

"End of the hallway."

"Why don't you read the file while I'm gone. See if you have any questions." Murphy took the file from his briefcase, set it on the glass-topped table, and went inside.

I had read half of the file when Murphy returned. The file confirmed the information Snoop had already obtained, plus it had Kelly and Bigs' investigation notes.

"Sorry I took so long. I had spicy Thai for lunch. It always affects me that way." He laughed.

"I can relate."

I finished reading the file while Murphy finished his third beer. I wrote the vital stats on a notepad and shoved the folder back toward Murphy. "Thanks for this, Dan."

"Oh, you can keep it."

Chapter 43

Clint and I finished our workouts at Jerry's Gym. Clint did the same exercises I did, but fewer repetitions or lighter weight. Ken and I both told him that the amount of weight was less important than the number of repetitions, but Clint obsessed about bench pressing over two hundred pounds and curling over seventy-five pounds. I figured he'd ease off on the weight once he hit those goals.

Clint had gained ten pounds, all muscle. He ran two miles a day.

We walked across the street to Java Jenny's for iced coffee.

Clint said, "Can I have a chocolate chip cookie?"

I gave him a twenty. "Go crazy. Get me one too."

Clint returned to the table and handed over the change. "Thanks."

He added a spoon of sugar to his coffee. "Why you be a detective?"

I raised an eyebrow at him and waited.

He smiled. "Excuse me. Why did you choose to become a police detective?" He pronounced it PO-lice.

"I wanted to make the world a better place. Removing bad guys from the world seemed like a good place to start." I unwrapped my cookie. God help me, I love those things.

"Why you start with the cops? Everybody hate the cops."

"Not everybody. Maybe you don't know the right people."

"You got that right." Clint bit off a chunk of cookie.

"I also needed a certain amount of qualifying experience to get a PI license. The police job qualified." I took a pull of coffee. "You given any thought to what you want to do with your life?"

"Don't know. Maybe I be a private investigator too." Clint laughed and sipped his coffee.

"I was your age when I decided to become a PI."

"No shi—no fooling?"

"I was a junior at Theodore Roosevelt High School in Adams Creek, Texas. The guidance counselor asked me what I wanted for a career. I'd never thought about it, but the instant she asked me the question, I knew the answer."

"What did you tell her?"

"I told her I was going to be a PI, like Spenser."

"Like who?" Another bite of cookie chased with a sip of coffee.

"Spenser. He's a fictional PI created by Robert B. Parker. I'll buy you a few of his books. If you like them, I'll get more. These cookies are righteous, aren't they?"

"More books? You already give me a lifetime supply."

"I have already *given* you a lifetime supply."

"Sorry. You have already *given* me a lifetime supply. But to the real question: Why'd you tell the guidance counselor the truth?"

"Why not?"

Clint dropped his eyes. "She might laugh at you, or somethin'."

Was this a clue to Clint's personality? "As a matter of fact, she did laugh at me."

Clint nodded as if that proved a point, but he didn't say anything.

"You want to know how it felt?" I set my iced coffee on the table and put both fists down on either side of it.

"Yeah."

"I hated it." I smacked the table. "She made me feel small as a person, as a… a human being. Like, if she wasn't going to respect my answer, why did she bother to ask?"

Clint frowned. "You got that right."

"When I got home, I discussed it with my parents."

"How'd that go?"

"Dad asked me if she would've laughed if I'd wanted to be a farmer like him or a veterinarian like my mom. I said, no, she wouldn't have laughed. Then Dad asked me if she would've laughed if I'd said an accountant or an auto mechanic or something more conventional. I said, no, she wouldn't have laughed."

I watched his eyes. He was following every word.

"Dad said maybe she was trying to manipulate me by laughing if I didn't answer right.'"

"You got that right."

I picked up my glass again. "The funny thing was, she was trying to help me. The counselor was a good person. She wanted what was best for me, but only what *she* thought was best—not what *I* thought was best. It was ingrained in her mind that people need to be and do what everyone else expects of them."

Clint broke a piece of his cookie. "What did you do?"

"Do? I didn't do anything. I didn't need her help. My parents were my real guidance counselors. That's what parents are supposed to do. That's what you'll do someday when you have kids."

"What you mean?"

"It's a parent's responsibility to guide his or her child in the right direction. Help them make good decisions. My parents helped me research the private investigation field and select the right high school courses to prepare for the future."

Clint's gaze wandered around the coffee shop. "You think they have any more of those cookies?"

"Best idea I've heard today." I handed him a twenty.

When we finished our second cookies, I said, "Clint, I want to spend the night with Terry tonight. I haven't seen her in over a week."

Clint grinned. "You getting horny, ain'tcha?"

"Social skills learning opportunity: We don't talk like that about people we care about. It's disrespectful."

"Sorry. I should have said that you don't want to get crosswise wit' you woman."

"That's much better. I'm glad you understand. I hate to leave you alone. What are you going to cook for dinner?"

Clint grinned. "Spaghetti and meatballs." That was the first meal I taught him to prepare. The bachelor's standby.

"When we get home, you check the pantry and make sure you have everything you need."

"Already did, man. We good."

"I feel like I'm abandoning you."

"I lived alone a long time. I'm used to it."

I spent a quiet evening at Terry's apartment waiting for the other shoe to drop. The evening went well enough, but she never said what she thought about my arrangement with Clint.

I let sleeping dogs lie.

In the morning, I left early to take Clint to school on time. Terry said she understood, but I wondered.

Chapter 44

I hoped that Ted Rayburn was feeling smug after he won the pissing contest with Kelly and Bigs. Maybe he had lowered his guard a little. It would help if that were true. I was getting nowhere fast, and I needed a break in the case.

Rule Two: *When in doubt, follow somebody.*

I walked the near-empty halls of the Everglades Mall, a shopping mall from the twentieth century that the big anchor stores had deserted. It didn't take long to spot Rayburn's office.

The sign on the door said *Rayburn Investigations*, but it didn't say *Private Investigator* anywhere, so it squeaked inside the letter of the law. As a convicted felon, he couldn't regain his PI license. Rayburn could claim he investigated UFOs or paranormal phenomena. Or not. But what the hell was he doing for money?

Rayburn's office occupied the space of an extinct used bookstore in a lonely corner of the mall. I could still make out *Play It Again Used Books and DVDs* where the letters had etched faint outlines on the plate glass. I picked the nearest mall exit to start the search for Rayburn's car. Snoop had given me vehicle information for Rayburn's minivan and car. I found them both in the parking lot and stuck GPS trackers under the rear bumpers.

Sometimes I can't place a tracker. If the target vehicle is parked in plain sight, I won't risk someone spotting me. When I do attach a tracker, it's so easy to follow that it's boring. In the PI business, boring is good. Boring was not getting caught or shot at.

Why did Rayburn keep both vehicles at the mall instead of leaving one at his apartment? Maybe parking was tight at his apartment so he kept whichever vehicle he wasn't using at the mall. Lots of parking space at the half-empty mall.

I moved to another lot at the back of the mall where I couldn't see his vehicles. That meant Rayburn couldn't see me either.

I watched the tracker screen from my Caravan and waited for either red dot to move. It was like waiting for an income tax refund. I listened to my favorite music downloads from the last fifty years. At five o'clock, the red dot for Rayburn's car blinked into motion. When he was two hundred yards off the mall lot, I slipped the minivan into gear. *Game on.*

Rayburn crossed the Beachline Causeway and swung north up State Highway A1A. An hour later he pulled into a neighborhood bar opposite North Beach. I knew the neighborhood well because Terry and I often went to North Beach on the weekend, but I'd never been in this bar.

I'd never met Rayburn. Nevertheless, I stuck a worn Pilots baseball cap on my head and headed inside.

Rayburn slid into a booth toward the back corner where he could watch the front door.

I picked a barstool where I could watch Rayburn's reflection in the mirror behind the bar. He ordered a drink, but it was obvious he was waiting for someone. I watched the closed-captioned sports news on the TV above the mirror while I kept one eye on Rayburn. I ordered a draft Port City Amber and sipped it while both of us waited for something to happen.

It didn't take long. A forty-something man in a two-thousand-dollar, pin-striped suit and three-hundred-dollar tie slid into the bench across from Rayburn.

I videoed Pin Stripes and Rayburn in the bar mirror with my phone. I left the beer and headed for the restroom. When I came out, I paused in the hallway and snapped a couple more shots of the two before I returned to the barstool.

They had an intense but quiet conversation. At least Pin Stripes acted intense. He scowled when he talked and ignored his white wine. His face reddened while he tried to make a point without raising his voice.

Rayburn sipped his Scotch with a small smile, a man calm and in control.

When Pin Stripes paused for breath, Rayburn placed his left hand on the man's right forearm. He said something to Pin Stripes that I couldn't make out. His last words were "…the way it is. Your call." Rayburn leaned back and dropped his hands below the table, eyes cold as a glacier.

Pin Stripes tugged at his collar. He started to raise a hand but stopped with it an inch off the table. He opened his mouth but nothing came out. He placed both hands on the table to steady himself. Even in the bar mirror, I could tell that he was shaking.

Rayburn waited, motionless and silent as the Sphinx.

Pin Stripes dropped his head. His hands relaxed. I read his lips in the mirror. "Okay." Pin Stripes reached inside his jacket, extracted a thick envelope, and pushed it across the table.

Rayburn must be up to his old tricks. That was my cue to leave.

I dropped a couple of bills on the bar and returned to my van to wait for Pin Stripes.

Rayburn's victim walked out like a half-deflated balloon. He drove off in a Mercedes S600 Sedan. List price: *Oh-my-God.*

I followed but I didn't have far to go.

Within minutes, the S600 reached North Bay Road and paused at an ornate, wrought-iron gate in a terra cotta masonry wall with broken glass inset on the top. Well-maintained landscaping filled the area between the winding two-lane street and the wall. The gate swung open, and Pin Stripes drove down a brick driveway that led to a Mediterranean-style waterfront mansion on the shore of Seeti Bay.

It was the sort of house God would own, if he had the money.

I pulled onto the grass verge and looked up the license number of the Mercedes. The owner was Charles Headley Morrison III. An online search located his photo. He was the guy in the pin-striped suit.

I researched the house on the Atlantic County Property Appraiser's website. The assessed value was mid-eight-figures. A search of the *Press-Journal* online subscription service and three social media websites revealed that Morrison's fashionable friends called him Trey. High society, politically well-connected. Married for ten years to Allison Throckmorton McIntosh, also high society.

Prime blackmail prospect indeed.

Chapter 45

Morrison's private money management firm occupied a four-bedroom condo on the twenty-fifth floor of a beachfront high-rise. He probably hadn't run afoul of zoning laws because he didn't have a sign on the door. The firm had almost no online presence and presumably did not accept or solicit outside investors.

I rang the bell, took two steps back, and put my hands in my pockets. I didn't want to appear intimidating to whoever opened the door.

The sexiest woman I had seen all day opened the door. Of course, it was first thing in the morning and I had not yet seen Terry, but this woman ran a close second and I hadn't even seen her naked. Professionally highlighted blonde hair, tight raw-silk skirt, a cream-colored silk blouse with a scoop neck that accentuated her world-class cleavage.

"Chuck McCrary to see Mr. Morrison. I don't have an appointment." I handed her a business card.

"Come in, Mr. McCrary. I'll see if he's available." Her smile hinted that if Morrison wasn't available, she might be. Sexy Woman pirouetted like a dancer, not easy in four-inch heels on a plush carpet. "Please have a seat."

She glided like a gondola toward the door behind her. Her skirt was so short that I hoped she would drop my card and bend over to pick it up.

Alas, she did not.

I admired the skill of her performance, and the view of her derrière made the trip worthwhile. I didn't know what Rayburn was blackmailing Charles Headley Morrison III for, but I would bet a bottle of thirty-year-old Scotch against a six-pack of Seven-Up that it involved Sexy Woman.

I wandered over to the window wall and gazed at the sailboats on Seeti Bay. Some yacht club was throwing a regatta, and most of the boats flew their racing spinnakers in a kaleidoscope of patterns and colors.

Sexy Woman returned. "Mr. Morrison asks what this is in regard to."

I pulled a sealed envelope from my jacket pocket. "It's confidential. Please give him this envelope."

"Of course." Sexy Woman pirouetted again and sashayed through the same door. This time I detected a whiff of Halston fragrance in her wake.

I enjoyed her performance again.

It took five minutes for Sexy Woman to return this time. Maybe he had trouble opening the envelope. Or else he and Sexy Woman had a quickie on the office couch. Maybe not.

She postured like a model, one foot forward, hip swung out slightly like she was showing a car at the Texas State Fair. "Mr. Morrison will see you now." She gestured gracefully toward the open door behind her.

Morrison didn't stand when I entered his office, nor did he offer his hand.

Maybe they don't teach manners at Stanford. Or maybe his arms weren't long enough to reach across a walnut desk the size of a ping-pong table.

The desk matched the walnut side chairs, walnut coffee table, and walnut bookcases decorated with books no one had ever read or ever would. The interior decorator must have selected them for the color of their bindings. They looked impressive though.

"How'd you find my office?" he barked. "It's not listed anywhere."

"Yes, thank you. I'll be happy to sit down." I sat in a white silk visitor's chair that cost more than my suit. "I was outside your home at 2056 North Bay Road at six o'clock this morning. I followed you when you left in your Mercedes S600 Sedan. When you drove into the parking garage here, I researched the

Atlantic County Property Appraiser's website from my car to see if you owned an apartment here. Turns out you own two. I tried this one first. *Voila.*"

"*Humph.* What's this about you helping me with my Ted Rayburn problem? Who's Ted Rayburn?"

I pulled out my phone, leaned across the desk, and showed Morrison a picture of him with Rayburn that I took the previous day. "If you don't like this picture, I have others. Or I could show you the video I took of you handing Rayburn an envelope stuffed with cash."

His shoulders slumped. "What do you want, Mr. McCrary?"

"A cup of coffee would be good."

He punched a button on his desk and Sexy Woman opened the door. "Please tell Helena how you take your coffee."

I did and Helena blazed a dazzling smile in Morrison's direction before she left.

"Now what else do you want, Mr. McCrary?"

"Call me Chuck."

He studied my card. Maybe I should add a logo of the Lone Ranger sitting on Silver.

"You're a private investigator. You followed me from home. Are you in the same business as Ted Rayburn?"

"God, no. Rayburn was convicted of a felony and lost his PI license when he was sentenced to ten to fifteen years in prison for blackmail. We are not in the same business. Rayburn causes people problems; I solve them."

He placed the card on his desk and steepled his hands.

Stanford must have taught that steepling your hands made you seem intelligent, like having lots of books in your office.

"I repeat. What do you want, Chuck?"

"Rayburn is blackmailing you. I can stop him."

"And if he were blackmailing me—and I'm not saying he is—how would you stop him?"

I told him.

Morrison seemed satisfied with the plan and gave me a fat retainer.

"What do I do now?" he asked.

I flipped open a notepad. "First, tell me what he's got on you. I presume it's a girlfriend. Helena at the reception desk?"

He seemed embarrassed. "Uh, she's one of them."

"Of course, I should have thought of that. If one girlfriend's good, two's better, and three is…"

"Exhausting." His lips twitched in an almost smile. "But I work out, and I'm in good physical shape."

"So, do the three include the wife or is it three in addition to Allison?"

"Why do you need to know this?"

"You wouldn't begrudge an ordinary man a little vicarious thrill, would you?"

He laughed. "Okay, I guess I'll have to trust you. I have three girlfriends, but Rayburn knows about only two. Helena is what you'd call a conventional mistress. Barbra Bamby in Chicago is a girlfriend."

"Helena's last name?"

"Josephson."

"Spell both their names."

He did. "Please don't make the obvious 'Bimbo' joke about Barbra Bamby. She's a successful real estate broker. I give her a little money to subsidize her apartment in Chicago."

"How much a month?"

He told me. I had paid less for my used, late-model Caravan. "Chicago rents are very high."

"I'll bet. How long has this been going on?"

"Maybe six years or so. We met at an investment conference in Chicago."

I wrote that down. "What about Helena?"

"She lives in a two-bedroom condo on the twenty-seventh floor." He pointed toward the ceiling.

"Very handy. How long has that been going on?"

"Ever since I bought the two condos—about four years ago. Helena was a sales agent for the condo developer. I intended to buy this one condo for my office."

"But…?"

"Helena was so… so… friendly and approachable that I asked her to lunch and things progressed from there. I decided to hire her and bought her a condo too."

"Now you're living the dream, huh?"

"I crave variety. I get bored easily." Morrison grinned. "What's the good of having money if you can't enjoy it?"

Mentally, I bit my tongue. It wasn't my business if this guy was a perpetual adolescent. "*Hmm.*" I used a wordless grunt to acknowledge that I'd heard him without necessarily agreeing with him.

"I also have a less frequent girlfriend in Atlanta—she's more of a 'friend with benefits.' I travel to Atlanta on business occasionally, and she comes down here once in a while to escape Atlanta winters. As far as I know, Rayburn doesn't know about her."

Charles Headley Morrison III stared at the desktop. "I'm not proud of it."

"You could've fooled me."

"Okay, I guess I am proud of it, but it's not like I neglect Allison. I do love her. I'm always there for anniversaries, birthdays, dinner with her parents, stuff like that." He regarded me with a straight face and added, "I'm a good husband."

Chapter 46

One of the many things I learned from my father is "The deal's not done until the check *clears* the bank." I went straight to the bank with Trey's retainer. The amount was too large to deposit with a cellphone app anyway. I don't have to like or approve of someone to do business with them; I figured Ted Rayburn was the greater evil.

Back in the Caravan, I called my computer researcher. "Flamer, I've got two jobs for you."

"Who?"

"First is Charles Headley Morrison III. Just a routine client background investigation."

"Spell it."

I did. "Next is Theodore P. Rayburn. He's the target. He's a former PI here in Port City." I spelled Rayburn's name and recited his office address. "Get me a top to bottom report. Everything in the public records, of course. And your specialty, everything private."

"How soon?"

"No hurry. The client's check won't clear until tomorrow."

Flamer's logo disappeared from the screen. No "goodbye," no "okay." That was Flamer. What he lacked in social skills, he made up for in spades with computer savvy.

Chapter 47

I sat with Terry at a waterfront table sipping Pinot Grigio and watching the occasional boat slide by on the Intracoastal Waterway. She stabbed a coconut shrimp with her fork. "How's Jorge's case coming?"

"Dan Murphy—"

"Jorge's partner?"

"Right. Murphy put me onto a guy named Ted Rayburn. Rayburn has a grudge against Jorge. He's a former police detective with the smarts to frame Jorge for murder. Say, I'll swap you a taste of my grouper for a bite of that coconut shrimp."

Terry stabbed a shrimp and placed it on my plate. "Is Rayburn involved?" She cut off a bite of my grouper and stuck it in her mouth. "*Mmm*, that's good."

I cut the shrimp into two bites and forked one. "Can I dip it in that orange sauce?"

She slid the dish across. "Help yourself."

"I don't know whether Rayburn's involved in Franco's murder, but I followed him and discovered that he's blackmailing at least one wealthy man."

"How wealthy?"

"Wealthy enough to own a seventy-foot yacht and a North Bay Road waterfront mansion with 150 feet of frontage on Seeti Bay."

"Wow. Who is the guy?"

I told her. I treated Terry like a professional colleague—which she was. She wouldn't violate the client's confidence any more than I would.

Terry laughed. "I could stand to be a victim like that."

"Now he's my client."

"Your client?"

I smirked. "He hired me to get Rayburn off his back."

"You found him while you worked on Jorge's case and now the victim is also paying you to work this case?"

"Separate case. Rayburn may not be connected to Jorge's case. Dan Murphy told me that Rayburn *could* be after Jorge. Morrison is a separate case. Besides, Jorge's not paying me right now. Maybe he never will—not that I care. At least this other case pays. I gotta make a living, and it might help Jorge's case."

"What's Rayburn got on this guy?"

"A couple of girlfriends."

"More than one?" She laughed. "Is he running a harem?"

"Sort of. He gave me a big retainer today, and it hasn't cleared yet." I took a bite of grouper.

She picked up the Pinot Grigio bottle and topped off her glass. "And how's Clint coming along?"

"Pretty well. His tutor tells me that he's quite smart. He has maybe a ninth or tenth grade education. I'm thinking about enrolling him as a resident student at Port City Prep once school starts."

"That can't be cheap."

"Fortunately, the Simonetti case paid off like hitting the lottery so I can afford to indulge myself in a little missionary work."

"If he's willing to go to school."

"Yes, that."

Chapter 48

Flamer emailed me the report on Morrison first.

Charles Headley Morrison III had hit the lottery when he picked his ancestors. His grandfather had earned the family fortune. The old man came to Florida in the last century and developed vast swaths of citrus groves and processing plants, creating hundreds of jobs for the locals and millions of dollars for himself and his investors.

Charles Headley Morrison, Junior, my client Trey's father, took over the family business and decided that running a business was too much work. He sold the groves and processing plants and put the fortune into tax-exempt bonds in the early 1980s, when interest rates were above ten percent. As interest rates dropped in the Reagan years, the value of the bonds soared. Whether it was luck or business acumen that he hit the interest rates at their peak, the move made Junior a billionaire.

When Trey went off to Stanford, Junior and Mrs. Junior became world travelers. They traveled to the San Francisco Bay area for mini-vacations around Christmas and for Trey's birthday. They would fly into San Francisco, rent a suite at the St. Francis, and spend a few hours with Trey between trips to Monterey and the wine country.

His sophomore year, Trey Morrison was arrested and charged with statutory rape of a high school girl. The girl and two of her high school BFFs crashed Morrison's fraternity party, got drunk out of their minds, and invited half the fraternity to help themselves. One girl's family filed charges and sued the fraternity, Morrison, Stanford University, and the fraternity dog for all Flamer knew. Morrison's fraternity brothers were mostly wealthy and came from all over the world. It was everybody-into-the-pool for defense lawyers from all over country.

Mr. and Mrs. Junior flew back from Portofino, Italy or the French Riviera or someplace equally yucky and bailed Charles Headley Morrison III out of jail. Junior settled Trey's part of the rape with the girl and her family out of court. The girl refused to testify against Trey and the rape charge was dropped. Morrison managed to squeak by with a Bachelor of Arts in Humanities. It took seven years. Some people would describe his GPA as a "gentleman's C."

In spite of his inauspicious start, he received an internship at a major investment bank in Tampa. Of course, Junior was a major customer of the bank. That might have helped him get the job. *Nah,* it must have been Morrison's sterling academic record.

Morrison wanted to learn how to manage money—specifically his multi-million-dollar trust fund. Within a year, he had made managing that fund a full-time occupation.

Apparently, he had hidden talents. His fortune kept growing until, according to Dun & Bradstreet, it had now reached ginormous proportions. After four years as a playboy, he married Allison Throckmorton McIntosh in a lavish society wedding covered by *People* magazine and various Let's-All-Watch-the-Beautiful-People TV shows.

Early in my PI career, I decided that I didn't necessarily have to like or respect a client to work for them, and I did not like or respect Morrison. But people are complicated and marriages even more so. My own relationship with Terry demonstrated that. I felt it skidding toward a cliff on a rain-slicked highway with no guardrail.

The bare facts seldom tell the whole story. If a client were not an active criminal, I would cut him a little slack. I didn't hold Morrison's wealth against him, nor did I blame him for being born a child of privilege. I had served in the Special Forces with numerous wealthy people and children of privilege. Most people would be amazed to know how many sons and daughters of wealthy families join the U.S. Army. Later, I learned that many of my fellow students at the University of Florida, a public university, were from rich families. For the most part, rich people are like anybody else. The majority are good folks; a few are jerks.

What I held against my client was that he thought with his prick instead of his mind. That, and that he hadn't taken his wedding vows seriously.

At least he paid top dollar.

Flamer's email on Rayburn's background had six large attachments, which I read on my computer monitor before selecting which ones to print.

Rayburn was not a nice man.

In order to print all the data, I had to reload the printer.

I like to read books on an e-reader, but for analyzing data, there's nothing like paper. I flip between pages, put pages side by side, make marginal notes, even spread four or five across the desk at the same time. I taped the most relevant ones on my wall with blue masking tape, and began to plan.

Step one of the plan: Call Snoop.

Snoop sat in the client chair, reading the pages spread on my desk and taped on the wall. "Okay, bud. Dazzle me with your brilliant analysis."

"It's not enough to find out what dirt Rayburn has and where he keeps the proof," I said. "I can burgle his office to get that. In the digital age, his backups will have backups. Even if I find and delete all the dirt he has on Morrison, it would remain hidden in the Cloud where he can recover it from any computer anywhere in the world."

"I'm sure you've got an answer for that problem, right?"

"Not yet. Just thinking out loud. We need to uncover some crime other than blackmail to hold over his head. Something so big that the cost to Rayburn if we reveal it would far outweigh any benefit he gets from blackmailing Morrison."

"Blackmail's a crime," Snoop said. "Why not simply threaten to expose his blackmail and send him back to prison?"

"Not good enough. We would need a victim willing to testify against him. The idea is to protect the victims—keep them out of it."

"Or we could kill him."

"Don't joke about that, Snoop."

"What makes you think I was joking? He murdered Armando Acevedo as revenge for the sting that landed him in prison. That's a death-penalty-type crime. How about this? We find proof of the murder to hold over his head."

I waved off the idea. "Kelly and Bigs already tried to nail him for the Acevedo killing. Even if we did a better investigation than they could do—which I doubt—I wouldn't sit on murder evidence. It would eat my guts out to let a murderer go free. Eat yours out too."

"Yeah, you're right. So, if you're not willing to kill him—correction—to *execute* him, what are we gonna do?"

"We're back to our original idea of proving that he's still blackmailing people. We know he's blackmailing Morrison. It's a good bet there are other victims out there. We hold that proof over his head. That stops his current blackmail schemes, and it's win-win all around."

"But he wouldn't go to jail for the blackmail, Sir Lancelot. Can your high-and-mighty morals live with that?"

I leaned back and clasped my hands behind my head. "Putting Rayburn in prison again might require a trial. At least one of his current victims has to testify or be willing to if push comes to shove. Whatever Rayburn blackmailed them about would be made public, so the victims get punished again. These poor schlubs made two mistakes: whatever misconduct they did that Rayburn is blackmailing them for, and paying Rayburn in the first place. Let's not punish them again. Yeah, I can live with letting him skate on the new blackmail charges."

"And if you can't find a victim willing to testify?"

"I'll think of something."

Chapter 49

Clint and I were enjoying the view from the balcony when the front door opened. Two knocks and a distant "hello" followed.

"We're on the balcony, Snoop."

In a few seconds, my mentor joined us.

"Snoop, may I present my friend Clint Watkins. Clint, I'd like you to meet Snoop Snopolski. Before he retired from the job, he was the best cop I ever knew. Now he's a fellow private eye, and he works with me sometimes."

"How do you do, Mr. Snopolski? I'm Clint Watkins. Chuck's told me a lot about you."

Clint had remembered his lessons on polite introductions. I had coached him on his handshake, so it wasn't limp. He had developed more self-confidence, and his handshake had strengthened along with his confidence.

"Are you Chuck's sidekick, Mr. Snopolski?"

"Call me Snoop." He laughed. "No, Chuck is *my* sidekick. I'm Batman; he's Robin."

"You mean, you're Beavis," I said, "and I'm Butthead."

"No, I'm the Lone Ranger, and you're Tonto."

Clint held up a hand. "I get it. I get it."

I fetched drinks from the fridge and handed Clint a soda. "Did you finish *Rocky*?"

Snoop raised his eyebrows. "*Rocky*? As in Rocky Balboa and Apollo Creed's 1976 bicentennial fight?"

"I'm exposing Clint to positive role models."

"Who's supposed to be the positive role model? Rocky Balboa, the leg breaker for the loan shark?" Snoop picked up a Diet Coke and popped the top.

"Rocky turned his life around, Snoop. Also, Apollo Creed is a good guy. I want Clint to see that Bryant Gumbel and Barack Obama aren't the only black men who speak good English. I suggested he watch Denzel Washington in *Antwone Fisher* next."

"Denzel Washington was a bad guy in *Training Day*," said Snoop. "So was John Travolta in *Broken Arrow* and Tom Cruise in *Collateral*. Just saying."

"That only shows that they are versatile actors." I told Snoop how I met Clint and began to fill him in on Clint's history.

Clint interrupted. "I already know this stuff, Snoop. I mean, I was *there*, man. I'm gonna go finish watching *Rocky*." He left us alone.

When I finished, Snoop said, "I never figured you for a bleeding heart, bud."

"Underneath this gruff exterior beats a heart of 24-carat gold."

"*Humph*. You and the Pope. Why'd you take this kid in?"

"I'm as surprised as you, Snoop. I figured he might be a witness to the Franco murder. At first, I did it to gain his trust. But now..." I shrugged.

"I know you want kids, bud. But most people begin with a baby, not a teenager." He laughed. "How long you gonna let him stay here?"

"Not permanently. I guess for as long as it takes to teach him how to get along in the real world—the civilized world."

Snoop scoffed. "The real world ain't civilized, bud. If it were, you and I would be out of a job. And 'as long as it takes to teach him how to get along' could be all the way through college. Did you think about that? What's your exit strategy with this kid? Where does it end?"

I took a swig of my Diet Dr Pepper before answering. "He's a good kid. Maybe it doesn't end..."

Snoop raised an eyebrow. "How does Terry feel about all this?"

"She's not too crazy about it."

"I could've told you she wouldn't like a third person in the middle of a cozy love affair."

Chapter 50

Sexy Woman smiled when I walked in. I was practically one of the family now. "Good morning, Chuck. Trey is expecting you."

"Thanks, Helena." I waited for her to show me in.

She pointed over her shoulder. "You can go right in."

"I'd rather you show me in like you did last time."

She giggled. "You want to stare at my tush."

I bowed. "Guilty as charged."

She smiled, rose smoothly from her desk, did the amazing pirouette, and paraded toward Morrison's office door. She gave her tush an extra wiggle while she opened the door.

"You make my day, Helena."

She winked and shut the door behind her.

This time Morrison shook my hand and led me to his best-friends-only casual conversation grouping on the north side of his office. "Good morning, Chuck. I have to tell you: I Googled you."

"That's okay, I Googled you too."

"Happens a lot nowadays."

"Yeah."

"I know about the Special Forces, and the attack on Ghar Mesar in Afghanistan. And the Bronze Star."

I waited. He thought he knew about the battle for Ghar Mesar, but only the men who were there understood what it was like. A Bronze Star is a good acknowledgement and a nice credential to have on my office wall, but every time I see it, it reminds me of duty and valor and blood and death. Maybe those are good things to be reminded of.

"I know you've killed people."

"That's what soldiers do."

"I know about the shootouts over the Simonetti case. You killed people there too."

"They tried to shoot me. It wasn't a good time to reason with them."

"I know what you're capable of."

"Do you have a point to make?"

"I agreed with your original plan to handle Rayburn because I didn't know there were other, ah, options available. But after I learned about your background, I think there is a much more, ah, direct way to handle the Rayburn, ah, situation." He lapsed into silence.

I waited. Morrison had asked for this meeting, not me.

He tired of waiting first. "I want you to take direct action against him."

"I am taking direct action."

"No, I mean, ah, action that is, ah, *more direct* than that. Much more direct."

"You want me to murder him." I stood and took a step toward the door.

Morrison waved his hands as if to ward off evil spirits. "No, no, no. It's just that... if he disappeared, say, it would be awfully convenient for everyone." He narrowed his eyes. "I know you own a large cabin cruiser. Capable of going all the way to the Bahamas."

He dropped his hands. "People have vanished from boats and never been heard from again."

"I'm a private investigator, not a hired killer. If you think you can solve your problem that way, I'm not your man. If you want, I'll quit, subtract what you owe me for what I've already done, and refund the rest of your retainer."

"No, no. Don't do that. I thought I'd see what you thought about the idea."

"Now you know what I think of it. I'm here to solve your problem, not create a bigger one. Believe me, killing

Rayburn—or making him disappear—would create a much bigger problem."

In a miracle of good timing, Helena brought in coffee. Both of us watched her leave. After she closed the door, we gazed at each other and grinned, the tension broken.

"Just so we're clear, I'm going to negotiate with Rayburn." I poured my coffee. I didn't pour his; I was pissed off.

"What can you offer in a negotiation? I've already paid him a truckload of money."

I set down the carafe. *Let him pour his own damned coffee.* "I won't murder him. I'll use other incentives. I can get physical—to a certain extent—if I have to."

Morrison smiled at that.

Chapter 51

Renate Crowell's story exposing the corruption among foster parents hit the *Press-Journal's* front page with Clint's former foster parents pictured on their perp walk. They had both pulled their jackets up to cover their faces.

I felt a twinge of pride while I read the newspaper at the breakfast table.

I was halfway through the article when my cellphone rang. Renate's picture flashed on the screen. "Congratulations, big-time reporter. Another front-page byline."

"You can kiss the hem of my robe later, handsome, and then you can keep on kissing if you want. I didn't call to let you dazzle me with your charm."

"I thought you called so I could stroke your ego."

"Listen, big guy, if I ever get you to stroke me again, it better not be my ego. This is business. This story has legs. I can do a five-part series on this. I need to interview the kid for a follow-up piece on the effect this corruption has on the children it's supposed to help."

"I'll ask, but I can't promise anything."

Clint finished reading Renate's article about his foster parents. He laid it on the breakfast table. "You want me to talk to this bitch, Chuck?"

"Clint, the word 'bitch' is not a substitute for 'woman' or 'girl.' It is demeaning and disrespectful. Only call someone a bitch if they are a malicious or unpleasant person. Renate Crowell is neither."

"Sorry. You want me to talk to this woman?"

Clint needed to learn to make good decisions to become a functioning adult. Decision making takes practice, starting with little ones. This decision couldn't hurt him no matter which way he decided. It was a good one to practice on.

I took the paper back. "It's your life, your privacy, and your decision. I don't want you to do it; I don't *not* want you to do it. Even if I had an opinion, it's your call."

He thought about it. "I'll meet the lady, but I don't promise nothing."

"You don't promise *anything.*"

"Right. I don't promise anything." He grinned.

It was progress. Maybe someday he would learn to pronounce "ask."

Renate was to meet Clint and me at the Day and Night Diner, Clint's favorite restaurant. Maybe Clint chose the diner for the meet because he viewed Veraleesa as a surrogate mother. He could have done a lot worse.

When Clint and I exited the Avanti, I recognized Renate's flaming red hair through the picture windows at the front of the diner. The familiar doorbell dinged when we walked in. I gestured toward the booth so Clint could lead. I hung back a couple of steps.

"Pleased to meet you, Ms. Crowell. I'm Clint Watkins."

Renate shook his hand. She usually wore designer jeans and today was no exception. Today's jeans were purple, accented with hot pink running shoes, and topped with a bright yellow polo shirt. Her ubiquitous reading glasses hung on a gold chain around her neck.

As we slid into the bench across from her, she eyeballed me and raised an eyebrow.

Clint saw it. "Chuck's been teaching me proper manners. And he takes me to Port City Preparatory School for regular remedial tutoring." He pronounced *remedial* carefully. "He feels my education has been lacking." He nudged me with his elbow and grinned.

I shrugged and smiled at Renate.

Veraleesa stepped up, order pad in hand. "Welcome to the diner, ma'am. Hey guys, nice to see you again. What can I get y'all?"

I ordered last and pointed at Renate. "She's paying."

Veraleesa laughed heartily.

"How do you like it at Port City Prep?" asked Renate.

"It's okay, I guess."

Renate interviewed Clint while we ate. I celebrated with a second piece of pecan pie.

Chapter 52

Snoop hung out at the mall's food court for three days and watched Ted Rayburn's operation. His errand-boy thug visited all three mornings, fetched lunch at the food court, and left after lunch all three times. The rest of the time, Rayburn was alone.

The fourth afternoon, Snoop called Chuck after the errand-boy left. "Rayburn's assistant thug has left for the day. Now's a good time to deal with Rayburn. Besides, my butt is bruised from sitting on these hard chairs, and I can't take another day of the food court's coffee."

"I'll do it tomorrow. Is he armed?"

"Rayburn's a convicted felon, bud. He can't legally own or carry a gun."

"That's not what I asked. There are lots of unhappy people out there in addition to Trey Morrison who would like Rayburn's scalp."

"It's too far for me to tell from the food court. I'd be armed if I were in his business."

"Me too."

I relieved Snoop and waited at the food court until Rayburn's errand-boy left. It was after three o'clock on a Saturday.

I walked through the entrance to Rayburn's tiny reception and closed the frosted glass door quietly. After locking the deadbolt from inside, I closed the blinds on the windows. I carried the sports bag I'd brought with me back to Rayburn's office.

Rayburn frowned up from his desk. "Didn't hear you come in. I'm Ted Rayburn." He stood and stuck out his right hand. Mr. Congenial Businessman. His left hand snaked toward his desk drawer.

I grabbed his right wrist, jerked him toward me, and pounded the blackmailer's nose with a hard right.

Rayburn opened the desk drawer and grabbed a small pistol with his left hand. I hacked his wrist with the edge of my hand and the gun clattered across the tile floor.

I stretched across the desk and punched him on the nose again, spattering the desk and my suit with blood. The blow knocked him over his chair. It rolled across the floor and slammed into the wall as Rayburn's forehead smacked the tile.

I kicked him in the ribs, and he skidded across the floor, his nose trailing a bloody streak. I followed and kicked him again when he tried to rise to his feet.

He rolled away and I kicked him in the kidneys.

Rayburn tried to cover his ribs, his stomach, and his kidneys at the same time—hands and forearms flapping wildly.

I stomped his right hand and felt a couple of the metacarpals break. He wouldn't shoot anyone with that hand for weeks.

I leveled a Glock at his midsection while I picked up his pistol, a Browning .380. Returning to the desk, I opened the other desk drawers. I found a .45 automatic in the top right drawer. "You got any more, Rayburn?" I dropped both guns in the sports bag.

"No, no, no. That's all. Who the hell are you? What the fuck do you want?"

"Teddy, Teddy, such language. It demonstrates a lack of breeding, don't you agree?"

"Who the fuck are you?"

I struck him hard with a right cross. "Please, don't use such language, scumbag. I have tender ears. If you don't know who I am, why'd you try to pull a gun on me?"

"I saw you in the bar taking my picture the other day. I knew this weren't no social call. Who are you?"

"That's not important."

"What the fu—hell do you want?"

"If I find another weapon when I search, I'll hurt you again. If you lie to me, I'll hurt you again. Do you believe me?"

Rayburn wiped his bloody nose on his jacket sleeve and grunted.

"Assume the position."

Rayburn struggled to his feet with a groan and leaned against the wall. His broken right hand hung limply. I let that slide.

I kicked his feet farther apart and frisked him. I pulled his cellphone and wallet from his pockets and tossed them on the desk along with a key ring.

"What about the file cabinet? What will I find when I open it?" The file cabinet was locked.

Rayburn's eyes darted around the room. "Switchblade in the top drawer."

"Which key?"

"The little one."

"Sit on the floor and cross your legs."

I opened the file cabinet and ransacked the drawers. I stuck the switchblade in the sports bag and sat in the office chair.

Rayburn moaned and held his bloody nose. "For crissakes, what the hell do you want?"

"You are no longer in the blackmail business."

"I'm not blackmailing anybody."

I strolled over and kicked him in the head, not hard. I didn't want to put him in the hospital, but I wanted his undivided attention. "I told you not to lie, scumbag. Don't lie to me again. I know all about you."

A variety of expressions passed across Rayburn's face while he considered the possibilities of what I meant.

I opened the file cabinet again and sorted through its contents.

Rayburn raised his hands. "That's private property. You don't have a search warrant. You can't do that."

"Just your luck. I'm not a cop, so I don't give a crap about your rights."

The top drawer held expense files: office lease, telephone and electric bills, and other administrative bits and pieces. I had two drawers like that in my own office. I found his cellphone bill file and laid it on the desk.

Second and third drawers were for office supplies. The bottom drawer had more than a dozen folders with no names on them. Each folder contained sheets of paper and notes and a stick drive.

I set those folders on the desk. "Is this all the data on your blackmail victims?"

"I'm not black—" He stopped and pressed his lips into a thin line. He sat on the floor and stared at me.

I opened his laptop and turned it on. "What's the password?"

Rayburn told me.

I wrote it on the cover of one of the victim folders. I clicked through the icons on the desktop and found his internet Cloud backup service. "Login ID for your Cloud backup?"

Rayburn hesitated.

I regarded him. "Really, Rayburn? I don't have your undivided attention yet?"

Rayburn dropped his head and gave me the login and password. I jotted them on the file cover beneath the computer password.

I went online and deleted all Rayburn's Cloud backups. I used the Account Setting to cancel the account. That would at least slow Rayburn down if he tried to go back into business.

An automatic window opened. The company was "oh so sorry" to see Rayburn go and wondered if he would be good enough to tell them why he had closed the account. I read the message aloud. "I'll tell them that Rayburn Investigations has gone out of business."

Rayburn glared at me wordlessly.

I opened the chat window and asked the backup service to refund the unused portion of the subscription. I didn't even want Rayburn's name in their records as a creditor, either. "Don't worry, Rayburn, they'll send you a partial refund."

Rayburn groaned and started to get up.

"Don't. I'll tell you when to move. Roll over on your stomach. Hands behind you." I took a plastic tie from the sports bag and fastened Rayburn's hands behind him. "Sit up."

When I reached for another plastic tie, Rayburn tried to kick me. I backfisted him. "Not smart, Rayburn. Play along and I'll let you live."

The back of my hand oozed blood from where it had scraped across Rayburn's teeth. I would need to apply disinfectant when I got home.

I fastened Rayburn's ankles together. "Where's the other cellphone?"

Rayburn glared at me.

I waved the cellphone bill at him. "You have two phones. I want them both."

"In the glove compartment of the van."

"I'll get it later."

I switched the phone on. "What's the password?"

Rayburn told me and I listed it with the other passwords.

I scanned Rayburn's contacts list and text messages. Lots of good stuff for Snoop to analyze.

I took the keys off the key ring. Rifling through the office supply drawers, I found a pad of scratch paper and a tape dispenser. "What are these keys to?"

As Rayburn told me, I labeled each one and dropped it in the sports bag—all but the van key and the office key. Now I had keys to his apartment, his office, his car, a cargo van, the file cabinet, and his safe deposit box.

I shut down his computer and stuck it and the power cord in the bag.

I tested the plastic ties—tight enough, but not too tight. "I found a pair of scissors in your file cabinet. You can use them to get out of those plastic ties. I'll put them in the top desk drawer." Shoving the scissors to the back of the drawer, I closed the drawer and locked it, leaving the key in the lock. I wanted to slow Rayburn down, not starve him to death. Worst case, someone would cut him loose Monday morning if he didn't free himself before then.

I locked the office door behind me and retrieved Rayburn's other cellphone from his van. I flung his office and van keys far across the empty parking lot.

Ted Rayburn's whole life was open to me. I had had a good day—the Army way.

Chapter 53

I slid a stack of bundled pages across the desk to Snoop. "The top bunch is the people in Rayburn's address book on his computer."

"I won't ask how you got this."

"A good fairy dropped them off anonymously."

Snoop grunted. "Of course."

"The second group is the contacts from his cellphone and the log of his calls and texts."

Snoop picked up the papers. "Same good fairy?"

"The good fairy was feeling generous. The fairy gave me the third bunch, which is a log of calls from his second cellphone."

I handed over the last sheets of paper. "It's not a smart phone; you'll have to research the numbers to see who they are. Compare all three lists. Anybody on two or more lists, run a quick-and-dirty background check to see what their relationship to Rayburn is. We want to find his current victims. And find out if he has any other legmen. I wouldn't want to be blindsided by an extra thug I don't know about."

Snoop butted the papers into alignment on the desktop. "Can I use your laptop?"

"Take it into the conference room and help yourself. I've got other stuff I need to do here." I didn't tell Snoop that I'd invaded Rayburn's office, nor about the victim files I'd found. In case the police ever asked Snoop anything, he wouldn't have to lie about what he didn't know.

An hour later, Snoop opened a manila folder on my desk and showed me a sheet of paper. "Here are the names and contact info on two probable blackmail victims. You may recognize one name."

I read the names and whistled. "Is this the famous one?"

Snoop grinned. "Maybe he'll give you the secret to how he cooks his ribs."

Hank's Bar & Grill & Bodacious Ribs was a "must visit" in the South Florida guidebooks. Convention managers shipped in tourists by the busload. Hank's occupied prime waterfront overlooking the cruise port and the ship channel. It coined money like the U.S. Mint.

Hank Hickham, the owner, was a Port City legend. I Googled the colorful restaurateur before making my approach, but that didn't prepare me for meeting the legend himself. Sixty years old, partially bald, and grey, Hank stood five-foot-nine and weighed over three hundred pounds, but he bounded to his feet like an Olympic gymnast doing a handspring. He hustled around a desk the size of an aircraft carrier with his hand extended, grinning broadly.

"Everybody calls me Hank." He pumped my hand like a Texas oil well, while he led me across the expansive office to a coffee table with leather chairs grouped around it. The view was impressive. "You hungry, Chuck? I'll hustle us up a mid-afternoon snack."

"Just coffee, Hank. A little cream, no sugar." I hadn't expected the red-carpet treatment when I showed up without an appointment. I'd given Hank's receptionist my business card and an envelope containing a letter addressed to him. That envelope lay unopened on his desk.

Hank tapped the intercom. "Would y'all please bring us coffee for two and, uh, three or four of them big Danish pastries? Thanks." He sat across from me. "What can I do for you, son?"

"You didn't open my letter."

Hank leaned back and laughed. His laugh was as big and friendly as he was. "You don't need no letter of introduction, son. Hell, I musta read every story about you and that orphan girl in the *Press-Journal*. I admire how you saved that little gal and had that shootout. I'm a fan."

"Thanks."

"The pleasure's mine. Something I always wanted to ask: Was you afraid?"

"Which time?"

"When that sniper shot at you from the parking garage."

"Sure. Anytime somebody points a gun at me, I'd be a fool not to be afraid. But that doesn't change anything; I still have to handle the danger. In that case, I handled it by running like a scalded dog."

Hank laughed and slapped his massive thighs. "I know better than that, son; I read the paper. Still, your way makes a better punch line: 'ran like a scalded dog.'" He stopped laughing while a man in a waiter's uniform carried in a loaded restaurant tray and placed it on the coffee table. "Thanks," he said and handed me a cup. "So, what's on your mind, son?"

I waited for the server to leave. "I'm here to talk about Ted Rayburn."

"Who?"

"Ted Rayburn. The guy you paid five thousand dollars a month for the last four months. And last month he raised you to six thousand." I tasted the coffee. Man, it was delicious.

"You know about that Rayburn weasel?"

"I'm a private investigator. It's what I do. The good news is: I'm here to help."

Hank offered the dish of pastries to me and raised an eyebrow. I waved it away, and he picked a Danish before setting the plate down. "How do you think you can help me?"

"I have another client who is also one of Rayburn's victims. That person hired me to stop him."

"The best way to stop that chicken shit bastard is with a bullet between his eyes."

"That won't be necessary."

"What else can you do?" Hank bit off a giant chunk of pastry.

"You're not the only person he's blackmailing." I explained my plan to hold proof of Rayburn's new crimes over his head.

"That's all well and good, son, but to put Rayburn in jail again, the facts of the blackmail would have to come out." He took another bite of Danish, washed it down with coffee.

"Probably."

"I'm sure as hell not gonna hang out my dirty laundry. Hell, that's why I paid the scum-sucking bastard in the first place. I'll tell you what: I'll make my own deal with you to get Rayburn off my back."

"I'm listening."

"Get Rayburn off my back and everybody else's back at the same time. You get my drift?"

I held up both hands. "I'm not a hired killer. Even if I were, the 'dirty laundry,' as you call it, wouldn't disappear, even if Rayburn did. He uses another thug to collect payments from victims. That guy could access the same information. Removing Rayburn wouldn't change that."

"But it might make the other guy think twice."

I expected Hank to laugh after that line, but he didn't crack a smile. He was dead serious.

"Tell me what he's got on you," I said.

"You don't know?"

"I read Rayburn's cash transactions file. Whatever he's got on you is none of my business unless you want me to know."

"How'd you get his cash file?"

"I'm the world's greatest private eye."

"Well I'm sure as hell not gonna tell you my secrets."

"For me to help you, Hank, I need to know what I'm up against. If your secret doesn't involve a current or ongoing criminal act, it would come under my confidential client relationship—if you were my client."

"It's something I did about forty years ago."

"Okay. Pay me a dollar so you'll be my client, tell me what it is, and I'll give you a dollar's worth of advice. Then we'll go from there. Fair enough?"

"No. You get what you pay for, and I want better advice than that. I'll pay you one thousand dollars." He pulled out a checkbook. "Who do I make it to?"

"McCrary Investigations."

I stuck the retainer in my pocket. "What did you do?"

"I robbed a bank."

"Where?"

"A small town in South Carolina."

"Anybody killed or wounded?" I asked.

"Nope. I got away clean as a skinned grape."

"How do you think Rayburn found out about it?"

Hank shrugged. "Maybe he traced the money I used to pay it back?"

"Pay what back?" I asked.

"The bank. A few years ago, my conscience got to bothering me something awful. It was about the time I set up those trust funds for my kids. It got so's I'd lay awake at night feeling guilty, so I discussed it with my preacher, and I paid back the money I stole—anonymously, I thought. It made all the newspapers in South Carolina."

"What did you do, send along a letter of apology?"

"Practically. There was this church across the street from the bank. It was still in the same place when I went back all those years later. I went to the church and confessed to the preacher what I done. I give him the money in cash, plus interest, so he could give it to the bank with my apology."

"The newspapers must've loved a story like that."

"They did." Hank lifted the plate with the remaining pastry and offered it to me.

"I'm good, thanks."

Hank shrugged and took the remaining pastry.

"The good news is that after so many years, the statute of limitations has expired," I said. "You're home free."

"I know that. That ain't the problem, son. What I really worry about is my liquor license. You know what would happen to my business if I lost my liquor license?"

"You can't run a tourist restaurant without a liquor license, and a felon can't have a liquor license. But the statute has run. You're no longer a felon. The county can't take your license."

"But think of the politics." He rapped the table for emphasis. "The damned politics would kill me."

"Politics is beyond my area of expertise. You want your check back?"

"Keep it." He waved a hand dismissively while he rose and stood beside the window. "Consider this a therapy session. If my past came out, them scaredy-cats on the liquor board would suspend my license while they considered the issue long enough to get their pictures in the paper. They'd hold hearings and issue statements to get on the TV news. They'd appoint investigators, gather public comments..." He sighed. "All that crap."

He rapped the table again. "It would be a damned three-ring circus that'd take a year before I reopened, even after I won."

"I see what you mean."

"It's no secret that I make over a hundred grand a month here, more in the busy season. You may think that I'm scared of losing a million dollars while we're closed, but that don't scare me none."

"Then what is it?"

Hank sighed. "I got more money than Hall's has cough drops, and my kids and grandkids is well took care of in case anything happens to me or the business. Hell, I could shut down tomorrow and it wouldn't affect my living standard or theirs by so much as a bowl of chili." He raised a finger. "I don't say the money ain't important; money's always important. It's just that I don't need it no more."

He leaned toward me. "I'll tell you what scares the crap out of me."

He put both hands on the coffee table. "One hundred seventy-five people would lose their jobs if we closed. Boom." He slapped the table. "Those jobs—gone with the wind. Some of them folks have worked for me for thirty years, and they live paycheck to paycheck. And the damage to our reputation. Oh, no. This can't come out."

Hank snapped his fingers. "Tell you what. I understand that you're not a hired killer, even if the bastard deserves it."

"I stay within the law, Hank." That was 99 percent true. Okay, 90 percent anyway.

"With God as my witness," the restaurateur raised his right hand as if taking an oath, "if anything happens to Rayburn that removes that scumbag from the land of the living—if he is unlucky enough to be run over by a drunk, or struck by lightning, or if anything else—no matter how far-fetched—happens to him, I will send you a check for $50,000."

Oh shit, I thought, *this loveable legend has stepped in it now.*

"Hank, you can't do that."

"It's my money and I can do anything I damn well please with it."

I raised both hands. "If anything happens to Rayburn, it'll have nothing to do with me. I don't operate that way. You could get us both thrown into jail."

"How so?"

"Rayburn has other victims. There are other people out there who want to see him dead too. You with me so far?"

Hank squinted. "Okay, go on."

"Suppose one of his other victims does something stupid like hire a hitman to kill Rayburn. The police will investigate his death. You see that?"

"Yeah. So what?" A frown marked his round face.

"I confronted Rayburn in his office a few days ago. He pulled a gun, and we had a fight over it. That's when I took all his files, by the way. For a thousand bucks, you deserve to know that. A homicide investigation would turn up my fight with Rayburn. It would also reveal his connection to you." I lowered his voice. "It would also reveal your secret."

"I didn't think of that."

"How would it look if you sent me fifty grand right after Rayburn died? It would appear as though you hired me to kill him, even though we'd both be innocent."

Hank frowned. "I could send a cashier's check—anonymously."

"Anonymous doesn't exist anymore. Every check is digitally stored in the bank's computer system. And the banks make a record of every cash withdrawal of that size. The banks record the purchaser of every cashier's check. The cops would trace the money to you in ten minutes. Same thing if you tried to use a money order."

I wasn't sure I'd gotten through to Hank. This well-meaning millionaire could get both of us in trouble up to our eyebrows.

Chapter 54

I watched Beverly Restrow push an empty basket from the parking lot into the Target store. She was a good citizen, bringing in a basket. Restrow didn't act like a blackmail victim—not that I knew how a blackmail victim was supposed to act. Suburban housewife, two teenage sons, married for twenty-two years to the same man. Her husband Doug was a successful real estate broker and a deacon in their church; she was president of its women's club and charity foundation. Pillars of the community.

I lingered at the Starbucks inside the store while she shopped.

After she cleared the cashier and headed toward the exit with her shopping cart, I approached. "Mrs. Restrow? I'm Chuck McCrary. Do you have a minute to discuss a donation to your church's charity foundation?"

I stood ten feet from her cart, outside her personal space. I wanted her to feel safe even though she'd been approached by a strange man, even one who wore a suit and tie.

"Do I know you, Mr.—?"

"McCrary. Chuck McCrary. Please call me Chuck. I've seen you and Doug at church. I'd like to discuss making a donation. Can I buy you a cup of coffee?" I pointed at the Starbucks fifteen yards away. She often bought coffee there, and I knew why.

She painted a social smile on her lips. "Of course."

Restrow wheeled her full cart to a table toward the back. She sipped her coffee.

I handed her my card. "Mrs. Restrow, I know about the regular withdrawals you've made from the foundation's bank account to pay Ted Rayburn."

Her face blanched white, her eyes widened, and her pupils shrank. "Wha—what are you talking about?"

I raised my hand an inch in a calming gesture. "I'm here to help you get out of this mess, Mrs. Restrow."

Her cheeks colored. "I don't know what you're talking about." She pushed her coffee cup a millimeter to one side.

I stared at her for a few seconds. "You have withdrawn five hundred dollars from the foundation's bank account every week for the last three months. Sixty-five hundred dollars so far. The same money you gave to Ted Rayburn at this very Starbucks."

I sipped coffee and studied her reaction.

Her gaze dropped to her hands clasped in front of her. "I'm ruined. My life is over." She fumbled with her purse as she started to stand.

I raised my hand a little more. "I'd like to get you out of this trouble if I can. Please, sit." I picked up my coffee to appear less threatening.

"Who are you and why do you care?" she blustered, but she sat back down.

"I'm a private investigator. I was hired by another of Rayburn's victims. You're not alone. My client is paying me to get him or her out of the same mess. I don't need any money from you. You've heard of collateral damage?"

"Of course."

"Think of me as a collateral benefit."

She forced a tiny smile. "Who is this other client who is so generous with his money?"

"It's not necessarily a 'he,' but the client's identity is confidential."

"But you'll tell your client about me."

"No. I'm not here to make any more trouble for you. You have enough trouble as it is. What I want is to nail Ted Rayburn, and stop him from blackmailing you."

"It's hopeless."

"Dum spiro spero," I said. *While I breathe, I hope.*

Her lips traced a hint of a smile. "Are you a fan of Cicero, Mr. McCrary?"

"Call me Chuck. Nothing is ever hopeless. Let's talk somewhere more private. You pick it."

I followed Restrow to a neighborhood library. She walked into a small, unoccupied reading room separated from the main lobby by a glass wall.

I admired her thought process. Private, but a safe place to meet with a strange man.

"You may as well call me Bev. Everyone else does." She sat down. "Now what do you propose?"

"Rayburn went to prison once for blackmail. He won't want to go back. I have proof that he's blackmailing people again. I intend to convince him that if he continues to blackmail anyone, I'll send him back to prison."

Restrow sighed. "For that threat to work, he must believe you will actually do it. Which would require one or more victims to testify. A victim such as I. Am I correct?"

"Yes."

She crossed her arms. Never a good sign. "That, of course, would expose the very secret I'm paying him not to disclose. My secret must remain secret, or I'll lose my husband, my children, my position at the church. I may as well be dead if that happens."

"Bev, your secret may come out anyhow. Your daughter may decide to try to find you the same way you found her. I discovered her identity in a couple of hours. Secrets have a way of coming out." I waited for her to process this.

The woman clasped her hands in her lap. "How did you find out?"

"I obtained Rayburn's file on you, and it was a big one. He had hacked your credit cards and your bank accounts, both your joint ones with Doug and your personal ones. He found the online birthday presents you sent to your daughter and the contributions you made to the adoption agency as well as the checks you wrote to your attorney."

"How did you get Rayburn's file?"

I waved a hand dismissively. "That's not important. What's important is that you left a trail to your daughter that any skilled PI could follow. I advise you to admit the mistake you made when you were a teenager and ask for everyone's understanding. Then it's all over. Rayburn will have nothing on you."

She examined her hands, shoulders slumped. "I can't. My life would be over."

"Bev, times change. Attitudes change. Doug will understand. Your other children will still love you, and the boys might enjoy having an older sister. Your church members will understand. If you pay it back, I'd bet they'll even forgive you for embezzling the foundation money."

"No."

"If you come clean, you can pay back sixty-five hundred dollars. It'll take time, but you'll manage it. The longer you delay, the deeper you dig the hole. Remember that old rule: When you find yourself in a hole, stop digging."

"No, no, no. That's final."

Chapter 55

"So how did it go with Beverly Restrow?" Snoop took another pull on his beer. We were sitting on my balcony watching the sun set.

"Same way it went with Hank Hickham."

Clint came out of his room. "What did you think of *Antwone Fisher*, Snoop?"

"Never saw it, kid. What did you think of it?"

"I think I'm not the only one with troubles. I also think that Denzel Washington deserves an Academy Award." He pivoted my direction. "Can I have a beer?"

"Help yourself. And Denzel Washington has won two Academy Awards—so far. If you want, we could rent the movies he won the Oscars for."

"That would be good."

The three men sat in companionable silence, sipped beer, and watched the sun slide toward the distant Everglades. The blue Florida sky transformed into multiple shades of rose, gold, and pink.

Snoop set down his empty bottle. "Bud, you're 0-for-2 getting victims to cooperate. Are we seeing a trend here?"

"Yeah, we go back to the drawing board."

I had to tell Snoop about the victim files.

I handed Snoop a portion of the victim files I'd taken from Rayburn.

"Another good fairy gave you these?" Snoop sat on the other side of the dining room table.

I plugged in the first stick drive and opened the first folder. This man was not yet a victim. Rayburn had investigated him, found a little dirt, but nothing significant enough to warrant blackmail.

The second folder was on Trey Morrison. Rayburn had the criminal records from the rape case at Stanford. Morrison hadn't mentioned that Rayburn knew about that. Maybe Rayburn was holding that in reserve in case the two mistresses ever blew up on him. He knew Morrison's financial position to the nearest ten million dollars based on reports he had filed with the Securities and Exchange Commission. Rayburn knew how much to ask for without jeopardizing the goose who laid the golden eggs.

The next folder was Bev Restrow's.

Then I opened the fourth folder. "Oh, jeez."

Snoop lowered the file he was reading. "Must be big."

"It is. Check out this one."

Snoop opened the folder. "Oh, jeez indeed."

The fourth folder was for Morrison's wife, Allison Throckmorton McIntosh Morrison.

Chapter 56

"You never hired me for legal advice before," Victoria Ramirez said. She spoke to me in Spanish, as she always did when we were alone. We sat at a medium-sized walnut table in her small conference room. Seeti Bay sparkled in the distance.

"This is the first time I've needed legal advice."

Vicky Ramirez was a name partner with a top-notch, boutique law firm in Port City. She specialized in corporate and family law, not criminal law. She and her firm had sent me a boatload of clients. She had also been my friend with benefits before I got involved with Terry. She reminded me of Condoleezza Rice, but with curly hair. The same aura of intelligence, style, and class.

She pulled over a fresh legal pad. "Tell me all about it."

I related the events of my investigation of Franco's murder, my interest in Rayburn as possibly framing Jorge Castellano for that murder, and Rayburn's blackmail of various victims. I told her how Murphy had put me onto Rayburn, how I followed Rayburn, and how I met Morrison.

"I've got three, uh, situations that I'm not sure what to do about. Morrison hired me to stop Rayburn from blackmailing him."

"What is Rayburn blackmailing him about?"

I told her about Morrison's three girlfriends. I also told her that Rayburn knew about the Stanford rape charge and that Morrison was not aware that Rayburn knew about it. I told her I had confronted Rayburn in his office and stolen his files and computers.

I waited while she finished writing her notes.

"Rayburn pulled a gun on you before you stole his files and office equipment?" she asked.

"Yes."

Vicky's secretary, Carmen, knocked on the door and entered with coffee service.

Vicky thanked her and continued making notes.

I poured us both coffee and waited for her to stop writing.

When she finished, she regarded me. "Since I'm not a criminal attorney, if you should encounter criminal charges over your altercation with Rayburn, I'll refer you to a criminal defense lawyer. You understand that?"

"Of course. That's not why I came to you."

"Then what's your legal problem?"

"It's an ethical problem. When I reviewed the files on Rayburn's victims that I took from him, I found a file on Morrison's wife, Allison. She's cheating on him, and Rayburn's blackmailing her, too."

Vicky laughed. "Oh, the delicious irony. He's cheating on her: she's cheating on him, and Rayburn is blackmailing them both. There's an elegant… symmetry to the whole mess." She made a couple more notes. "Okay, what's the ethical problem?"

"Do I have to tell Morrison about his wife's infidelity?"

She pursed her lips while she thought. "What exactly did Morrison hire you to do?"

"To get Rayburn off his back."

"Do you have a written agreement?"

"For a sensitive case like this one, I decided to go with a verbal agreement. Especially since he paid in advance."

"Getting Rayburn 'off his back' is not very specific."

I shrugged. "You know my business. Often, that's as specific as I get."

"And are you trying to get Rayburn off his back?" She made air quotes.

"Of course."

"Then you're earning your money." She put down her pen and added sugar to her coffee. "In my view, you don't have to tell him his wife is cheating." She snickered. "Although I'd love to see his expression if you did."

"Okay, that's good. Now about the second problem… is there any reason I couldn't take on Morrison's wife as a client too?" I added a little half-and-half to my coffee and stirred it in.

Vicky chuckled. "You have balls a bull elephant would be proud of."

"Excuse me while I blush modestly. If I don't have to tell the husband about his wife, then logically I wouldn't have to tell the wife about her husband, right? Which means I could represent them both."

"If you couch the terms of your engagement the same way you did Trey's, yeah."

"Okay. Then the third problem is that I have this other guy who is technically my client."

"Technically?"

"It was more of a joke that anything else. Rayburn is also blackmailing Hank Hickham."

"*The* Hank Hickham? The guy that owns Hank's Bar & Grill & Bodacious Ribs?"

"The very one."

"I love his ribs."

"Don't we all. Anyway, Rayburn is blackmailing Hank too."

"This Rayburn guy gets around. Go on."

"I visited Hank and told him to pay me a dollar so he'd be a client, and I would give him one dollar's worth of advice."

"I'm not sure that would hold up in court if anyone challenged it." Vicky smiled and sipped her coffee.

"He said he wanted better advice than that. He paid me $1,000."

Vicky wrote on her note pad. "That's enough to convince a jury he was a serious client."

"Hank offered me $50,000 to kill Rayburn." I told her the whole story of Hank's offer.

"Oh, jeez."

"You can say that again."

"Oh, jeez."

"That's not all."

Vicky set her cup down with a clink on the saucer. "There's more?"

"Oh, yeah. Trey Morrison also asked me to kill Rayburn. In fact, he said it before I ever met Hank Hickham."

"Surely he wasn't serious."

"He pussy-footed around the issue and dropped hints, but he was as serious as a heart attack."

"Oh, jeez again."

I related my conversation with Morrison as best as I could recall, which was pretty well. "I said there was no way that was going to happen. I think—I hope—that he understood that I would never do such a thing."

Vicky put a hand to her chin and frowned. She picked up a spoon and idly stirred her coffee.

I stepped to the window and contemplated Seeti Bay. "Vicky, I don't trust Trey Morrison."

"What are you worried he might do?"

"He's got more money than Fort Knox. He's led a life of privilege since he was born with a silver portfolio in his brokerage account. He's buddy-buddy with the top dogs politically, and he feels entitled. Hell, Vicky, the guy keeps three girlfriends. In my book, that qualifies as a harem. If that's not evidence that he feels entitled to break the rules, show me a better example."

"He feels invincible. I got that. Go on."

"Now that the idea of killing Rayburn has occurred to him, I'm worried that the SOB will hire someone else to make the hit. If that happens, my, ah, confrontation with Rayburn would be uncovered during the murder investigation. The fact that Morrison is a client might also come out. It would look bad for me."

"And then Hickham—" Vicky said.

"Right. If Hank sends me a check for fifty grand in spite of my warning him not to…"

"That would be a gold-plated motive for murder. You'd be in trouble up to your eyebrows."

"Bingo." I spread my hands. "How do I protect myself from this?"

Vicky leaned back in her chair and steepled her hands. On her, it looked intelligent. She stared at the ceiling then lowered her eyes to me. "The short answer is: You can't. If someone else kills Rayburn, you'll be a prime suspect."

"Then I'll just have to pray that nothing bad happens to Rayburn."

Chapter 57

I researched Allison Throckmorton McIntosh in the Notre Dame *Dome* yearbook at the downtown branch of the Atlantic County Library. She'd been captain of the lacrosse team and earned a broken nose in the NCAA championship semi-finals, which the Fighting Irish lost ten to nine. One of her teammates described her in the student newspaper as "the most competitive b---- I've ever known, and I mean that in the best possible way." As co-captain of the Notre Dame tennis team, her yearbook photo showed a slender, rather flat-chested, brunette with a chipped tooth and a crooked nose.

The next day I tracked her down.

The Allison Morrison that I studied through my binoculars was a busty, athletic, thirtyish, ash blonde with brown eyes. She pranced from the Wessington Club like a gazelle to reclaim her red Tesla Model S. The smile of thanks she flashed the parking valet revealed perfectly capped teeth. Her hair hung loose and she wore no makeup. Probably came straight from the shower after her tennis game. White linen shorts revealed tan legs with highly defined muscles above white leather sandals with gold trim. The hot pink, sleeveless top showed off her well-muscled arms.

After college, she must have invested a chunk of McIntosh family money in a new nose, capped teeth, and a top-of-the-line boob job, no pun intended. One thing hadn't changed: She looked like she could run a half-marathon without breathing hard.

Allison's cellphone number had been in Rayburn's file. I
drafted a text while she tipped the valet and got in her car.

> I can solve your Ted Rayburn problem. I am in
> the silver Avanti behind you. If you want to talk,
> call me or pull into a coffee shop. Your choice.
> Chuck McCrary, Private Investigator.

After following her Tesla down the street for a half mile, I
pressed *send*.

Ahead, Allison glanced down.

She was reading my text while she drove. *For crissakes,
don't have an accident.*

She turned her head to the rearview mirror, waved a hand,
and pulled the Tesla to the curb. My phone rang.

"I'll do both," she said. "How about that Starbucks up
ahead?"

"Fine."

Allison bought an iced coffee and picked a table outside, far
away from other customers. "How do you know about my Ted
Rayburn problem?"

"I have his file on you." I gave her a business card. "I'm
Chuck McCrary."

She read the card and shook my hand. "Obviously, you
know my name."

"I do. May I call you Allison?"

"Of course." Her mouth flashed a smile that didn't reach her
eyes. "Prove to me that you have Rayburn's file."

"Reynaldo Mateo is your tennis pro."

"So?"

"Also, Rayburn's file is where I got your cell number."

"Then you should know how much I'm paying him." She
stared at me with a hint of a smile while sipping her coffee.

I told her.

"Right on. How the hell did you get the bastard's file on
me?"

"I have magical powers. What matters is that the
information is still stored on the internet and Rayburn can
recreate it in a matter of minutes from any computer. In fact,

he's probably already done it. Losing his file might inconvenience him, but it won't stop him."

"What will, short of a bullet to the brain?"

"That's a professional secret until you and I reach an arrangement."

"Arrangement?"

"For me to help you, you need to hire me as your PI."

"Well, I've heard of ambulance-chasing attorneys. This is the first I've heard of an ambulance-chasing private detective."

"Detectives are sworn police officers. We call them LEOs: Law Enforcement Offices. I used to be one. Now I'm a private investigator."

"Sorry. An ambulance-chasing private investigator." This time the smile reached her eyes.

"This is a first for me too. It seemed like the easiest way to meet you without your husband getting suspicious."

"Okay, so you know how much I'm paying the blood-sucking prick. How much will you charge to get him off my back, and how do I know you won't turn around and blackmail me too?"

"I take it that my boyish good looks and trustworthy face aren't enough of a guarantee."

Her eyes took in my face, arms, and what she could see of my body above the table. She smiled. "You're better looking than Reynaldo, but I still need references."

"How about a lawyer, a police detective, and a couple of former clients?"

"They'll tell me your heart is pure as the driven snow?"

"Hardly, but they'll tell you I keep my word, and I can be trusted."

She took a long pull on her coffee. "Maybe later, certainly before I give you any money. Right now, let's talk terms."

Allison was a tough negotiator. Then I remembered her college teammate's assessment of her as highly competitive. I guess she still was.

Allison called Lieutenant Weiner and asked her if I could be trusted. Then she called Vicky Ramirez and asked the same thing. Two other clients had given me permission to use them as references, and she called them too.

She returned her phone to her purse. "Okay. We're in business. You check out."

Chapter 58

When I opened the door to my small office suite, Allison swept into my conference room like an invading army. She sprawled across the love seat as if she owned the building, the contents, and all the occupants. Her outfit could have come from an expensive fashion magazine. Her hair was done up and her makeup expertly applied. She placed her cup in the center of the coffee table, taking possession of it also. "What do you want to know?"

"How did you meet Reynaldo Mateo?"

She studied the Bronze Star citation on my ego wall before answering. "I lettered in both lacrosse and tennis at Notre Dame, but you know that."

"I do."

"I'm that rare combination of a girly-girl and a jock. I liked satin and lace and makeup as well as any teenage girl, but I've always been a jock. I stay in shape, and there's not much opportunity to play lacrosse in Port City." She laughed at her own not-so-funny joke.

I smiled back. When a client is talking, it's a good idea to listen, especially since her retainer check had cleared.

"I joined the Wessington Club to find women tennis players who could give me a good game. Tennis isn't like golf, where you're both playing against the golf course. To have a good tennis game, you have to play an opponent with comparable skills."

"I'd guess that few women members at the Wessington Club are in your league."

"The number is exactly zero." She sipped her coffee.

"So why not play a male member?"

"Too controversial. Having a regular game with a male member would raise eyebrows. Most of the male members are married, and the single ones are mostly trying to get laid. Or they're gay, and still trying to get laid."

"Any gay men that could give you a good tennis game?"

"Unfortunately, no."

"So it would appear even worse if you played with a hetero bachelor."

"That would get back to Trey pretty quickly. I can't risk that."

"Yet you took Reynaldo Mateo as a lover."

"That's different."

"How?"

Allison sat up straighter. "In our social circle, you don't screw another member's husband. Word gets around. I'm no home wrecker. It's simply not done." She drank more coffee, again setting the cup in the center of the table.

"But it's socially acceptable to boff the tennis pro?"

Allison laughed. "Believe it. You see, Rey's not a club member; he's an employee. It doesn't raise eyebrows to screw the help. It's like I'm using Rey for stud—which I am."

"The other members wouldn't see you as a home wrecker."

"Right. Just a horny woman cruising for recreational sex. Like a British Earl who screws the upstairs maid."

"So, Rey Mateo...?" I prompted.

"I signed up for lessons to have a good game of tennis," she smirked, "and was delighted to learn that Rey is also good at other games."

"How long has this been going on?"

"Six years. Since right after Trey took up with that chippie in Chicago."

I stifled my surprise and made another note. "Tell me about that."

Allison filled me in on every detail of her husband's relationship with Barbra Bamby, including how much of Bamby's rent Trey paid.

I wrote it down like I was hearing it for the first time. "How did you discover Trey's affair?"

Allison laughed. "I hired a private investigator."

"Excuse me for asking, but why didn't you hire the same PI to help you with Ted Rayburn?"

"Two reasons." She held up a finger. "First, the guy is in Chicago. And second—" She held up another finger. "He's old—a retired Chicago cop. I don't think he's tough enough to do what might need to be done."

Omigod, I thought, *not another contract killing offer.* "And you think I'm tough enough."

Allison lifted her coffee cup. "I'm empty." She raised an eyebrow.

I called Betty on the intercom and ordered more coffee.

When I hung up the telephone, Allison said, "I'm a good judge of character." She peeked again at my Bronze Star. "I Googled you before I came. I know how you got that medal."

I raised a hand. "Let me tell you what I have in mind. Rayburn's already served one prison term for blackmail. Now that I have his files, I have proof that he's back in the blackmailing business. I'll send him to prison again if he doesn't stop. That will be sufficient motive for him to leave you alone."

Allison shook her head. "One problem with your plan. Putting Rayburn back in jail would require that one of his other victims testify. Am I right?"

"Not necessarily. If Rayburn believes that I have a victim who will testify, he'll cave."

"You'd have to run a bluff."

"Yes," I admitted.

"If he calls the bluff, you don't have a hole card." She waved a hand. "The whole reason I came here was to discuss how you can put Rayburn out of business. *Permanently.*"

She leaned back. "And I do mean *permanently.* I know your history, and I know your skills. I know that Rayburn is no match for you. And you know it too."

"I'm in the information business, not the punishment business. That's for a judge and jury. I'm an investigator, not an assassin."

"Bullshit. I know better."

"Why do you care if Trey finds out you've been shtupping your tennis pro? Do you have a prenuptial agreement?"

Allison was about to answer, when a knock on the door stopped her. Betty brought in the coffee.

When she left, Allison waited while I poured her coffee. "Let me tell you about rich people—or people that you think are rich. My mother's family, the Throckmortons, and my father's family, the McIntoshes, are what most people would call rich, but we don't think of ourselves as rich. We say that we're *comfortable*. Trey's family, the Morrisons, they're super-rich. Do you know what the difference is?"

"I can't wait to hear."

She smiled. "People who are comfortable have enough money to do practically *anything*. But they don't have enough money to do *nothing*."

"In other words," I said, "they still need to work at something—not live off the interest or dividends."

"Right. Our fortunes seem large compared to the middle class, but with our lifestyles, we could lose them or outlive them unless we manage them prudently. The alternative would be to live in a house instead of a mansion and drive a Chevy instead of a Tesla." She smirked. "And we'd have to vacation at Disney World instead of St. Tropez."

"And the super-rich?"

"That's Charles Headley Morrison III's family. Trey has so much money, he could buy a small Central American country. Trey could do anything or nothing. He chooses to manage his portfolio of stocks and bonds and real estate—that's a hobby, nothing more." She blew on her coffee and took a sip. "Plus, he can get into Helena Josephson's pants whenever he feels like it."

Again, I concealed my surprise. "Helena Josephson? Who's that?"

"Helena is Trey's so-called office assistant."

I picked up the notepad again. "Tell me about that."

Allison filled me in with the same information her husband had told me.

"You're remarkably well-informed. Did your Chicago PI get this information too?"

"No, that stuff I found out on my own."

I raised an eyebrow. "How?"

Allison laughed. "My blonde hair may come out of a bottle, but I'm not dumb. Despite the boob job..." She cupped her breasts with both hands, "and the dyed hair and the capped teeth, I'm no bimbo. I graduated with honors from Notre Dame in business, not fine arts. I'm quite intelligent."

"I never doubted it."

"My detective in Chicago wrote a report detailing the investigative steps he took to uncover the truth about Barbra Bamby."

"You used his report as a textbook."

"Right. It was my template."

"I'm impressed. Most people would not think of that."

"Thanks." She sipped coffee. "Anyway, I followed the procedures that my Chicago detective did, but the subject was Helena Josephson right here in good old Port City instead of the Windy City. Josephson—now there's a textbook example of a bimbo."

"Trey is cheating on you with two different women, and you have the proof."

"In my personal safe deposit box."

I set my notepad on the table. "The way I see it, there's no harm in you letting me run the bluff on Rayburn. Worst case, Trey hasn't got a leg to stand on legally or morally if he tries to divorce you. He wouldn't have what lawyers call *clean hands*."

Allison stood. She was as graceful as Helena Josephson but in a different way. Helena moved like a model; Allison moved like a lioness.

She paced the room. "You asked if there is a prenuptial agreement. No. Believe it or not, Trey and I had a passionate whirlwind courtship. We were married within six months of our first date."

She stopped pacing for a moment. "You think I'm rich, and I guess I'm a member of the so-called 'one percent.' But remember, we McIntoshes are good Catholics, and I have six brothers and sisters. My parents' money will be split seven ways. That's why I had to marry well."

"I see."

"No, you don't see. I spotted Trey a mile away and stalked him like a deer in the forest. Trey thinks he swept me off his feet. Poor schlub. He thinks with his gonads; he never knew what hit him."

"You mean the whole whirlwind courtship…?"

"I orchestrated the whole thing. You know my degree is in business administration?"

"Yes."

"I minored in marketing." She grinned. "Don't look at me like that. I did my research before I picked him for my future husband. It was a marketing campaign for a good business arrangement. I even interviewed three of his former girlfriends, so I knew I would like him—no sense spending fifty or sixty years shackled to someone you can't stand. I knew I'd be fond of Trey, but I fell in love with the guy."

"He must be pretty loveable."

"Oh, he is. Mother raised me with the idea that it's as easy to fall in love with a rich man as a poor one—easier in fact, since you can overlook so many faults. So, I focused on rich men from the time I was in high school. With Trey, everything clicked into place."

"I admire your focus," I said to hold up my end of the conversation.

"Trey's net worth is literally a hundred times more than mine. He's number 296 on the *Forbes 400* list of the richest people in America, for crissakes. My parents don't even make the list."

"You've got to keep him happy."

"Trey gives me more money than I know what to do with. I have a brokerage account and I've squirreled away a few hundred thousand of my own for emergencies. But, if he wanted to, Trey could cut off the money in ten seconds. That's why I won't give him an excuse to divorce me. And why him boffing a mistress or two wouldn't do me any good in a divorce fight. Trey could cut me off without a penny and hire high-priced attorneys that I could never touch with my own resources." She smiled. "Besides, Trey's not a bad guy; he merely thinks with his dick. And I love him."

"And you've been married ten years now. You have an investment in the marriage."

"So far, so good." She smiled. "I keep Trey happy and I have mind-blowing sex with Rey Mateo about once a week."

"This is not something I need to know, Allison, but I'm curious. If Trey 'thinks with his dick' as you put it, and keeps two mistresses, he must like sex a lot. If he likes sex that much, why can't he keep you satisfied?"

She smirked. "Trey likes sex all right. His way. I knew that from my interviews with his former girlfriends that he would be, ah, unoriginal in the bedroom. There are certain, ah, desires that I have that Trey won't... doesn't particularly care for. Rey happens to love those things. Okay, I'm not proud of it, but it's not like I neglect Trey. I always remember our anniversary. I throw him a great birthday party every year. We have dinner with his parents every couple of weeks."

Her sincerity amazed me. I couldn't believe it, but she was going to echo her husband had said.

"I'm a good wife."

Chapter 59

My cellphone rang the next Monday morning while I made breakfast for Clint and me. I clicked off the stove burner and answered the call. "Hey, Snoop. What's up?"

"Ted Rayburn's been murdered."

My throat tightened, and I fought down the sick feeling that churned my gut. "Oh, God. When?"

"Last night or early this morning."

"Where?"

"In his apartment."

My legs wobbled and I sat down at the breakfast bar. I could barely breathe. "Who found the body?"

"Rayburn's pet thug shows up at the apartment this morning and can't get in. The apartment manager opens the door for him and they find Rayburn—dead."

"Who's got the case?"

"My guy at the precinct didn't say."

"Whoever it is, they'll find my fingerprints in Rayburn's office and apartment, and surveillance video of me from when I visited his office a few days ago."

My mind raced with possibilities. I was riding an emotional rollercoaster, being hauled inexorably up the first incline. When the car reached the top, it would pitch over and begin a steep, curving dive that I couldn't stop or change. My mind filled with visions of disaster after disaster.

"You there, bud?... Chuck, are you still there?"

"Just a minute, Snoop. I've got to think." I took two or three slow breaths before speaking. "Anything else I should know, Snoop?"

"That's all I've got."

"Thanks for the heads-up." I rang off and stared sightlessly out the window. I took the elevator down to the garage, completely forgetting that Clint was still getting dressed for school.

I sleepwalked to the Caravan and yanked on the door handle. It didn't move and I tried it again. Why wouldn't the door open? Oh yeah, it was locked. I found that very funny and laughed aloud.

A passer-by in the garage gaped at me and hurried to his own car.

I pulled a set of keys from my pocket and stared at them, trying to remember which one was for the Caravan. It wasn't a key; it was a big clunky thing. Yeah, it was a remote. I punched a button and the horn honked rhythmically while the headlights flashed on and off. I had hit the panic button by mistake. That, too, was funny and I laughed again. Gotta concentrate. I shut off the panic alarm and punched another button. The door locks thunked open.

I climbed into the vehicle, slammed the door, and breathed deeply. I waited for my heart rate to slow before backing from my reserved parking space.

I drove without thinking. After a mile, I realized where I was going. I pulled to the curb and called Kelly Contreras. "Who's got the Rayburn homicide?"

"It's not on the news yet. Where'd you hear about it?"

"Snoop called me."

"Where'd he hear about it?"

"I didn't ask. You know Snoop; he hears everything."

"Where are you now, Chuck?"

I stopped at a stop sign, surveyed all directions before proceeding. "I'm on my way to the crime scene."

"How'd you know where it is?"

"Snoop said it was Rayburn's apartment."

Kelly asked, "You know something we don't?"

"Yeah. Who's got the case?"

"Bigs and me."

"You there now?"

"We are. How far away are you?"

Not far enough, I thought. I wished I were lost in the wilds of the Amazon jungle, or maybe the Australian Outback. Anywhere but Port City, Florida.

"I'll be there in ten minutes."

Chapter 60

Kelly put away her phone. "Bigs, Chuck McCrary says he knows something about the case. He's on his way over. I'll have Casey stop him at the door. I'll interview him outside."

"Good. We don't want him to compromise our crime scene."

Patrolman Casey Cassidy was the uniformed patrolman guarding the door. "Casey, you know Chuck McCrary, don't you?"

"Everybody knows Chuck."

"He's on his way here. Remember that he's a civilian, even though he acts like he's still a detective. Don't let him into my crime scene. Stop him at the door and come get me."

"Will do."

Kelly was taking pictures of Rayburn's bedroom when she heard Casey's voice from the front door.

"Hang on a sec, Chuck," Casey said, "Kelly wants to talk to you out here. I'll get her."

Kelly handed the camera to her partner. "Bigs, I'll take Chuck. Back in a few."

Casey saw her coming and twirled around.

Chuck stood in the hall.

"Hey, Chuck, let's walk." She put her hand on his shoulder for a second longer than necessary. Then she and Chuck went to the front yard and stood near the apartment entrance.

She flipped open her notepad. "What do you have for me?"

"Did you know that Ted Rayburn had a thriving blackmail business?"

That's news to me, Kelly thought. "You gotta be kidding. That's what he went to prison for."

Chuck shrugged. "Rayburn wasn't the sharpest knife in the drawer. Maybe it's the only thing he was good at."

"How do you know this?"

Chuck acts nervous. I've never seen him nervous. I hope to God he's doesn't lie to me.

"Remember Rayburn's history with Jorge," Chuck said. "If he wanted revenge, he was smart enough to frame Jorge for Franco's murder. When you and Bigs released Rayburn, I investigated him myself. That's when I uncovered the blackmail business."

Kelly wrote on her notepad: *Chuck discovered Rayburn blackmail business.* "Bigs and I figured you'd go after Rayburn. What happened?"

"Rayburn was blackmailing several powerful people. People with the money and the motivation to hire a hitman. And I learned the identity of one of his blackmail victims."

Kelly asked, "Who's the victim?"

"You'll find out anyway, but I promised I wouldn't tell anyone. Anyway, this person hired me to get Rayburn off their back."

She wrote that down. "Go on."

"In the course of my negotiation with Rayburn, I went to his office Saturday a week ago."

"So? Bigs and I went there when we investigated him too."

"The CSIs will find my fingerprints all over that office, and, unless Rayburn did a good job of cleaning his office last week, they'll find his blood spatter. I had a fight with him when he pulled a gun on me. I didn't want you and Bigs to be surprised."

Oh, jeez. That's a motive for murder. "You fought with Rayburn?"

"Like I said: He pulled a gun."

This gets better and better—or worse and worse. This poor bastard suddenly became a suspect. Kelly shook her head and sighed. *Better not take any chances with an inadmissible confession.* She took the card from her pocket and read him his

Miranda rights. "Do you understand these rights I have read to you?"

"What the hell is this?"

"Chuck, you're a friend and all that, but I have to put that aside. Once a person becomes a suspect, it's policy to read them their rights. You would have done the same thing when you were a detective."

"Kelly, this is me," he protested. "You can't be serious."

"As serious as a funeral." Her insides knotted up.

"Since I am apparently a suspect, I need to consult my attorney."

"Don't leave town."

Chapter 61

Vicky walked into the conference room looking like two million dollars. "You look like hell."

"Thanks for noticing," I said. "You look great as usual."

"Sorry. I'm pissed that you made me cancel an appointment to meet with you. What's the big emergency?"

"I know you're not a criminal lawyer, but when the shit hit the fan, you were the first person I thought of. It's Rayburn."

"Omigod, did something happen to him?"

"The worst. I'll probably be arrested for murder in the next few hours."

"Crap. What happened?"

"Someone murdered him," I answered. "They found the body this morning. It's not in the news yet."

"This is bad."

"It's worse than that."

"How so?" she asked.

"When I met with you last week, I didn't tell you that after my fight with Rayburn, I took his apartment key. I went straight to his apartment and searched it before he could get loose and come home."

Vicky frowned. "Why didn't you tell me?"

"Thought it wasn't important. Amnesia. Temporary insanity. Bad judgment. Take your pick. No excuse."

"Did you find anything useful?"

"Nothing, but I left fingerprints all over the place."

Vicky raised her eyebrows. "You did a B & E without wearing gloves?"

"In my defense, it wasn't a B & E, because I didn't have to break in order to enter. I had his keys. I didn't wear gloves because it never occurred to me that the police CSIs would ever need to process that apartment."

Vicky gazed at the ceiling. "So young, so naïve, so… so…" She nailed me with the evil eye. "…stupid with a capital S."

"Counselor, I could do without the lecture on how to be a better criminal. I promise I'll wear gloves next time I burgle someone."

She shook her head. "Did you tell Kelly you went to the apartment too?"

"I intended to, but she read me my rights immediately after I told her about the fight. I clammed up and called you. I need a criminal attorney."

"You need Abe Weisman. I'll see if he's available." She picked up the conference room phone. "Carmen, see if you can reach Abe Weisman for me." Her eyes were wet. She wiped them with the back of her hand. "No, not the estate planner; the other one. The criminal attorney."

She hung up, mascara smeared on her cheeks. "You look like you need a hug, baby. I know I do."

Chapter 62

Abe Weisman ushered me into his office and we touched all the courtesy bases: "Call me Abe," "Call me Chuck," and so forth. "Thanks for seeing me on short notice," "Any friend of Vicky's…," and "This is my associate, Diane Toklas."

Abe had reached the far side of sixty. Longish, gray hair. Yarmulke perched behind his receding hairline. Black, pin-striped suit. White shirt, red tie with thin blue stripes.

"Compared to Abe, the president of Israel seems like a gentile, but Abe's the smartest criminal defense attorney in fifty-three states," Vicky had told me before I left her office.

Diane Toklas was in her late twenties, professional pantsuit, blonde hair, eager blue eyes. An apprentice courtroom magician learning at the side of the master sorcerer. She could have been Darcy Yankton's younger sister.

The two attorneys sat on one side of the conference table; I sat across from them.

Abe took the lead. "Okay, Chuck. How bad is it?"

"Pretty bad. I'm their first suspect."

Abe held a Mont Blanc ballpoint pen over his legal pad. "Okay. Let's get it all down." He and Diane questioned and prodded and wrung out my memory like a wet sponge for two hours. Abe filled sheet after sheet with notes. Diane documented her comments on a laptop.

Abe paused as he placed his Mont Blanc parallel to his legal pad—a tidy placement by a neat man with an orderly mind. He steepled his hands and tapped his index fingers together as he thought.

I wondered if Harvard University taught hand-steepling in law school. Like Vicky Ramirez, and unlike Morrison, on Abe the gesture looked intelligent. "Now we can speculate. Who are your suspects?"

"There were a dozen people whom Rayburn was either blackmailing or planned to blackmail. At least three of them are wealthy enough to hire a hitman. All three are my clients."

Abe gestured. "Let's hear it."

I tapped my first finger. "First is Charles Headley Morrison III, known as Trey Morrison. He asked me in so many words to murder Rayburn."

Diane questioned me until she dredged up every bit of information on Morrison that I could remember.

I ticked my middle finger. "Second is Hank Hickham—"

Diane interrupted. "Hank's Bar & Grill & Bodacious Ribs?"

"The same."

"I love his ribs."

Abe gaped at her. "Aren't they pork ribs, Diane?"

Diane waved a hand. "You know I don't keep kosher. Especially when it comes to Hank's ribs."

"*Humph*," replied Abe, "you could at least order beef ribs." He turned to me. "Go on."

"Hank gave me a thousand-dollar retainer for general advice. Then he asked me to kill Rayburn too. He offered me $50,000." I related my conversation with Hank.

Abe frowned. "We'd better hope he doesn't mail a check to your office. The police are sure to get a search warrant. Go on."

"Should I call Hank and tell him to wait?"

"No. Don't contact him at all. The phone records last forever. If the phone call came out, it would appear like collusion."

"Okay." I ticked my ring finger. "Third is Allison Morrison, Trey's wife."

Diane suppressed a smile. "Is she a suspect too?"

I shrugged. "She's rich, smart, and motivated. I have seldom met anyone as competitive. If she decided to take matters into her own hands, she has the balls to either kill Rayburn herself or find and hire a hitman."

Abe flipped to a fresh sheet. "Names of the others."

I named a couple more from memory. "I'd have to refer to the files to give you the rest."

"Those are the files you, uh, liberated from his office?"

"Liberated, schmiberated. I stole them." *No point mincing words,* I thought.

"Where are those files now?"

"In my home office in the condo, bottom file drawer lying flat."

"Give Diane your keys to everything you own but the car you came here in. She'll fetch those files. The police will no doubt obtain a search warrant for your home, office, boat, and both your vehicles. I don't want those files found in your home. What else don't we want them to find?"

I raised a hand. "Isn't that concealing evidence?"

He and Diane peered at each other and laughed. "We're not concealing evidence, *boychik*. We're *gathering* evidence for your defense. Big difference." He and Diane laughed again. He winked at me. "What else did you, ah, liberate from Rayburn?"

Abe made a list. "Diane, bring that stack of files that have no names on the tabs. And remember the stick drives in each folder. Make sure those don't fall out. Take sealable bags and bag each folder separately. You'd better bring Chuck's own files on any of his clients that are connected to this case."

He put a notepad in front of me. "*Boychik*, write down the names of all your clients that have anything to do with this Rayburn fellow, no matter how remote."

"I have three: Jorge and both Morrisons."

"What about Hickham?"

"There's no file. When he became a client, it was more of a joke than anything else. He called the thousand dollars a fee for therapy because I listened to his story. I didn't really think of him as a client."

"Where do you keep client files?"

"Top two file drawers in my office in the executive suite."

Abe consulted his notes. "That would be McCrary Investigations on Bayfront Boulevard."

"Yeah."

"Did you make a note in Trey Morrison's file about him soliciting you to murder Rayburn?"

202

"No. I figured that wouldn't be prudent."

"What about Allison? Anything incriminating in her file?"

"No. Same reason."

Abe rubbed his hands together. "Okay. We won't touch your office. Let them find the normal stuff there; that will be less suspicious than if they found nothing. What about your cellphones?"

"I have three, two on me and one in my office desk. That reminds me: All Rayburn's stuff is in my desk at home. His laptop is in my bottom desk drawer on the left, and I have his tablet from his apartment and his cellphones. Same desk. He's had a week to replace those, so the homicide detectives may not know that they're missing."

"You heard that, Diane? Bring those too. Take Mel with you to help carry everything."

Chapter 63

By 11:00 a.m. the Medical Examiner's office sent someone to pick up Rayburn's body. The technician zipped the body bag and turned to Kelly. "We're a little backed up, detective. The ME said she'll try to get to this tomorrow. She asked me to tell you."

Kelly frowned. "Oh, great."

Bigs shrugged. "It is what it is."

"You keep processing," she said. "I'll go interview the manager."

She went to the manager's apartment. "Tell me how you found the body."

The guy eyeballed her up and down twice before deciding to look her straight in the boobs. *Maybe I should start thinking of it as a compliment,* she thought. *Nah. It'll make me want to kick him in the balls.*

The manager lit a cigarette without asking or apologizing. "Why don't you have a seat, doll? This may take a while."

"My name is Detective Contreras." She gave him a business card, then sat as far across the room as she could.

"Right. Detective." The manager put the card in his shirt and patted the pocket. He shifted his gaze to Kelly's crotch.

She wished she hadn't worn such tight pants. She placed her notepad on her thigh and pressed her knees together. "How did you find the body?"

"About seven o'clock this morning, one of Rayburn's employees come to me and asks me to let him into Ted's apartment. He tells me that he's supposed to meet Ted at six-thirty. Says he's been knocking on the door for a freakin' half hour and no one answers." He took a drag and blew the smoke out the side of his mouth.

Kelly crossed her legs and the guy decided to study her boobs again.

"Then the guy says Ted's van is in the garage so he knows he's home. Says he's worried about him."

She wrote that down.

"Funny thing, though. I let Ted into his apartment a week ago last Saturday night. He said he'd been mugged and the mugger took his keys and his wallet. You think there could be any connection?"

She shrugged and wrote that down. "Had you seen him since?"

"*Nah*. He comes and goes. He's a tenant. It's not like we was best buds or nothing. Hey, you wanna cup of coffee or something?"

"No, thanks. How did he appear after the mugging?"

"He looked like hell if you wanna know. Yeah, like hell. Said the mugger beat him up for no reason when he didn't even hafta. I asked him if he needed me to make him a new key. I got a slick new key-making machine in the shop back there." He gestured over his shoulder. "You wanna see it?"

"Did you make him a new key?"

"*Nah*. Ted said he kept a spare set in his apartment."

"How bad did he look?"

The manager thought for a minute. "He was bruised real bad on his cheek, right here. And he was already getting two black eyes, the kind you get when you've been smacked right on the nose pretty good. Oh yeah, and he had red marks around his wrists and his right hand was bandaged."

"Like he'd been tied up?"

"I dunno. Them marks was real narrow, not wide like a rope."

Kelly thanked him, then went to find the guy who'd discovered the body. She felt the manager's gaze burn her butt while she walked out. Nothing she could do about it other than wish he'd go blind.

The apartments had a tiny entrance lobby with two cracked plastic couches crammed against a wall. Rayburn's employee had been waiting there while Kelly interviewed the manager. They each tried to make themselves comfortable on the broken-down couches.

The guy struck Kelly as someone who would lie for the fun of it. He radiated a bad-guy vibe like he had been hired to be Rayburn's muscle. He said he hadn't talked to Rayburn since Saturday afternoon. Rayburn seemed okay when he'd left him at the Everglades Mall office.

"So how did you know to meet the victim at his apartment this morning?"

"He told me Saturday afternoon that he had this, ah, errand for me and that I should come see him at home this morning early."

"What kind of errand?"

The vibe got worse.

"I dunno. He didn't say."

"What did he want you to do?"

"He never told me."

"What kind of work did you do for the victim?"

He gazed around the room. Anywhere but at the detective. She waited.

"Oh, this and that. Run errands and stuff."

"What kind of errands?"

"Like I would bring his lunch from the food court sometimes."

"And—"

"Fill his car with gas, and get it washed, and like that."

"And what else?"

"And that's all."

"How long you worked for Rayburn?" Kelly asked.

"About six months, maybe."

"You must have some idea what he wanted you to do today."

"Nope. I dunno."

"Did anything strange happen to him about a week ago?"

"What you mean?"

"Like did he get mugged?"

"Oh, that. Yeah. And his office got burglarized. He had to buy all new computers and shit last week. New cellphones too."

The detective questioned him a couple of minutes more but got nothing. She took his contact information and returned to the crime scene.

She and Bigs and the CSIs processed the apartment most of the day Monday. Fingerprints, fibers, blood spatter, drains from the kitchen and bathroom.

"Bigs, you find a computer?"

"*Nah*. And no tablet and no cellphone, either. You think he kept them at his office?"

"Maybe. But still you would think he would have a computer at home too, right?"

"And no keys. I didn't find any keys. Why would the killer take his keys?" Bigs asked.

"Maybe he wanted to get into Rayburn's office, or car, or something else?"

"The guy who forced the door was almost certainly the murderer. I'll take an impression of the marks left by the pry bar."

There were no security cameras in the apartments. The two detectives canvassed the tenants, but no one had seen or heard anything unusual other than the manager.

Monday afternoon, Kelly and Bigs sent uniforms to seal the doors to McCrary's condo and office until they could get search warrants.

Kelly, Bigs, and the CSIs hit the Everglades Mall Tuesday morning. Mall security let them into Rayburn's office.

Rayburn's office appeared normal at first glance. Kelly moved into the back room and saw red splatters on the wall near the file cabinet and a couple more on Rayburn's chair. "Bigs, have the CSIs process those splatters. They look like blood."

The CSIs found lots of fingerprints. Kelly hated that part. The fingerprint dust stuck to everything: hands, shoes, pants, hair. *I'll have to wash my clothes twice when I get home.*

She knew it would take CSI a couple of days to identify all the prints. Some of them would be Chuck's. *No, I can't think of him as Chuck anymore,* she thought. *He's a suspect. They will find* McCrary's *prints all over the office.*

Chapter 64

Lieutenant Weiner's office called Kelly late Wednesday morning. The autopsy was complete.

The Medical Examiner was a brown-skinned woman in her forties. Kelly assumed she was Indian because she had a red dot painted between her eyebrows, a *bindi* or *bindu* if Kelly remembered correctly.

The gold earrings and necklace go well with her skin color. I would kill to have hair like hers. I'll bet she never needs conditioner.

Lieutenant Weiner waved the detectives over. "Doc, have you met Kelly Contreras and Arnie Bigelow?"

The ME shook hands. "I'm Dr. Anandi Mahajan. Call me Annie."

She referred to her notes. "Time of death was between 11:00 p.m. Sunday night and 4:00 a.m. Monday." She handed Kelly two evidence bags containing the two .45 caliber shells she'd pulled from the body. The detective signed for them.

"Both shells hit the victim in the stomach from close range, about three feet. The bullet holes were three inches apart. He was shot through his shirt; we found trace of the shirt fabric in each wound. The victim had numerous bruises and contusions and a broken right hand, all about a week old."

"Could it have been a mugging?"

"COD was the two gunshots."

"I meant the week-old bruises."

The ME shrugged. "Sure. He fought back. He had cuts and bruises on the knuckles on both hands."

Wednesday, Kelly and Bigs executed search warrants on McCrary's condo, boat, and office.

They hit his home first. Diane Toklas met the detectives there and opened the gun safe. They put his weapons into evidence bags. None were .45s.

A search of the basement storage rooms for McCrary's condo yielded nothing of interest.

By Thursday, the CSIs had identified the fingerprints from Rayburn's apartment.

"McCrary's prints were all over the place," Kelly commented while she read the report. "It seems like he searched Rayburn's apartment. What do you think, Bigs?"

"Yeah. Did Chuck tell you he'd been in Rayburn's apartment?"

"No, but in all fairness, I did Mirandize him before he finished telling me his story. Still, the evidence is leading to McCrary."

"He didn't do it, Kel. You know Chuck."

"Yeah, but evidence is evidence. We can't ignore it."

Diane Toklas unlocked the door to the McCrary Investigations office and stepped back while Kelly Contreras and Bigs Bigelow pulled on rubber gloves. Kelly gave a pair of gloves to Diane. "You better put these on too."

Kelly gestured Bigs to proceed. The giant detective removed the seals and led the group into the conference room.

Kelly twisted around. "There's nothing here we need, Bigs. Just take still pictures of all four walls and the furniture to show we looked." She pointed to the ceiling at one corner. "Make sure you get a picture of that video camera."

When Kelly opened the adjoining door to Chuck's office, Bigs raised his camera and began clicking.

She peered inside the office. "Jerry," she said to the police videographer, "record everything in this office in place, including that other video camera up there." She pointed. "We'll search the back storeroom before we do this office."

She stood aside while Jerry videoed the office. "You done?"

"Got it."

Kelly crossed the office and entered the storeroom. It contained an empty coat rack, a metal supply cabinet, a set of metal shelves, and two file cabinets. She opened the supply cabinet. "Nothing relevant here, Bigs. Just take a photo of the shelves." She opened both doors wide for her partner to photograph. When he finished, she closed the cabinet doors.

Diane had followed her into the room.

Kelly stepped back and saw a black metal box with a greenish-yellow display sitting on top of the metal shelves. "Is that where the security camera video and audio is recorded?"

"What you see is what you get."

Kelly motioned to Bigs. "Let's take the DVR with us. Bag it."

She asked Diane, "You have keys to the file cabinets?"

"Yeah. I'll unlock them."

Rifling through the file drawers, Bigs said, "I don't see any file with Rayburn's name on it."

Diane didn't say anything.

Bigs took the files into evidence anyway.

Back in Chuck's office, the homicide detectives bagged his computers and two cellphones.

Bigs asked, "You got keys to the desk too?"

Wordlessly, Diane unlocked the desk and stepped back.

Kelly began with the top left drawer. Her spirits fell even farther. "Jerry," she called to the videographer, "come video this before we move anything." A Craftsman pry bar lay diagonally in the drawer. She knew at once that it would match the marks on Rayburn's apartment door. "Bigs, you'd better bag this."

She opened the next drawer and stepped back while the videographer recorded everything. Kelly removed a Smith & Wesson Governor model revolver, .45 caliber, with two empty cartridges in the cylinder. She handed it to Bigs, who smelled the barrel.

"It's been fired recently and not cleaned."

"Figures." Kelly frowned. "Chuck—no—*McCrary* was a good cop; he wouldn't fire a weapon and put it away without cleaning it."

"I told you he didn't do it. It's a frame—just like the Franco murder."

"And a damned good one, so far."

"Kel, we have to run the ballistics."

She wiped her eyes. "I know, and we both know what they'll show."

Chapter 65

"**Chuck, it's Grandpa.** Grandma and I are coming to see you in a couple of days."

I put the phone on speaker. "Grandpa, I'm busy investigating a case. I don't have time to entertain you and Grandma. And I don't know if they'll let me back into the condo by then."

"We're not coming to be entertained, and don't worry about the condo. We'll get a hotel if necessary. We're coming because you'll need our support when you get arrested."

"What makes you think I'm going to be arrested?"

Grandpa laughed. "Get real, son. Grandma and I don't live in a cave. We get news feeds from Port City any time the local news mentions Carlos McCrary or Chuck McCrary or McCrary Investigations. We know all about the Franco case and the Ted Rayburn thing. At least we know everything that was in the paper or on the internet. We discussed it with your parents. Your mom called your *abuela* in Mexico. Somebody from the family has to come and we're retired. No argument—we're coming."

"I'd love to have you, Grandpa, but there's nothing you and Grandma can do to help me. You don't need to come. I'll be okay."

"Nonsense," Grandpa said. "If nothing else, we'll babysit that boy you took in. Your grandma will love someone new to cook for. And we'll cook your breakfast and evening meals. That'll save you time. And I'm a real good listener—much better than Grandma." He laughed. "She's a better talker, but you know that. Besides, we're retired. We've got nothing but time on our hands."

I might as well have tried to stop the Mississippi River on its way to the Gulf of Mexico.

Chapter 66

Clint sprinted ahead of me down the boardwalk. He had spent two nights with Snoop and his wife Janet until the Port City PD released my condo. He didn't seem any worse for the experience. Maybe the presence of Snoop and Janet's two teenaged daughters had helped.

I picked up the pace to overtake him. We had run four miles. Clint's legs were as long as mine and he was in good shape now.

For the first time, I couldn't catch him. Clint had outrun me.

When he hit the end of the boardwalk, Clint pulled up, grinning ear to ear. "What's the matter, old man? Can't keep up?" He did a Muhammad Ali shuffle.

I high-fived him. "This red-letter day deserves ice cream."

We stepped up to a beach kiosk. "Fudge Ripple and Walnut Crunch please, in a waffle cone," said Clint.

"I'll take a Peanut Butter Flip with Vanilla ice cream." I reached in the pocket of my sweat pants and extracted a wad of bills.

Clint took a bite of his cone. "First time I ever beat you."

"That's a big deal." I gave him another high five. "I never was a sprinter; I'm a long-distance runner. I knew the day would come when you'd beat me. I'm glad to see it."

Clint seemed surprised. "Why, man? I beat you."

"I'm proud of you. Of what you've become."

He took another lick. "And what have I become, bro?"

"Oh, that's a profound subject for a definite philosophical discussion. Probably not appropriate while we're having a male bonding experience."

"Is that what we're having here, a male bonding experience?"

"Definitely."

"And I thought we were eating ice cream." Clint smirked. "Oh, yeah, I can feel the bonding kick in right now." He licked his cone. "But I beat you good, didn't I?"

"You well and truly did." I clapped him on the shoulder. "You beat me like a drum."

Clint laughed and did another Ali shuffle. We wandered toward a bench on the boardwalk.

"You see that girl over there?" Clint gestured with his cone.

"I couldn't take my eyes off her if world peace depended on it."

"How old you reckon she be—she is?"

"Twenty-five, twenty-six. Whaddya think?"

"That would be my guess." Clint kept watching her while we talked. "Why don't the girls my age take off they tops? I never see no teenage titties on the beach. Why is it only the older ones?"

"Why don't you ask Terry?"

"I think I will ask her." He pronounced it "ask" instead of "ax."

There's a first time for everything, I thought.

We finished the ice cream and tossed the napkins in a bin. I picked up an extra napkin that had missed the bin. Clint picked up a couple too. I hoped he would follow my example in other ways too.

I curved south. "Let's start walking back."

We strolled in silence for a hundred yards.

"Clint, I expect to be arrested for murder soon."

"I know. You warned me about that."

"You can't stay in my condo without adult supervision. You don't have a car or a driver's license yet. And too many people, cops and others, know you're there. Someone would squeal to DCF and they would make you go back into foster care."

"I kinda figured that. You taking me back to the warehouse?"

"What? God, no. My grandparents are coming to visit. They'll take the other guest room. When I get arrested, they'll make you dinner, take you to school—all that good stuff."

"You asked them to come stay with me?"

"No. They called me yesterday and announced they were coming. In my family, you don't need to ask for help. They just do it." One more benefit of a close-knit family that Clint had never experienced. Grandma and Grandpa would be good for Clint.

Chapter 67

An unmarked car pulled into the visitors' parking lot. From my balcony on the fourteenth floor, I couldn't make out the faces of the two people who got out, but I didn't have to. One was huge and, from his sheer bulk, it had to be Bigs Bigelow. The other would be Kelly. They walked with slumped shoulders and weary steps, like they were each carrying a heavy weight, which, in a way, they were.

A black-and-white stopped behind the unmarked car. Its lights sent spears of blue and red streaking across the other cars in the lot. Two uniforms got out and formed up behind the two detectives. They all stared up at the balcony.

I waved at them.

No one waved back.

I called Abe Weisman. "It's time. They've come to arrest me."

"I'll meet you down at the precinct."

In less than two minutes, I heard a knock on the door. Kelly and Bigs entered with the two uniforms.

"Carlos McCrary, you are under arrest for the murder of Theodore P. Rayburn. You have the right to remain silent…"

Kelly recited the Miranda warning for the second time.

I about-faced and placed my hands behind me. I hadn't been handcuffed since police academy training. I didn't like it then, and I didn't like it now.

Kelly drove straight into the police garage. No perp walk. Abe had connections all over Port City and, apparently, I still had friends in the police department.

Abe met us in the interview room. "Detective Contreras, I have instructed my client not to answer any questions."

Abe had arranged bail with the prosecutor. Within two hours, I was fitted with a tracking anklet, and Abe drove me home.

By the time Abe arrived at my condo, a television news van had already staked out the front of my building. A blonde reporter with impossibly white teeth yakked breathlessly into a television camera as she stretched for the maximum drama from my arrest. A female vulture is actually called a "hen." That seemed too nice for a human carrion-eater. I thought of her as a "vulturess." I could imagine what she was saying: "Approximately three hours ago, former police detective Carlos McCrary was arrested, charged with the murder of an unarmed man during a home invasion…"

I rolled my eyes. At least my building's security would keep the blonde vulturess from knocking on my door and sticking her microphone in my face. If that had happened, I might have stuck her own microphone someplace she wouldn't like.

I shook hands with Clint and collapsed on the couch.

"Can I get you something, bro?"

"I'm good. I'm gonna call Terry."

Her phone rang twice and went to voicemail. That meant that her phone was on, and she had time to see who was calling. She had refused my call. Ever the optimist, I left a message. "It's Chuck. I'm out on bail. I'd sure like to hear your voice or talk to you or something. Please call."

Clint sat with me on the balcony watching the sun set. We hadn't said much in the four hours since I came home. There wasn't much to say.

My phone whistled. It was a text from Terry.

Terry knew how I felt about texting. Texting should be used for a simple conveyance of information to confirm an appointment or send an address or phone number to someone. It was a sterile one-way communication to someone you didn't need to talk to. Yet Terry had texted me instead of calling. The medium was part of the message. She didn't want to talk to me.

"Is it from Terry?" Clint asked.

I nodded.

Clint squeezed my shoulder.

I knew the substance of the message before I read it.

> Chuck, I can't take this anymore. I have mailed back your condo key. Please mail me mine. Good luck with the trial and good luck with Clint. All the best, Terry.

I handed the phone to Clint, then clasped my hands and leaned over my knees, sobbing.

The next day, Clint and I were waiting in the guest parking lot when Grandma and Grandpa arrived. They couldn't wait to meet Clint, so Grandpa stopped in the guest lot and they got out.

"Magnus and Connie McCrary, may I present Clint Watkins."

"Pleased to meet you, Mrs. McCrary, Mr. McCrary."

Grandpa shook Clint's hand warmly, and Grandma grabbed Clint in a bear hug. "Clint, you'll call us Grandpa and Grandma. All Chuck's friends call us that." She squeezed both shoulders and examined him from head to foot. "My, but you're a handsome young man. Okay, let's go up and get settled."

I gave them a portable remote to the parking garage gate.

It appeared as though I wouldn't have to put Clint in the Port City Prep dormitory yet.

Chapter 68

Two weeks later

"Chuck, examine the evidence from the jury's viewpoint." Abe Weisman frowned at a stack of stapled documents. "The DA gave me these transcripts of all their witness interviews, so we know what they'll say on the stand if this goes to trial. Trey Morrison said that you and he discussed the advisability of killing Rayburn."

"Morrison is so low that he could walk under a snake without removing his hat," I replied. "The guy's a weasel who won't take responsibility for his own idea."

"That may be true, but his testimony would be very damaging."

"Abe, he brought up the subject, not me, and I told him 'no way.'"

Abe plowed ahead as if I hadn't spoken. Maybe he was handling me like the prosecutor handles a jury. "Morrison says you mentioned that you have an ocean-going boat and that people sometimes fall off boats and are never heard from again."

"The weasel found out about my boat when he Googled me. I never mentioned it to him. He brought up that crap about people falling off boats, not me."

Abe regarded me without expression. "There's more. Hank Hickham asked you if you were going to kill Rayburn and you said 'That won't be necessary.' Did you say that killing him would not be necessary?"

I regarded Snoop before answering. "Yes; that much is true." Abe had hired Snoop as a defense investigator so Snoop's conversations with us would be covered under attorney-client privilege.

"That implies you would kill him if it became necessary."

"Bullshit. It meant that we could achieve our objective of stopping Rayburn without killing him."

Diane said, "Don't forget the cashier's check for $50,000 that Abe is holding for you in his desk."

"I told Hank not to do that."

"He did it anyway," Diane said. "At least he was smart enough not to volunteer that information to the prosecution."

"I warned him that it would look like he'd hired me as a hitman."

The check had arrived at my office the Friday after Rayburn's murder, the day after homicide finished processing the crime scene and released it. For once, I was happy for slow mail service. I hated to think what would have happened if it arrived when the PCPD still controlled my office and read my mail.

"If that payment surfaces," Snoop said, "Mabel the Marauder will crucify Chuck."

"That's why it's in my desk. Right now, that $50,000 is the least of our worries." Abe referred to another file. "Chuck, your fingerprints were on both of Rayburn's guns and his switchblade that the detectives found in your home."

"I disarmed him; you know that."

"Your fingerprints were on his file cabinet, desk, office chair, and door."

"I told you that."

"But think how that will appear to a jury. The prosecutor will say you accosted him in his office, and that you were the aggressor."

Abe perused his file. "Your fingerprints were on the barrel of the murder weapon that homicide found in your office. And on the cartridges found in the murder weapon."

"When I loaded the revolver, I left fingerprints on the cartridges. Then I held it by the barrel when I placed it in the nightstand. There were no prints on the handle of the gun because the killer wiped the handle to remove his own fingerprints."

I couldn't sit still any longer. I stood and spread my hands.

"Abe, I've been framed. I keep—I *kept* that revolver in the nightstand beside my bed. I didn't know it was gone until the cops found it in my office. I know I didn't move it. The last time I saw it was when I moved into my condo and unpacked. That was months ago."

"And Rayburn's apartment door was forced by a pry bar that homicide found in your office."

"Chuck had Rayburn's keys," Snoop said. "If anything, that's evidence of his innocence. Remind the jury that he didn't need to force Rayburn's door. The real killer did that. Then he planted the pry bar in Chuck's office when he planted the revolver. You'll tell them that Chuck's fingerprints were not found on the pry bar or the handle of the murder weapon."

Abe ignored Snoop's comments. "Chuck, unless you prove who entered Rayburn's apartment the next weekend after you searched it, and who planted the revolver and pry bar in your office, we won't win this trial. The DA could go for the death penalty unless we plea bargain."

"Abe, I won't plead guilty to something I didn't do."

"I think I can get you manslaughter. You'd serve ten years, out in eight on good behavior."

"I can't plead guilty; I didn't do it."

"Then you'd better find out who did, and you don't have much time. The judge could revoke your bail any time she thinks you might be a flight risk."

"I'm not going anywhere."

"But you have lots of money and lots of family in both Mexico and Texas. Don't count on the judge ignoring that."

I had confronted enemies before, but this was different. In Afghanistan and Iraq, enemies shot at me and my fellow soldiers or planted bombs in the road, but we had trained to handle that. I knew how to spot IEDs buried in the road and where to look for ambushes.

My trained brothers, fellow Green Berets, were in the same boat. We had each other's backs.

This was different. Snoop was doing the best he could, but he couldn't help anymore. My friends on the Port City police couldn't help. Some of them thought I did it and the rest weren't sure.

I left Abe's office in a daze.

Chapter 69

I found myself at Vicky's front door. I don't know how I got there. I must have called her from my new cellphone. The police still had my old phones in the evidence locker. I remembered trying to call Snoop to apologize for the way I'd left him in Abe's office, but the call had gone straight to voicemail.

Vicky stepped back and held her apartment door open. Her eyes were wet and her mascara had run down her mocha cheeks leaving black tracks behind. Again.

I stepped inside and she hugged me like she was holding me during a hurricane. The door slammed behind us. She must have kicked it closed. I didn't pay attention to anything except the warmth of her embrace, the caring, the acceptance—and the trust.

Ever since Rayburn's murder, I had held myself together with duct tape and baling wire, worrying about Jorge and Clint and Snoop and my parents and grandparents. Everyone but myself. I had always been the tough guy who handled anything life threw at me, but Abe, my own attorney, had urged me to plea bargain. It was too much to carry any longer.

Tears spilled down my cheeks the minute Vicky led me into her bedroom. We hadn't said a word; none was necessary. We fell on the bed and held each other as if the world were ending. For me, it seemed like it was.

After a while, she held my face in her hands and gazed into my eyes. "It will be all right, baby. It will be all right." She kissed my eyelids and wiped my tears with a tissue. She held my face in her hands again. This time she didn't say anything.

She kissed my forehead, each cheek, my chin. She stopped and peered into my eyes, as if for a signal.

Whatever she saw there, she kissed me on the mouth.

I felt my libido stir. Survival instincts are amazing.

"I'd better watch out or I could lose my Macho Man Membership."

Vicky smiled. She had given up on the mascara and removed all her makeup.

All afternoon we had alternated between making love and simply lying in each other's arms.

I didn't exactly feel better, but at least I had stopped feeling worse. "Vicky, you've recharged my batteries. I can return to the fight."

She laughed and squeezed my hand.

I lay back against the pillow, my arm draped around her shoulders. I gave her an affectionate squeeze and smiled. "I suddenly remembered that I have a secret weapon," I said. *If it works…*

Chapter 70

Abe Weinstein and Diane Toklas handed Snoop and me copies of the rest of the discovery documents that the prosecutor had provided them.

I flipped to the list of items taken from my office under the search warrant. "Abe, I haven't told you this before, but I have a secret weapon."

"A secret weapon?"

"Yeah. The police didn't find my other office surveillance system."

"You have more than one?"

"I have a manual system that I turn on to document meetings with clients. The detectives found that and took it into evidence. But there's a second system."

Abe's eyes opened wider. "What is this? You have a surveillance system you didn't tell me about?"

"I do."

"Why don't I know about this?"

"Frankly, I'd forgotten about it until yesterday. I installed it three months ago. After my initial tests, I never needed it again. Until I examined the videos this morning, I didn't know if it worked."

"What area does it cover?"

"My office and conference room. I installed one hidden microphone and two pinhole cameras in each room." I tapped the prosecutor's discovery file. "Apparently, the installers hid them well enough that the detectives didn't find them. Either that or they didn't think to search for a second system after they found the first one. The new system sends a wireless signal to a computer hidden above the ceiling in my storeroom. It is motion- and sound-sensitive. It records everything whether I tell it to or not."

"Can you play the recording?"

I grinned. "You bet. I played it in my office this morning. The guys who installed it said I can access it from any computer attached to the internet."

"You mean you can access it here in our office? Now?" Diane asked.

"Bring me a laptop and I'll download the files from the system onto your computer so you'll have a copy."

In minutes, Diane set a computer and stick drive on the conference table. "How far back do the recordings go?"

"Theoretically 24/7 for one year."

"You'd run out of storage space on the hard drive."

"Not really. When there's no motion or sound in my office, it's not recording. When it does record something, it backs up to the Cloud every night and starts new files every day at 2:00 a.m."

"I'm impressed. Show us."

Diane, Abe, and Snoop stood behind me.

I logged into the surveillance company's website. "These guys installed the system. I had them do it after midnight on a weekend so no one in the office knows I have it. In fact, until now, no one else in the world knew I had it, not even Snoop."

The McCrary Investigations account popped up on the screen. "Here's the file directory." I clicked my way through more commands and a list of files materialized on the screen. "The autopsy said the murder occurred after 11:00 p.m. I watched the videos from my home this morning. The killer broke into my office about 3:00 a.m."

I keyed in the command and held my breath while we waited. It seemed to take longer to load than it had in my office. I hoped Abe's office had a slower connection than mine. If not, I was toast.

"I installed two pinhole cameras and a hidden microphone in the conference room and another set in the office. The cameras are in opposite corners where the walls meet the ceiling.

The microphones are in the light fixture. The surveillance company modified the ceiling tiles so the cameras can see out. The monitor is supposed to show all four pictures."

The silence was tense.

"It's taking too long," Snoop said. "It's not gonna work."

"Keep your shirt on, Snoop. These high definition files take a lot of bandwidth. It takes time for the files to buffer. Give it a minute."

The screen lit with four dim images, and I resumed breathing. "The system started recording when the microphone heard the killer pick the lock. When we see something to investigate further, I can zoom to the whole screen with any of the images."

"Why is the picture so dim?" Diane asked.

Snoop pointed at the monitor. "Middle of the night. The lights were off, so the picture's lousy."

Diane said, "I hope the killer switched on the lights when he came in. Otherwise, it's gonna be impossible to identify anyone from that."

"Unfortunately, he left the lights off. This picture is as good as it gets. But don't worry—I know who the killer is."

The three others spoke at the same time.

I held up a hand in a *stop* motion. "Just be patient. You'll see what I saw in a minute." The monitor showed my office door opening.

"Hold it," Snoop said.

A figure moved across the screen.

"I see it." I reversed the video and the figure moved backwards until it left the frame. "Okay, I'll show you what happened."

The screen index said 03:22:21. The hall door to my office opened inward. I clicked on the upper left image from the camera behind my desk and it expanded to fill the screen. "Here he is."

The figure was tall. Moved like a man. He seemed too hefty to be a woman. It definitely fit the description of the man I now knew was the killer. The figure was dressed like the mysterious jogger from the Day and Night Diner surveillance tapes, except he wore a ski mask. The unknown jogger wore what appeared to be a watch cap. It was a ski mask rolled up like a cap. He carried a shopping bag hooked over his left forearm.

"Pause that." Snoop leaned closer in his seat.

I paused the video. "I'll blow up the shopping bag." With three or four clicks, I zoomed the image and dragged it to where the bag filled the screen. I zoomed it more. "I studied this earlier. As you see, the back side of the bag is blank." A click sent the image to Abe's network printer. "For evidence."

Diane moved toward the door. "I'll get the print."

"Wait," I said, "there will be more we'll want. The other camera got a good shot of the front of the bag."

I clicked back to the four-image screen and clicked on the upper right image. It was at the same time index. I zoomed the image.

"I can't make that out," said Diane.

"I'll enhance it." I clicked a couple of links and dragged the enhanced image to the center of the screen. "It's from Harry's Handy Hardware. I'll print that." I sent the next image to the printer. Restoring the image to full-screen, I tapped *play* again.

"He's wearing white gloves," Abe said.

"No, those are latex disposable gloves. Cops wear them at crime scenes."

Diane asked, "The killer's a cop?"

"I've suspected that all along. But when I saw the video this morning, it all fell into place."

"Who is it?"

"It's Dan Murphy."

Chapter 71

I played the video again.

Murphy waved a small flashlight and walked around the desk. He opened the top left drawer. The camera angle showed the view over his left shoulder. He reached into the Harry's Handy Hardware bag and removed a pry bar, holding it by the blade. The Craftsman name showed on the handle.

I zoomed in, enhanced the picture, and printed the image. "I'll bet a Cadillac against a candy bar that that's the pry bar he used to break into Rayburn's apartment. Maybe we'll get lucky. Maybe he even bought it at Harry's Handy Hardware."

"We're overdue for some luck," said Snoop.

I ran the video again. When Murphy pulled the S&W handgun from the bag, I paused the image. "Dan dropped by my condo unannounced a few weeks ago." I told them about Murphy's visit. "The reason he was gone to the bathroom so long is that it took him five minutes to find my revolver."

I zoomed the image of the handgun, enhanced it, and printed it. "Now, Diane, you can go get the prints."

"How did he get Jorge's gun?" Snoop asked.

"I'll have a skull session with Jorge and we'll figure it out."

"I'll brainstorm that with you both."

"I've got a different assignment for you. Now that we know when Dan broke into my office, I want you to recheck the other surveillance cameras in my building, the parking lot, and the route between Rayburn's apartment and my office. I bet Murphy drove straight to my office after he killed Rayburn. He needed to plant the evidence before dawn. You're going to be busy."

Abe made a face. "You seem awfully sure it's Murphy. Where's the evidence?"

"It's the one explanation that makes sense. Murphy is the one person that had access to my gun and the smarts to pull off both of these murders. And don't worry about the evidence. Now that I know who the killer is, I'll focus like a laser on Murphy. Snoop and I will find the evidence."

Abe asked, "What's Murphy's motive?"

"I don't know yet. But you can take this to the bank: Dan Murphy murdered Ted Rayburn, maybe even Garrison Franco."

"I can understand why he'd kill Franco," Abe said. "But why would he frame Jorge Castellano?"

Chapter 72

I pulled up Google Maps on my new computer. Homicide had kept the old computers for evidence. I asked the app for directions from Rayburn's apartment to McCrary Investigations.

"Okay, Snoop, I'll print this." I dragged the blue line over to highlight two more routes and printed them.

"Kelly and Bigs already reviewed the surveillance from my office parking lot, but they didn't know what to look for or when. Review it again from 3:00 a.m. on that Monday morning. See what vehicles Murphy and his wife Jessica own. See if you can spot one of their cars."

"Relax, bud. This ain't my first rodeo."

"Sorry, Snoop. I didn't mean to insult you."

"I earned every gray hair and wrinkle I've got, bud. After I figure out which car Murphy used, I'll canvass those three routes, beginning with this one." He tapped a Google Maps printout. "If, for any reason, I can't identify Murphy's car from your office end, I'll start from Rayburn's apartment and trace it from there. That's a lot of territory to cover. This could take a while."

"Well, it's not like my life depends on it or anything."

Chapter 73

Jorge leaned back in my conference room chair. "Dan has the smarts and the guts to kill Franco. And I understand his motive. He heard Franco threaten Karen, and he wanted to protect her. And he knew I could never gun down anyone in cold blood, even if he deserved killing."

"You think Murphy could kill someone in cold blood?" I asked.

Jorge frowned. "I hate to say it, *amigo*, but, yes, Dan could kill someone if they needed killing." He stopped. "But what's his motive to frame me? Why would he pin a murder on me? That's not going to protect Karen."

"Whatever his motive, Dan wasn't trying to protect Karen. He killed Franco for another reason. He killed two birds with one stone and you were the other bird. From the get-go, he had it in for you; that was his real motive for the murder. That's why he framed you, and he did a slick job of it."

"But why?"

"Maybe it's something you know, but don't know you know. Think about it. Anything going on with you and Karen?"

Jorge's eyes flicked to one side. His lips moved and then he froze.

"You thought of something."

"It was nothing, really."

"In my experience, when someone says, 'It was nothing, really,' they mean 'It was *something*, really.' What crossed your mind when I asked you about Karen?"

"Dan and I have been partners for three years. When we first teamed up, we took our wives and went out on a sort of double date to get to know each other, you know?"

"I did that when Snoop and I partnered up. Except I'm single and it was Snoop and Janet and me."

"Right. Anyway, Karen and Dan's wife Jessica hit it off right away. Turns out, they both played tennis in high school. Jessica was four years older so they never met each other when they were competing." He hesitated.

I waited.

"Karen began a regular tennis game with Jessica." He stopped again.

"So?" I prompted.

"They've played every week for the last three years."

I waited again. Sometimes you have to let people answer in their own way, in their own time.

Jorge spread his hands and shrugged. "It's strange."

"What's strange about a regular tennis date? I know guys who play poker or golf every week for years with the same bunch of guys."

Jorge leaned his elbows on his knees. "Karen and I used to play tennis a lot. Most weekends we played for two hours at a public court right next to our apartment."

I scoffed. "And Karen doesn't play with you anymore. What, you're jealous?"

"No, no, it's not that. When Karen and I finished playing, we'd race each other home. It was a hundred yards, and we'd come in all sweaty. We would take a shower together. And then…" He stopped, swallowed, then continued, "we'd make love like we were on fire. It was like the exercise of playing tennis made us both so horny we couldn't keep our hands off each other."

"What's your point?"

Even though we were alone in the conference room, Jorge leaned toward me and lowered his voice. "Since Karen began playing with Jessica, when she comes home from a match, she's always too tired for sex." His eyes seemed too bright. "That happens every week now, and Karen and I don't… We just *don't* very often anymore."

I waggled a finger. "When I told Dan about you and I meeting on the boardwalk near the topless beach, he made a comment about maybe you weren't getting enough sex at home. He said that was why you were stepping out on Karen. I thought he was joking at first. Are you stepping out?"

"Dan had to be joking."

"He wasn't joking."

"I don't tell Dan all my troubles, so he doesn't know about my situation with Karen, but I have never cheated on her."

"Then why would Dan think you had?"

Chapter 74

There were over three hundred hardware stores in Atlantic County. Probably two hundred of them carried the Craftsman brand of pry bar used to force Rayburn's apartment door. No matter how many uniforms the PCPD used to canvass hardware stores, and even if I had bought the pry bar, their chances of finding evidence of that were slim to none.

Judging from the prosecutor's discovery file, I figured they hadn't even tried. Kelly and Bigs found that pry bar in my desk, the DA declared the case a slam dunk, and that was enough for the prosecution. It was rare, sloppy police work by Kelly and Bigs. I figured the DA's office had told them to stop investigating the murder—the case against me was solid as the Rock of Gibraltar.

Harry's Handy Hardware had ten stores in Atlantic County and a whiz-bang computerized perpetual inventory system.

I drove to their regional headquarters in southwest Miami where I had an appointment with the company's security director, Wallace Townsend.

"Come in, Mr. McCrary. You want coffee?"

"That would be great, and please call me Chuck."

Townsend's secretary asked, "How do you take your coffee?"

I told her and she left.

"You said something about a criminal investigation?"

I gave him a business card. I would've flashed my PI license too, but Bigs took it when he and Kelly arrested me. "The Public

Defender's Office in Atlantic County retained me to investigate a homicide."

When I was arrested, Darcy Yankton had seized the opportunity to fire me, but she had, at one time, retained me, so that statement was *true-ish*. I didn't tell Townsend that the homicide Darcy had hired me to investigate was for a different victim.

I handed Townsend the pictures of Dan Murphy and the pry bar. "I need to find out if this man bought this pry bar from one of your stores within the last few months."

Townsend placed the two pictures on his desk. "Can you narrow down the time frame?"

I told him the date of Rayburn's murder. "Sometime before that. I'd like to start then and work backwards. And this guy..." I tapped Murphy's picture, "lives closest to your store number 717 on Southwest 44th Boulevard near 67th Avenue. Could you check that store first?"

"Sure. Pull your chair around over here."

Our coffee came.

Townsend adjusted his keyboard. "I'll pull up this SKU number first. We carry pry bars in several different lengths. I can't tell from this photo which one this is. How long is the actual bar?"

I referred to the official police crime scene photo that had the black and white scale laid next to it. "It's seventeen inches."

Townsend tapped the keyboard. "That's part of a three-piece set of 12- , 17- , and 25-inch pry bars." He wrote down the SKU number on a Post-It Note and stuck it to the edge of his monitor. He punched in the number and studied the screen. "Oh, that SKU is very popular." He smiled. Then he frowned. "Of course, that's not good for your investigation, is it?"

"Whether it is or not, I want the truth."

Townsend examined the screen again. "Since the first of the year, we've sold thirty-seven of those pry bar sets at that store." He hit another key. "Four were sold for cash. The other thirty-three used credit cards. Would it help if I gave you the names of the customers who bought them?"

Like Snoop said, I was due for a little luck.

Chapter 75

Sunday morning, I parked in the shade of an ancient live oak across the street from the park and opened the side windows of the Caravan. I had a good view of the tennis courts through the windshield. I knew Karen, of course, but I'd never met Jessica. I watched them through binoculars while they played a hundred yards away. Karen had a strong, two-handed backhand. Jessica was a lefty with a powerful serve-and-volley game.

Karen worked as a bank teller and always had Sunday off. Jorge said Jessica worked five days a week in the office of the Gladesview Apartments, a large complex on the western edge of town.

The two women played for twenty minutes then grabbed their gear and left the court. They walked to Jessica's car, a late model blue Corolla sedan. Both women got in and left Karen's car at the tennis court.

I followed at a respectable distance.

Fifteen minutes later, Jessica's Corolla pulled into the Gladesview Apartments. It was a large complex with dozens of three-story buildings arranged around rectangular recreational areas. I followed them to the back. Most of the parking spaces were filled, and the other vehicles hid my Dodge from view when the two women climbed the stairs hand-in-hand. They had left their tennis gear in Jessica's car, but Jessica carried am overnight bag.

She used a key to open the door to an apartment and both women went in. I zoomed my camera and snapped a telephoto picture as they entered. I switched to binoculars. The number on the door read *2274*.

I booted my tablet computer. The apartment complex had its own website. Apartments ranged from one to four bedrooms. The 2200 building featured all two-bedroom apartments. I called the leasing office and spoofed as a prospective tenant. I learned that Unit 2274 was vacant. And furnished.

An hour later, Karen and Jessica came out arm-in-arm, and I followed them back to the tennis courts. Before Karen got out of the Corolla, she kissed Jessica. This was not an air kiss between good friends. This kiss was on the mouth. For a long time.

Poor Jorge. Poor Dan.

Chapter 76

Abe Weinstein joined Diane Toklas and me in a conference room. "Sorry to keep you waiting. Long telephone call. Some people don't know how to say goodbye."

We shook hands.

"What have you got for me, Chuck?"

"I have the credit card receipt and the cash register tape where Murphy bought the pry bar three months before Rayburn's murder."

"That's great. How did you find that?"

"I'm the world's greatest detective." I told them about Wallace Townsend and his magic inventory system.

"Why didn't Murphy pay cash for the pry bar? Using a credit card was dumb. He left a trail for you to follow."

"Because he bought the pry bars long before he decided to murder Rayburn."

"Why would Murphy buy the pry bar so soon? You said he didn't know Rayburn was out of prison until a couple of weeks before he killed him."

"People do buy pry bars for legitimate reasons," Diane said. "Maybe he wanted to pry something."

Abe laughed.

I said, "I'll call Kelly and Bigs with this so they can get a warrant to search Murphy's house. Maybe they'll find the other two pry bars from the set. If we're really lucky, the store's security cameras have a video of him buying it."

Chapter 77

Jorge raised his beer and took a long pull.

He and I both had our feet propped on the rail of my balcony. "Jorge, have you been running around on Karen?"

"Like I told you, *amigo*, I admit that I've been tempted. Karen's not there for me anymore, but I haven't strayed off the farm. Yet."

"Dan said you did."

"I told you before and I'll tell you again: Dan's wrong."

"Okay. That makes what I'm gonna tell you a lot harder for you to take."

Jorge dropped his feet to the deck. "You followed Karen and Jessica, didn't you? I figured you would when you asked me where they play tennis."

"Yeah, I followed them. I've got bad news."

Jorge set his beer bottle on the table so hard I thought either the bottle or the glass tabletop would break. Fortunately, neither one did. "Jesus H. Christ, I was afraid of this. At some level, I guess I already knew: She's having an affair with Jessica, isn't she?"

"Sorry, buddy."

He jerked to his feet and paced across the balcony. "Goddammit. Goddammit. Goddammit."

"You want the details?"

"No… yes… I don't know." He stopped and the pain in his expression was as plain as a flashing neon sign. "Do I want the details?"

I shrugged. "I always figure it's better to know than not know, but that's me. It's your call."

Jorge closed his eyes. "Tell me."

"Jessica works in the office of the Gladesview Apartments. She knows which furnished apartments are empty. Last Sunday, she and Karen played tennis for twenty minutes, then took Jessica's car and drove to the Gladesview. They went into a vacant furnished apartment. Jessica carried a small suitcase with them. It was large enough to hold sheets for the bed. They stayed for an hour before returning to Karen's car."

Jorge smashed a fist into his other palm. "Goddammit."

"*Amigo*, don't go off half-cocked on this. You need Karen in your corner right now. Play this close to your chest until I clear your name."

Jorge started to protest.

"Karen can't help who she is. Until she met Jessica, she may not have realized she was a lesbian. You gain nothing if you blow up your marriage. Just cool it, okay?

"Okay."

"Now, the big question: Does Dan know?"

Jorge pursed his lips in thought. "I don't think so."

"Dan thinks you chase girls. Suppose something is wrong with his marriage to Jessica. Suppose he thinks Jessica is being unfaithful." I snapped my fingers. "Perhaps he thinks she's cheating with you. That could be his motive to frame you for Franco's murder."

Chapter 78

I called Snoop and Jorge to my condo for a strategy session. My grandparents had gone to a movie matinee.

Clint was studying in his bedroom. He walked into the living room.

I was pacing by the glass doors while the three of us discussed the case. "Okay, we have to consider that since Murphy framed me for Rayburn's murder, he also framed Jorge for Franco's murder."

Jorge eyeballed Clint. "Guys, we shouldn't discuss this in front of Clint. He doesn't need this in his life."

Clint said, "Jorge, my younger sister was killed in a drive-by shooting when I was eight."

"Oh God. I'm sorry to hear that, Clint."

"I watched her bleed to death, man. I can take hearing about this. Besides, maybe I can help you."

All three of us spoke at the same time. "How?"

Clint sat on the other end of a couch from Snoop. "A few weeks ago, Chuck asked me about the night Franco was killed."

He pronounced "asked" correctly again. Was he finally out of the ghetto in his mind? I gave myself a mental high five and gestured for him to go on. "And...?"

"Maybe I did see something that might help you."

Jorge started to say something.

I motioned him to stay quiet. "Go on."

"Something woke me up that night. I didn't know what it was, so I switched on the light. I looked around my room, but I didn't see or hear nothing—I mean, *anything*—out of the ordinary. I decided to go back to sleep when I thought I'd take a quick peek out the window."

"What did you see?"

"This dude dressed in black ran to the middle of the street where some other guy was lying on the ground beside this car. I watched the dude in black shoot the guy on the ground. Then he robbed the dead guy. He went through the dead guy's pockets and took his wallet and stuff."

"Was he wearing gloves?"

"I don't remember."

"Close your eyes. See the man again in your mind. Watch him run to the center of the street. See him bend down."

"Yeah." Clint opened his eyes. "His hands were as black as his shirt, but he had a white face. He must've worn gloves."

Clint moved to the center of the room and squatted. "He leaned over like this." He demonstrated. "He pointed a gun at the building where I was crashing and shot it three times. *Bang, bang, bang*." Clint returned to the couch. "Then he ran to the building next door and pulled out a flashlight."

"The building next door?" I asked.

"Yeah, the one to the south. Closest to that car that was in the street."

"I knew it, Snoop. When I first visited the crime scene, I thought the place with the bullet holes in the building was not the best place to shoot from. It was the next building south."

I focused on Clint again. "What did he do there?"

"I couldn't tell, man. He shined that light around a bunch. For maybe a minute. Then he run off down the street."

"Which way did he run?"

"South."

"Toward 84th Street," Snoop said.

"Where we found the surveillance video of him before and after the shooting."

Chapter 79

It was late afternoon when the four of us arrived at the crime scene. The parking lot was half full. "Show us where the shooter was."

Clint walked to the curb. "The dude was standing here." He peered up at the window of the room where he used to sleep to get his bearings. "Yeah, about here." He rotated toward the street. "Then he jogged out here."

Clint moved to the center of the street and dropped to his knees. "He shot the guy again." He mimed the action. "Then he robbed the guy." Clint leaned over and pointed both hands back at the building where he used to live. "Then he fired three times at my building."

"He must have put Franco's gun in his hand after he was dead," said Jorge. "He used Franco's finger to pull the trigger."

"Jorge, you investigated Franco for months," I said. "Was he right-handed or left-handed?"

Jorge closed his eyes and his head moved while he recreated a scene in his mind. "He was right-handed."

Snoop nodded. "That's right, bud. The autopsy report."

"The gunshot residue was on Franco's left hand," I said.

Jorge grinned. "My dumb bastard partner used the wrong hand."

I high-fived Jorge and then Clint. "Okay, we're on a roll. Clint, show us where you saw the flashlight."

A middle-aged man wearing a sports coat and slacks exited the building. "I'm the office manager here. Can I help you folks?"

I handed him a card. "I'm Chuck McCrary and these are my associates. We're investigating the shooting that happened in front of your building a few weeks ago, right out there in the street."

"I remember that. But I thought the police finished their investigation."

"I work for the defense attorney. The police may have to re-open the case."

The manager frowned. "This won't block my entrance, will it?"

"I think we can make our investigation without blocking the entrance."

"Okay, I guess." He went back inside.

Clint pointed. "The dude was shining his light all over this area here."

I clicked on a Maglite and dropped to my hands and knees. "I'll take the steps. Jorge, you begin at that end of the wall with Snoop's Maglite. Snoop's too old to get on his hands and knees."

"I am not, but I'm too smart to be crawling around when I have one of you youngsters to do it." He handed his Maglite to Jorge. "Go for it."

I had examined six or eight feet when I saw a flash of brash wedged between the concrete step and the asphalt paving. "I found what Murphy was searching for. It's a brass casing."

I regarded the other men gathered around. "Call Kelly and Bigs."

Bigs walked over with traffic cones and crime scene tape.

"I promised the owner we wouldn't block his entrance," I said.

"I'll punch his TS card." Bigs unrolled the crime scene tape and blocked off the entrance to the building from the edge of the parking lot to the front door.

Clint whispered to me, "What's a TS card?"

I chuckled. "An old Army joke. It means *tough shit*. If you get twenty-five punches on your TS card, you get a free visit with the chaplain."

Bigs frowned at me, but he suppressed a smile. "Okay, Chuck, show me what you found."

Chapter 80

Mabel Magruder, proudly known by friend and adversary alike as Mabel the Marauder, sat on one side of the conference table with Assistant DA Tomás Estacado, Bigs, and Kelly. Abe and Diane sat with Snoop and me across the table from them. Offensive line versus defensive line, with Jorge Castellano's and my futures as the football.

Darcy Yankton and Jorge Castellano were wedged into one end of the table. Jorge gave me a thumbs-up. Darcy seemed uncomfortable, but she always seemed uncomfortable around me. Bad chemistry.

Kelly smiled at me for the first time in weeks.

Handshakes all around, friendlier than I expected, except for Darcy. She didn't look at me. I winked at her, but she didn't see it.

Snoop saw it and smirked.

Magruder cleared her throat. "There have been new developments in the Garrison Franco murder case and the Ted Rayburn murder case." She motioned to Estacado, who passed around a thin stack of papers.

"Let's see the top sheet first," Magruder said.

It was a "ten set" of fingerprints. Dan Murphy's name was at the top and a single exemplar was at the bottom, a partial print.

"Detective Contreras, please tell us the results of your analysis of the shell casing found at the site of the Garrison Franco murder."

"Three days ago, Carlos McCrary called us from the building at 8524 Northwest Second Avenue. He had found a shell casing that he believed was evidence in the Franco murder."

She read from a notebook. "Detective Bigelow and I went there with a CSI team. We extracted a nine-millimeter shell casing from a crack in the pavement. It was consistent with the bullets used to kill Garrison Franco. On the casing, we found a partial fingerprint. See the first page for the comparison. It had enough points of similarity to determine that the print came from Dan Murphy's left little finger."

"And what else did you discover about that shell casing?" Magruder asked.

Kelly eyed me and grinned. "We determined from the firing pen mark that it was not fired from Jorge Castellano's service pistol."

Kelly referred to her notes. "We obtained a search warrant for Dan Murphy's service pistol, a Glock 17. We compared its firing pen mark and proved that Murphy's pistol had, in fact, fired the shell. See page two of the sheets you were given earlier."

"Wait a minute," Abe interrupted. "You mean the shell casing was fired from Murphy's pistol, but the bullet that killed Franco came from Castellano's gun?"

"Not quite, Abe," I put in. "Murphy switched the barrel from Jorge's Glock with the one from his own Glock. The barrels are interchangeable; it takes less than ten seconds. Murphy used his own gun to shoot Franco and the lead bullet had the markings from Jorge's gun barrel."

Jorge smacked himself in the forehead. "*Estupido, estupido, estupido.* Dan offered to clean my gun after we went to the firing range a few weeks ago. That's when he switched the barrels. Then he bided his time until he could kill Franco."

Abe said, "But Murphy had to switch them back before the ballistics test."

"He did that after Jorge was arrested," I said. "Jorge's gun was in the evidence locker. As a detective, Murphy had access to the locker."

I swiveled to Kelly. "I suggest that you examine the security footage for the evidence locker. I'll bet you a steak dinner to a day-old French fry that Murphy went into the locker right after Jorge's Glock was logged in."

Kelly eyed Bigs. "Make a note to do that."

Magruder perused her notes. "Detective Contreras, please tell us the results of the search warrant you executed at Dan Murphy's residence."

"Page three is a picture of a tray found in Murphy's garage. The tray is slotted for a set of Craftsman 12- , 17- , and 25-inch pry bars. As you can see, the 12-inch and 25-inch pry bars were in the tray. The 17-inch slot was empty. We made a diligent search for the 17-inch pry bar but did not find it."

She moved her head in my direction. "Chuck gave us evidence that Dan Murphy purchased an identical pry bar set from Harry's Handy Hardware store earlier this year. Pages four and five are copies of the credit card slip and cash register tape for the purchase. The credit card slip and the cash register tape are not originals. We obtained them from the computerized records at Harry's regional headquarters in Miami."

She waited for everyone to find the copies. "You all may remember that we found a 17-inch Craftsman pry bar consistent with the missing pry bar in Carlos McCrary's desk."

Kelly looked at Magruder and Estacado. "It had no fingerprints on it. That pry bar matched the impressions we took of the marks left when the killer broke into Rayburn's apartment."

She smiled at Snoop before turning to Magruder. "Raymond Snopolski sent us this office surveillance footage from McCrary Investigations' office." She played the video. "Mr. Snopolski also found footage from four different surveillance cameras along the route from Ted Rayburn's apartment to Carlos McCrary's office."

Snoop authenticated the videos he had found as Kelly played each recording.

"These videos show a blue Corolla sedan belonging to Jessica Murphy," Kelly continued. "We confirmed that from its license plate. The Corolla drives from the vicinity of Rayburn's apartment   to   the   intersection   a   block   from   McCrary

Investigations. A traffic camera caught the Corolla turning right seven minutes before the intruder broke into McCrary's office."

Magruder closed the folder. "Mr. McCrary, we are this close," she held her thumb and forefinger an inch apart, "to dropping the charges against you. It would help if we knew Murphy's motive. We thought you could enlighten us."

I said, "Murphy had no motive to kill Rayburn, other than that Rayburn was a scumbag parasite who leeched off other people, and he deserved whatever retribution he got. I was Murphy's target when he killed Rayburn. I was this close," I held my thumb and forefinger an inch apart and smiled at Magruder, "to proving that Murphy killed Franco. Murphy didn't know that. He still doesn't, as far as I know, but maybe he thought that it would be a good idea to distract me. That's why he killed Rayburn and framed me."

I eyed Yankton. She twisted her face away.

"Murphy pretended to help me with Jorge's case. He sent me after Rayburn to distract me from the real killer. It worked. I chased Rayburn like a hound after a raccoon. When I talked with Murphy about Rayburn, he offered to help and brought a copy of the PCPD file to me at my condo. He did this so he could get inside my condo. That's when he stole my Smith & Wesson revolver from the nightstand. Then he killed Rayburn with it and framed me for the murder."

Magruder jerked her chin at Estacado. "Drop the charges against McCrary."

"Not yet," I said.

Magruder's eyebrows raised a couple of millimeters. "You don't want the charges dropped?"

"Ma'am, right now Murphy knows he's under suspicion for something because homicide cops executed a search warrant against him. He knows you took the pry bars, because they're not in his closet anymore. However, he may not know you suspect him of Franco's murder too. He doesn't know what else we found or how strong the case against him is. I'd like it to stay that way until I nail down his motive for killing Franco."

She motioned to Estacado. "You heard the man. Leave the charges active."

Magruder regarded me again. "Let's talk about the Franco murder. How do you think that went down?"

I spoke to Darcy Yankton. "Darcy, you want Jorge to tell this?"

She shook her head. "Until the charges are dropped, my client doesn't say anything." She still wouldn't face me.

"Fair enough." I focused my attention on the DA. "After Murphy switched gun barrels with Jorge, he bought three burner phones from three different discount stores. He paid cash."

"You have evidence?"

"Evidence is my middle name." Nobody smiled. Sometimes comedic talent goes unrecognized and unappreciated.

"I analyzed the cellphone records for Jorge and Franco and discovered that they both received calls a few minutes apart from two different numbers originating at the same cellphone tower near Murphy's home. And the anonymous 9-1-1 call that reported the murder later came from a third number. That call originated at a tower between the murder site and Murphy's home. Kelly and Bigs had all three phone numbers in the murder book they gave me, but they didn't realize they were connected. They hadn't tied them together. The next two pages are the phone records."

I waited for the others to find the copies before continuing. "I went to the cellphone company and got the Electronic Serial Numbers for all three phones. From the ESNs, we found the manufacturer and the time each phone was initialized. The manufacturers provided us with the stores each phone was shipped to. Based on the driving time between each store and the activation time, the buyer drove directly from store to store."

Bigs waved at Snoop. "Tell the DA how you know Murphy bought them."

Snoop cleared his throat. "I went to each discount store where the phones were sold. I watched the surveillance video at each store's electronics counter at the time the phones were activated. The videos showed all three purchases. The next three pages are screen grabs from the videos showing Murphy buying each of the phones."

Snoop waited for us to study the photos. "I provided Detectives Bigelow and Contreras with copies of the videos. The same guy bought all three phones and he wore a Tennessee Titans hat—not very common around here—and sunglasses at each store, but it was Murphy all right."

"How can you be sure?' Magruder asked.

Bigs answered. "When Snoop gave us the videos, we went to the discount stores' parking lot cameras. We found one good picture of a guy Murphy's size wearing a Titans hat getting into Murphy's car."

I asked Kelly, "Did you and Bigs take any of Murphy's clothes into evidence?"

"Yeah. No Titans hat. We tested all his dark clothing and gloves for GSR too. Nothing."

"He must have dumped the clothing." I swiveled back to Mabel the Marauder. "Murphy used a burner phone to call Franco first and told him to meet him at the 8500 block of Northwest Second Avenue."

"Why would Franco fall for that?"

I shrugged. "Any number of reasons. Murphy may have threatened him. Murphy's a tough cop. Or Murphy could have told Franco that he had evidence to put him away for drug dealing, but that he would take a bribe. You could construct several scenarios which Murphy could use to lure Franco to the murder scene."

Magruder said, "Then he called Castellano and pretended to be the informer?"

"Right. He used an electronic voice changer to disguise his voice. You can get them online. He had to set the meet with Franco before he called Jorge. After he and Jorge set up their stakeout near the bogus meeting site, Murphy muted his phone so Jorge wouldn't hear him while he was killing Franco. He jogged to the murder scene—we found surveillance video of him running down 84th street—and he laid in wait for Franco with Jorge's gun barrel installed in his own gun. The next two pages are screen grabs from those videos but the picture quality is terrible. After the shooting, he policed his brass."

I eyeballed the two detectives. "Fortunately for us, one shell casing fell in a crack. That's why Clint Watkins saw him use that flashlight. He was searching for his brass. He must have seen that shell in the crack, but he couldn't reach it. He took his glove off to make his finger smaller and tried to reach it again. That's when his little finger left the print."

I peeked at Darcy. She still wouldn't face me.

"Then he jogged back to his car on 84th Street, where we found the second surveillance video of our mystery jogger. The next page is another screen grab of that video. And on his way home, Murphy used the last burner phone and called 9-1-1 to report the murder he had just committed."

"What was Murphy's motive?" Magruder asked. "Why did he have it in for Castellano?"

"I don't have the whole story."

I cut my eyes to Darcy and Jorge. "If Jorge and his counsel approve, I'd like to ask you not to drop the charges against Jorge. Same reason I don't want you to drop my charges."

Darcy regarded Jorge. He shrugged. "Okay, *amigo*. I trust you."

Chapter 81

Clint and I finished another five-mile run on the boardwalk.

"Clint, I'll have this murder mess cleared up pretty soon."

"I figured you would."

"After I do that, Grandpa and Grandma will go back to Texas."

"I figured that too."

"Let's get ice cream. What do you want this time?"

"Fudge Ripple and, uh, Black Walnut." He grinned. "Black like me."

"And I'll take a double scoop of Dark Chocolate. Dark like you."

Clint clapped me on the back.

We walked while we ate our cones.

"Bro, I can tell that you have something on your mind."

"You're right. I do." I licked a drip off my cone.

"You tell me not to delay the inevitable."

I had to laugh. "Clint, how are things at Port City Prep? They treating you okay?"

"Yeah, they're okay. You're stalling, dude."

"You know that your living with me was never intended to be permanent. My goal was to help you prepare for the real world. You've made great strides."

"Yeah. So?"

I stopped walking. "Port City Prep has a resident student program. They have dormitories, like at a college."

"Yeah, I know."

"How would you feel if I enrolled you as a resident student?"

"Dude, that would cost a ton of money. Who's gonna pay for that?"

"I will."

Clint finished his cone before answering. "Man, that's pretty drastic."

"I talked to your tutor. She says you'd fit into their sophomore academic program. They'll test you and you might even make it as a junior. They have a good basketball program too. You're tall enough and, God knows, you're fast enough."

Clint did the Ali shuffle that he had done when he first outran me. "I'd like that."

"The thing is, you've attended the school as a tutoring customer. No red tape. I pay for the tutor's time. Enrolling you as a residential student requires paperwork."

"So?"

"I have no legal standing with you. I'm not a *guardian ad litem*, I'm not a foster parent, and I'm not a relative. I'm just a good friend."

Clint frowned. "What's a *guardian ad litem*?"

"That's a guardian appointed by a court to protect the interests of a minor."

"What you getting at, man?"

"We need your mother to sign the enrollment application."

Clint's lips tightened. His eyes narrowed. He stopped and gazed out over the ocean. Tears welled in his eyes.

I waited.

"We got no choice, do we, bro'?" The tears spilled down his cheeks.

Chapter 82

The block started with an abandoned parking lot surrounded by an ancient hurricane fence topped with rusty barbed wire.

Hand-lettered signs on a nondescript building had been painted on the faded gold paint. "We buy Rims, Amps, TVs. Buy and Sell Gold." The narrow steel door was barred and padlocked.

The sole signs of life were at the second building. Numbers *8010* and *8012,* where The Uptown/Downtown Pawn Shop featured *E-Z Check Cashing, 10% Loans, Tools, Jewelry.* The remainder of the building at *8014* was a nameless "Coin Laundery" with a misspelled hand-painted sign. The barred windows and doors looked off-putting. Nevertheless, two women sat inside watching their clothes tumble in the dryers.

The last time I had been on that block was to take pictures of Rasta Man Ashante Derringer dealing drugs on the sidewalk in front.

Clint pointed. "Stop at the pawn shop. Old Mose runs it."

I parked our rented Lexus in front of the shop where four men in assorted ghetto attire were having a half-hearted conversation on the sidewalk.

They ignored Clint and stared at me with dead eyes.

"Good afternoon, gentlemen," I said. "It's nice to see you too." I followed Clint inside.

An old black man sat on a high stool behind the barred counter. "Hey, Sneakers. I ain't seed you in a while. You looks all growed up now. How you been, nigga'?" He noticed me standing by the entrance and froze.

Clint gave his head one slight shake. The message was clear: Don't say anything.

I didn't.

"He cool, Mose. He work for me."

Mose surveyed me up and down. "Doing what?"

"He my bodyguard."

"What you need a bodyguard for, nigga'?"

Clint spread his hands in a *ta-da* motion and lowered his gaze to his new clothes. Now I understood why Clint had insisted we both wear suits and ties and drive a shiny new Lexus. We were imitation gangsters. "Things is different for me now, Mose. Whitey work for *me* now. Get it?"

"Uh, you, uh, in the business now?"

"I'm doing fine, Mose. I'm looking for my momma. You seen her around?"

"Not lately."

"Where she gettin' her shit from now?"

Mose squinted at me; I stared at Clint, ever the attentive employee.

"Mose, I asked you a question." He pronounced it "axt." Clint was back in the ghetto and needed to fit in.

I narrowed my eyes at Mose and made a small movement with my right hand.

Mose cleared his throat. "Last I heard, she hanging 'round at Pipefitters Hall. Ask for Cricket." He pronounced it "ax" too.

"Mose, you see my momma 'fore I do, you tell her I have money now. I wants to help her out, you catch my drift?"

"I do, that I do."

Clint stuffed a hundred-dollar bill in Mose's hand before we left.

Fifty years before, Pipefitters Hall had been a union hall. When the union moved to newer quarters, the building sat empty for decades. The city repurposed it as a community recreation center, complete with an outdoor basketball court on one side and a parking lot on the other. It gleamed with fresh paint and unfulfilled dreams.

I pulled into the freshly paved and striped parking lot. Ah, the wonders of taxpayer money. I followed Clint around to the front. Like a good bodyguard, I stationed myself with my back against a wall not yet defaced with graffiti.

A half dozen men of assorted races stood on the wide sidewalk, smoking and drinking from bottles concealed in paper bags. Clint walked up to the biggest man. "I'm looking for Cricket."

"And who would be looking for him?"

Clint gave him a dead stare. "I tol' you, *I'm* looking for him. You Cricket?"

"And who the hell are you, nigga'?"

Clint moved his chin a half-inch.

I walked over to the guy, knocked the cigarette from his hand, and hit him hard in the solar plexus. He doubled over. I grabbed his arms and slammed him against the concrete block wall. "Mr. Watkins wants to find Cricket. Are you him?"

The other men backed up.

"Be cool now, man. Just be cool now. Ever'ting all right. Nobody get excited now. I'm Cricket."

I released him and resumed my position by the wall.

Clint said, "I looking for Oralie Watkins. Where she at?"

Cricket raised both hands. "Don't get me wrong, man, but you not cops or nothin', right?"

"Oralie is my momma. You not in any trouble with me long as you straight with me. Now, where is she?"

"I ain't seed her since last night, man. Me and her done a little business and I ain't seed her since."

"Once she fixed up, where she like to go to relax and enjoy herself?"

"Usually she go down the next alley over dere." He pointed. "They's a little area 'bout halfway down where she like to crash."

Clint spun without a word and we returned to the Lexus.

I steered down the alley, dodging the trash. Half a block down, the alley branched. To the left, windowless walls with metal doors framed a dead-end dumpster alcove. I smelled the place before I finished opening the car door. It reeked of rotten food and human waste.

Clint's expression was as cold as a marble statue. God only knew what was coursing through his sixteen-year-old mind.

I followed him into the alcove as he peeked behind the first dumpster. Clint grabbed the dumpster and started to roll it away from the wall.

I helped.

A shapeless heap of rags lay sagged against the concrete wall. Two feet stuck out the bottom. One sandal had fallen on the asphalt, the other clung to her foot by one toe.

Clint moved aside the rags. "That's her. Let's see if we can wake her."

I picked Oralie up in my arms. I'd have to dry clean my suit to remove the stench. "Grab her sandals."

"Hey, do I know you?" she mumbled. "You give me some blow and I show you a good time, baby. You looking for a date, hon?"

Clint walked beside me, expressionless.

"Not right now, Oralie," I said.

I carried her to the car. "You want to take her to the emergency room?"

"No. I've seen her like this lots of times. She's past the worst." Clint opened the door and slid into the backseat first. I handed the semi-conscious woman in and we wrestled her into the other seat.

Clint reached over and fastened a seat belt around her. "She's coming down now. She'll be all right. Let's take her to the diner. She needs food and coffee."

Oralie was walking, sort of, by the time we reached the diner.

I left my smelly jacket in the car. I wondered what the car would smell like when we returned it to the rental company.

Veraleesa looked up when the front door dinged. She smiled, then saw we were half-carrying Oralie. "Put her over there." She pointed to a booth.

I shoved Oralie in first and pushed in beside her.

Veraleesa followed us. "How can I help?"

"Bring her black coffee and food—whatever today's special is, that would be the quickest, right?"

"Make the coffee with cream and three sugars," Clint added.

Veraleesa disappeared into the kitchen.

The other diners tried not to stare. We ignored them.

It was a long two hours.

I managed to feed Oralie a little food. I put a straw in the coffee and she sucked up a little. Gradually, she came back to life. She gaped around the diner blearily, head weaving from side to side while she steadied it. Oralie noticed Clint. She raised one finger and opened her mouth to say something, then stopped. She stared at her son for maybe a minute. She grasped her coffee cup in two hands and raised it toward her lips, watching Clint the whole time. "Do I know you?" she asked.

Clint stared at her.

"I used to know someone look jus' like you."

"Hello, Momma."

A series of emotions crossed her face. She set the coffee cup down and reached for Clint with both hands. "My baby. You're all growed up now. How long you been gone, baby?"

The diner crowd thinned and Veraleesa took Oralie to the bathroom. When they came out, Oralie appeared a little better.

I patted Veraleesa on the back while she helped Oralie back to her seat. "There's a special corner of heaven reserved for angels like you."

She smiled a sad smile. "You've got that right for sure. That's Clint's mother?" she whispered.

I nodded.

"Oh, that poor, poor boy."

I had Oralie practice signing her name on the notepad I always carry. It took her four tries before it looked like a real signature of a normal person. She signed the application papers for Port City Prep. Veraleesa and I witnessed her signature.

When we left the diner, I slipped two folded hundred-dollar bills into Veraleesa's hand. "You don't have to do that. It's my Christian duty."

I wrapped her fingers around the bills. "The Bible says: The laborer deserves his wages. You can give it to your church if you want, but saying 'thanks' is not nearly sufficient."

We buckled Oralie into the backseat. I cranked the engine and opened the windows to air out the car. "Port City Rescue Mission isn't far from here. Reverend Jim Holmes runs it, and he's a friend of mine. Let's take her there."

Clint regarded her with tears in his eyes. "That's been done and done and done again. Take her to the Pipefitters Hall."

"I won't leave her on the street. Not like this. We'll take her to the mission."

Clint stared at me for a moment. He shrugged. "Okay, but don't give her any money. It'll go right up her nose or into her arm, depending on which drug dealer she finds first."

"I'll give the money to Brother Jim. He'll know what to do with her, if anybody does."

"Believe me, bro', nobody does."

Chapter 83

I preferred the direct approach. I hoped I was a good enough actor to pull it off with Murphy.

I called him. "We need to talk."

"How about that bench on the North Beach Boardwalk, ten o'clock tomorrow."

"As good a place as any and better than most."

Murphy laughed.

Murphy was already there. His arms draped across the back of the bench, the picture of relaxation. His Panama hat tilted down to the top of his sunglasses. The sun hung halfway up in the east, climbing toward heaven. A line of pelicans glided north parallel to the shore. Altogether, a great day in paradise. The shade of the palm trees had not yet reached the bench.

Murphy wore old jeans and a bulky sports coat to conceal his pistol. His old Glock had been entered into evidence, but Murphy had another one now.

I knew he'd be armed; he was a cop. The search warrant that had been served on his home had not changed that.

I took the other end of the bench. "Scoping out the girls, Dan?"

He pointed. With his left hand. "Check out that babe in the red, white, and blue."

"Yeah, she's a keeper."

We lapsed into silence.

I watched a flock of pelicans make their way in formation up the coast. A few gulls bobbed on the Atlantic out past where the waves broke.

"Is this about that search warrant that Kelly and Bigs served on me at my house?"

"No. I heard about that, of course, but I wanted to talk about something else."

"What do we need to talk about?"

I cleared my throat. "This is painful, Dan. I'm having a rough time getting my mind around it."

"Around what?"

"You know that Jorge saved my life, right?"

"Oh, yeah. He told me that story a couple dozen times."

"You know I'd take a bullet for Jorge. Hell, he literally took a bullet for me."

Murphy took his arms off the bench. "I know he did, but what does that have to do with you and me?"

I coughed. "When Jorge came to me about this Franco killing and said he didn't do it, I believed him. When he says it's Christmas, I hang my stocking, y'know?"

"You'll believe anything he says. I got that. So what?"

I squirmed in my seat a little. I knew nothing about acting, but it seemed like a good idea. "The last time you and I sat on this bench, you told me that Jorge was stepping out on Karen. You said he was getting a little strange, maybe because he wasn't getting enough at home. You remember saying that?"

"Yeah. I said it because it's true."

"I didn't think anything of it at the time. I thought you maybe exaggerated about how much he enjoys watching the girls out here, y'know? But now I wonder." I tried to look him in the eye, but I couldn't because of his sunglasses. "Is he really cheating on Karen?"

Murphy pushed his hat up so he could see me better. "That's why you wanted to talk to me? To discuss Jorge's extramarital exploits? No kidding?"

"No kidding. How do you know he's stepping out on Karen?"

Murphy hesitated.

"Dan, Jorge's my best friend." I raised my voice a little and made what I thought was a sincere gesture. "I *need to know* if he's ever lied to me—about anything."

Murphy stared at me. The sunglasses hid most of his expression, but the corners of his mouth curved down.

I waited.

Murphy's voice sounded a little rough. "He *would* lie to you. He *did* lie to you. He's stepping out on Karen." He crossed his arms and stared out to sea. From the side, I saw his eyes behind the sunglasses. Were they wet with unshed tears?

I dropped my shoulders and lowered my gaze to my hands. I sighed. Some people do that when they're unhappy. "Frankly, I'm beginning to doubt Jorge's story about the stakeout the night Franco was shot. There's too much evidence against him. If he lied to me about one thing, maybe he lied to me about the Franco killing."

"That's why you asked to meet? To discuss how I knew he was stepping out on Karen?"

"How do you know that he is?"

Murphy took off his sunglasses. There were tears in his eyes. "Because he's doing it with my goddamn wife."

"Oh, God. I'm sorry to hear that. That's terrible." A few seconds passed. "How did you find out?"

"Jessica's cellphone. She calls Jorge's number several times a week. She goes out to 'play tennis' with Karen every week. But I know what they're doing."

The tears spilled down his cheeks. "She was everything to me. Without Jessica, my life is pretty much over."

Chapter 84

I followed Jessica and Karen from their tennis game the same as before. It was time to stir the kettle.

I waited for the two women outside Apartment 3117 in the Gladesview complex. I leaned against the railing near the door for nearly an hour.

The door opened and Jessica came out.

She flinched when she saw me. Then she saw I was a normal guy and flashed me a plastic smile as she walked a couple of steps past me. She stopped and waited for Karen.

Karen came out and did a double take. She cut her eyes at Jessica and back at me. Her shoulders slumped. She sighed. "Does Jorge know?"

"Yes. But Dan doesn't—exactly."

She gestured to Jessica. "Jessica, this is Chuck McCrary. He's a friend of Jorge's. He's investigating the Franco murder case for Jorge."

Jessica blushed. She didn't say anything.

"Why haven't you told Dan?" Karen asked.

"Dan is neither my friend, nor my client. Jorge is both."

"What did you mean when you said Dan doesn't know 'exactly'?" Jessica asked.

"Dan knows you're having an affair, but he thinks it's with Jorge."

Jessica put her hand over her mouth. "Oh, my God."

Karen twirled back to me. "What will you do now?"

"The question is not what will *I* do now, but what will *you* do now?"

"Jessica and I are in love. I know it's a cliché, but it's not something we planned; it just happened." Karen reached toward Jessica. "I didn't even know I was gay until I met Jessica."

Jessica touched Karen's outstretched hand. "I didn't know either—until I met Karen."

"How long has Jorge known?" Karen asked.

"A few days."

"He hasn't let on. Things have been pretty normal. Why is that?"

"I told him that you can't help who you are and that he needs your help and support until we found out who murdered Garrison Franco."

"And now?"

"I know who murdered Franco."

"Who?" Karen asked.

I glanced at Jessica before I answered. "Dan Murphy."

Jessica dropped the apartment key she had been holding in her other hand. "Oh no."

"Ladies, we need to talk. Let's go to my van."

"No," Jessica said. "Let's go back inside. It's more private."

Jessica Murphy and Karen Castellano sat beside each other on the couch, holding hands.

Jessica blinked; tears spilled and ran along her jawline. "Are you sure it was Dan?"

I nodded.

"How can you be so goddamned sure?"

I waved a hand. "Long story, lots of evidence. Just accept it. It was Dan and the police know it too."

"Why haven't they arrested him?"

"The case isn't solid enough yet. I told them I'd get Dan's motive so they could tighten the noose."

Karen said, "You? I don't get it. The last I heard, they arrested you for murdering Ted Rayburn. Why do the cops any favors?"

"It's the right thing to do. They're the good guys, remember? I'm no longer a suspect in the Rayburn murder."

"Since when?" Karen asked.

"Since I proved who murdered Rayburn too."

"Who was it?"

I eyeballed Jessica and didn't say anything. She bent over and covered her face. "No, no, no. Not Dan."

Karen put her arm around Jessica's shoulder.

Chapter 85

Assistant DA Tomás Estacado met me and my legal team at Abe Weisman's office. I had insisted that Abe invite Darcy Yankton and Jorge also. Mabel the Marauder chose not to attend the meeting. There would be no headlines today. Nothing to help her reelection campaign.

Diane Toklas passed out info packets to everyone. "You've got the floor, Chuck."

"The pictures on the first four pages of your exhibits are screen grabs of the video of Dan Murphy." I flipped a page for each item. "The first picture is when he signed into the evidence locker. Next is him entering the locker. The third shot is him leaving the locker five minutes later, and the last one is when he signed out. While he was in the evidence locker, he switched his gun barrel with Jorge's."

"Did you find any video of Murphy changing the gun barrels?" Estacado asked.

"There are no surveillance cameras inside the evidence locker, only at the entrance."

I flipped to the fifth page of the packet. "The next page is a ten print of Dan Murphy's fingerprints like the one at our earlier meeting, with one exception. After our last meeting, I asked Kelly and Bigs to send the CSIs back to my condo to examine inside my nightstand drawer for prints. At the bottom of the page are copies of Murphy's prints that they found in my drawer—the drawer where I kept my Smith & Wesson revolver—the murder weapon."

"Why didn't the CSIs find Murphy's fingerprints in the drawer the first time?"

"When homicide first searched my condo, they opened the top drawer of my night stand, found it empty, and didn't check it for fingerprints. They saw there were no fingerprints on the handle of the drawer and assumed the drawer had never been used. That's because Murphy wiped his prints from the drawer handle after he stole my revolver. But he forgot to wipe inside the drawer. CSI got prints of the middle and ring finger of his right hand, which he used when he picked up the gun."

I scanned around the table. "Other questions?"

"Why did Murphy frame Jorge for killing Franco?" asked Darcy Yankton.

"Revenge. Murphy believed Jorge was having an affair with Jessica, Murphy's wife. He murdered Franco and framed Jorge for it as revenge for the supposed affair."

"And was Jorge having an affair with Murphy's wife?"

"No, Abe, he wasn't."

"Then why would Murphy think so?"

"A tragic mistake. The next sections of your exhibits are copies of Murphy's cellphone bills. When Murphy read his own phone bills, he discovered that Jessica called the same number several times a week. He established that the number was listed to Jorge Castellano. Murphy thought Jessica had called Jorge. In fact, Jessica was phoning Jorge's wife, Karen."

Abe said, "Surely Murphy knew the phone number of his own partner."

"Not in this case. Murphy and Jorge always called each other on their police department cellphones. They never used their personal phones. Murphy didn't realize that Karen's phone was on the same family plan as Jorge's. It didn't occur to him that Jessica was a lesbian. He jumped to the wrong conclusion and murdered two people as a result."

Chapter 86

Jorge and I piled into my Avanti and dropped into Barney's, a cop bar and restaurant near the North Shore Precinct. I picked a table near the door.

I peered at my watch. It was four-thirty. "It is after five o'clock in Halifax."

Jorge laughed. "What and where is Halifax?"

"Either the capital of Nova Scotia or a city in Scotland. Take your pick. It's after five o'clock both places. It's time to celebrate." I ordered a bottle of champagne. Jorge had an imported beer.

We solved most of the problems of the world over drinks. I clinked my champagne glass against Jorge's beer mug. "*Salud.* It's amazing how much smarter you and I get when our consumption of alcohol increases."

Jorge lifted his mug in agreement.

A little after five o'clock, off-duty cops began to drift in. Word had gotten out that a warrant had been issued to arrest Dan Murphy for the murders of Garrison Franco and Ted Rayburn.

A stream of arriving cops approached to shake hands with Jorge and me and reveal that they always knew we were innocent. One was Barry Kleinschmidt, the sergeant who had brought Jorge into the visitation room when I first met him in jail.

I winked at Jorge before I smiled at Kleinschmidt. "Thanks, it was good to have your support, Barry."

Jorge considered me with a pained expression and took another swallow of beer. I smiled back serenely.

After three beers, Jorge leaned toward me and lowered his voice. "Most of these mooks thought I shot Franco and you shot Rayburn. Now they all say they never believed we did it." He frowned and raised his beer again. "It chaps my ass to see guys I thought were my friends lie right to my face." He chugged more beer.

I drank a swig of my fourth glass of champagne and belched. "*Amigo*, they're not lying, and they are your friends. Those cops believe that they always thought you and I were innocent."

I gestured over my shoulder with the champagne glass. "Take Barry Kleinschmidt. The last thing he said to you when he brought you to visit me in jail that first time was something like 'You did the city a favor. That bastard Franco deserved it.'"

"Yeah, he called Franco a 'rat bastard.' I remember everything about that meeting."

"Whatever." I waved the champagne glass, almost spilling some. "But Barry doesn't remember it that way. He remembers it as 'I know you didn't kill that bastard Franco, but even if you had, you'd have done the city a favor.' See the difference? He changed his memory to fit subsequent events." I had trouble saying *subsequent.*

"You think people change their memories?" Jorge signaled for another beer.

Barney came over to pick up Jorge's empty.

"Barney," I said, "you better bring us a plate of Buffalo wings. And we'll need a cab later." I belched and winked and handed Barney the Avanti keys.

"I asked you if you believe people change their memories," Jorge repeated.

"Absolutely," I replied. "I have a theory about that."

"You have a theory about everything."

"Indubitably and indeed." Why were those words so hard to pronounce? "I call it *McCrary's convenient memory hypothesis.* That has a nice ring to it, doesn't it?"

Jorge laughed. "*McCrary's bullshit theory* is more like it. *Amigo*, you're blowing smoke up my ass again." His next beer arrived and he took a long pull.

We each grabbed a chicken wing.

I took another hit of champagne and belched again. "You want to hear my hypo—hypothewhatsis—theory or not?"

"Go for it, big guy."

"People remember what is convenient for them to remember. Hell, we all do it. Right now, I remember Terry as shallow, because she broke up with me."

Jorge fingered his beer glass. "I think this better be my last one."

I poured the last of the champagne into my glass. "Me too." When I belched, I tasted champagne and chicken wings. "I hope I'm not gonna be sick later."

Kelly and Bigs strolled through the door.

Bigs's countenance lit up with a smile. The chair creaked in complaint when he sat at the table. "Kelly and I heard you all were over here. We wanted to come and congratulate you both."

They shook hands all around.

"We wanted to apologize for doubting you—either one of you," Kelly added.

Jorge jumped to his feet. "Aha! See, Chuck, not everyone has a convenient memory. High fives all around." He held his hands toward the two partners.

They each high-fived him, but they stared at Jorge and me like we were crazy.

Jorge and I burst out laughing.

"Sorry, Bigs. You and Kelly came in at the end of a long, philosophical discussion fueled by copious quantities of alcohol," I explained. "We're not crazy. We're just a little sozzled."

Chapter 87

Kelly cancelled the cab and the two detectives offered us rides home. "The least we can do, Chuck," Bigs said. "We took you away from home in an unmarked car. We'll bring you back the same way."

Kelly glanced over her shoulder. "Sort of an elegant symmetry there."

My grandparents were pissed that I came home drunk.

I grinned. "At least I didn't get drunk when Terry left me, Grandma. I don't drink when I'm sad, and not much when I'm happy." I could count on one hand the number of times I'd drunk too much to drive legally.

I wrapped an arm around Grandpa's shoulder. "But I've never been charged with murder before, and neither has Jorge. Getting murder charges dropped on both of us at the same time—that seemed pretty special. Jorge needed to let off steam, and we both wanted to give our cop friends the chance to see us and shake our hands. Barney's was perfect for that. Otherwise, those guys might feel guilty and take their guilty consciences out on us."

Grandpa smiled a little. "Are all your fences mended now?"

"No way to tell, but we did what we could."

The next morning, I convinced my grandparents that it was okay for them to return to Texas.

After Clint and I dropped them at the airport, I rang Kelly. "Have you taken Murphy into custody?"

"No. He wasn't at his house. Both cars were gone too. We don't know where Jessica is, either."

"With both cars gone, they may not be together. Did you search his house?"

"Do birds fly? We didn't find any guns or ammo. Bigs thinks he's going to do something stupid."

"I do too." I told her about my conversation with Murphy. "Jessica was everything to Dan. He said without her, his life was pretty much over."

"Jeez, that sounds ominous. We put out a BOLO for his car. It'll turn up."

"Yeah, but it might turn up with his and Jessica's bodies in it. Murphy is at the end of his rope, and the rope is unraveling."

Chapter 88

My phone rang. Karen Castellano's name and number showed on the screen.

"Hey, Karen. What's up?"

She was blubbering. "Jessica's in trouble."

"What kind of trouble?"

"We were talking on the phone and I heard her doorbell. She looked in the peephole and said it was Dan. She said that she'd get rid of him and call me back." She stifled a sob. "That was half an hour ago. She still hasn't called."

"Have you called her?"

"Of course," she snapped. "Her phone goes straight to voicemail. I sent her a text and she didn't answer. I know she's in bad trouble with Dan."

"Easy, Karen. Hold it together for a minute. Where's Jessica's new apartment?"

"She's staying at an apartment in Gladesview until we find a place more convenient for both of us."

"You two moving in together?"

"Don't start with me."

"I wasn't starting anything. I only want to know if you and Jessica are getting a place together. Friends like to know what's going on in other friends' lives. Just because you and Jorge are splitting up doesn't mean you and I aren't friends anymore.

Karen sighed. "You're right. I'm sorry I snapped at you. Will you help me?"

"Of course; that's what friends do. Do you have a key to the apartment?"

"Yes."

"Where was Jessica when you were talking?"

She told me.

"Okay. I'm heading over there. Bring the key to the bottom of the stairway that leads up to the unit. I don't want Dan to see you through the window. When you and I hang up, call 9-1-1 and tell them where Dan is."

Jessica had rented Unit 3117 in the Gladesview Apartments, the same unit where I had confronted her and Karen a few days earlier. *How ironic,* I thought. *At least I know the apartment layout.*

I picked up Snoop on my way to the apartment.

I stopped the van just inside the parking lot so we could prepare out of sight. I handed Snoop a Kevlar armored vest.

"You oughta give me hazardous duty pay for this, bud. Anytime a guy wears a bulletproof vest, it means he's likely to get shot at."

"If I get out of this alive, I'll buy you a Heart Stopper burger and a beer at the Fat Tummy."

"Close enough. Just don't get yourself killed; I'm looking forward to that burger." He held up the vest. "You're bigger than me." He adjusted the straps. "I don't know why I bother with this vest; you're the guy that's going in. I'm just hanging around as backup."

"I feel safer with you here, Snoop."

"You may not need a vest either. As good a shot as Murphy is, he'll shoot you between the eyes."

"Maybe Murphy will have the hiccups or something." I pulled a Florida Gator sweatshirt over my vest.

"He'll probably kill us both."

"That's what I like about you, Snoop; you're always an incurable optimist." I strapped a Browning .380 in an ankle holster on my right leg and stuck a Glock 26 subcompact in my belt in the small of my back. My Glock 17 went in a shoulder holster. I slipped on a raw silk sport coat to cover it all.

Snoop said, "I hope you don't get bullet holes in that nice jacket. Murphy will spot the 17 in a second, but maybe he'll miss one of the other guns."

"Or maybe I won't need a gun, Snoop."

Snoop scoffed. "Maybe the Federal government will balance the budget."

We got back in the van. I dropped Snoop where he couldn't be seen and parked the Caravan where I'd parked before. I studied the front of Unit 3117. Venetian blinds covered the windows. They were closed.

I rang Karen. "I'm in the parking lot. Did Jessica put up drapes in the living room?"

"No. Just the blinds. I'm at the bottom of the stairs. Snoop's with me."

"I'll be right there."

While I crossed the pavement, one slat of the blinds moved. Murphy had spotted me. I waved at the window. Good ol' affable Chuck was coming up for a nice, friendly chat. The slat closed.

I met Karen and Snoop at the bottom of the stairs. "Have you got the key?"

She handed it to me. Her hand shook. "Be careful."

I forced a smile. "That's why I'm still alive."

Snoop and I mounted the stairs to the third floor instead of taking the elevator. Snoop stopped at the top. I continued to 3117 and halted beside the front door with my back against the concrete block wall. It was as safe a place as any.

I gave Snoop a thumbs-up and rang the doorbell. Nothing.

I knocked on the door. More nothing.

I knocked again. "Jessica. It's Chuck McCrary. Are you in there?"

A muffled scream escaped from inside, quickly extinguished.

I called Murphy's cellphone. I heard his phone ring through the apartment door.

After six rings, it went to voicemail. I spoke loud enough for him to hear me through the door. "Dan, this is Chuck McCrary. I'm right outside the door. The SWAT team is on the way. Together, you and I can work this out so no one gets hurt. Let's do that, okay? You let me in, and I'll walk you out when the cops get here. No trigger-happy rookie will shoot you if you're with me. How does that sound?" I put my phone away.

Two black-and-whites and a SWAT truck rounded the corner of the building, red and blue lights flashing.

I hollered at the door. "Dan, the cops are here. I have a key. I'm going to unlock the door and come in. Let's talk, okay? Don't do anything you'll regret. And don't shoot. You can always shoot me later."

I stuck the key in the lock. If Murphy were going to shoot, he would shoot through the door when he heard me insert the key. But he would shoot through the center of the door to have the best chance of hitting me. Maybe my vest would protect me. I held my breath and twisted the key.

Pushing the door open, I lifted my open hands to shoulder height, and walked in.

Chapter 89

Dan and Jessica huddled at the dining room table at the far end of the combination living/dining room. Dan sat with his back to the wall on the long side. He had handcuffed Jessica's right wrist to his own left. She perched on the edge of her chair like a bird ready to take flight.

Two dining room chairs lay on their side across the room. One chair back had pulled loose from the frame. A jagged hole marred the drywall above where the broken chair lay.

An open bottle of cheap Scotch sat on the table. About four inches was gone. Dan's left hand was wrapped around an old-fashioned glass that held an inch of amber liquid. A new Glock 17 lay an inch from his right hand.

Just like the one he killed Franco with, I thought.

Murphy lifted the glass and knocked back half the whiskey, pulling Jessica's arm along with it. He set the glass down heavily. "Hello, dick-face. Welcome to the party. Or maybe this is a wake. I haven't decided. Close the door."

I had purposely left the door open when I entered. I ignored the command and instead took a step closer to the table.

"Close the goddamn door!" Dan snatched up the Glock and waved it in my direction.

"Okay, Dan." I sidestepped to the door, pushed it gently. It closed but did not latch. Maybe Dan wouldn't notice. "The cops are outside. How do you want to do this?"

"How do you want to do this?" Murphy mocked. "How do I want to do this? That depends on what you mean by 'this.'"

"We can work out a peaceful way where no one gets hurt. That's what I meant. I want to end this peacefully."

"Peacefully. What a beautiful word. You know my world was peaceful before Jorge became my partner. Jessica and I had a good life, a good marriage. We wanted to have kids. At least I did. Real peaceful." He took another drink.

"That's gone down the toilet with this Karen crap." He waved the pistol around the room aimlessly.

"Jessica, are you all right? Has he hurt you?"

Murphy pointed the gun at her. "Well, bitch? Why don't you answer him? Tell him I haven't laid a hand on you. In fact, I haven't laid a hand on you in weeks. Ha, ha. That's funny. I haven't laid a hand on you in weeks." He began to sniffle.

I moved a step closer. "Dan, why don't you uncuff yourself, and you and I can take a walk outside. I'll make sure no one shoots you by mistake."

Murphy laughed. It was not a happy sound. "Take a walk outside. Ha, ha! I've got a better idea. Let's take a walk on the *wild* side instead." He waggled the Glock in my direction, then he put it against Jessica's throat. Then he shoved it against his own temple.

I hoped he hadn't swilled enough liquid courage to pull the trigger yet, but if he kept swigging Scotch, it wouldn't be long before he reached that point.

I would have to make a hard decision. Soon.

Murphy extended the empty glass toward Jessica with his left hand. Jessica's right arm followed, tethered by the handcuffs.

She grabbed the bottle in her left hand. Her hand shook, rattling the bottle against the glass while she poured another inch of Scotch. Her lower lip trembled. Her breath sounded ragged.

Murphy gulped another half-inch, jerking Jessica's right arm toward his mouth. "Good for what ails you."

Tears streamed down her cheeks. She wiped her runny nose with her left forearm. Her whole body shuddered.

"Sit down, dick-face. This is a party—or a wake." He laughed, but it was a raspy, unhappy sound. "You should make yourself comfortable at a party. Sit down."

I picked up the dining chair that wasn't broken and carried it toward the table.

"That's far enough," Murphy rasped. "Sit right there."

I set the chair in the center of the room and sat.

Murphy pointed the gun at my forehead, his aim steady as an anvil. The black circle of the barrel loomed big as a mine tunnel. My gut tightened.

"Remove the pistol with the fingertips of your left hand and toss it over here."

I shrugged out of my jacket and dropped it on the floor to my right. Grasping the handle of the Glock 17 with my left thumb and first two fingers, I extracted it from the shoulder holster and dropped it on the floor.

"Dan, you haven't hurt anybody yet. Let's keep it that way."

Murphy frowned. "Haven't hurt anybody? What's that supposed to mean? What about that scumbag Garrison Franco? Wasn't he anybody? What about that other low life Ted Rayburn? Wasn't he anybody? It's too late for that hostage negotiations crap. I've already killed two slimeballs."

"Yeah, but they deserved it. You haven't hurt any *innocent* people. Let's keep it that way."

Murphy brandished his gun to emphasize his words. "I always wondered about murder-suicides. Jorge and I always joked: If he's going to commit suicide, why not do the suicide first? What's the point of killing someone else, if you're just gonna kill yourself afterward? I mean, what's the point anyway?" He dropped his gaze to the table. "What's the point of anything?"

Tears flowed down his cheeks. He raised his head. "Well, now I understand the murder part of murder-suicide. Jessica destroyed everything that made my life worth living. Some people don't deserve to live."

Murder-suicide. That was the key phrase I had listened for—all the while hoping he would never speak it. God, I hated to hear Murphy say that. He had made my decision for me.

I waited for an opportunity and prayed it would come in time. If Murphy didn't give me an opening, I would just have to make my own.

Murphy pressed the barrel against Jessica's neck. "You know, dick-face, it wouldn't be so bad if the bitch had left me for another man. Maybe I could compete with another man. I could kill the bastard in a duel. Or I could frame him for murder and send him away to prison." He laughed again. "Get it? I could frame him for murder." Murphy waved his gun around like a kid with a sparkler on the Fourth of July.

He waved the gun in my direction again. "But to leave me for a *woman*. A fucking *dyke*. How the hell do I compete with that?"

I kept my eyes riveted on the waving gun and his trigger finger, waiting for the right moment. For an instant, Murphy's gun pointed at the ceiling.

Now!

I dived to the left, grasping behind my back for the Glock 26.

Murphy's eyes widened as he brought his pistol down.

I plucked the compact gun from my waistband and rolled left.

Jessica screamed and yanked against the handcuff while Murphy pulled the trigger in rapid fire.

A sledge hammer hit me over the heart. Another round tore through my right thigh.

I put three rounds into Dan Murphy's chest.

Murphy kept firing. A bullet ripped my right bicep and spun my pistol across the floor.

Jessica kept screaming while Murphy tumbled off the chair, pulling her on top of him as he fell. Murphy's pistol fell to the tile and skidded inches away from his outstretched arm.

My right arm dangled uselessly. I tried to reach the ankle holster, but I couldn't pull my injured leg high enough to reach it with my left hand.

Blood spread like a rising red tide across Murphy's shirt when he stretched toward his dropped Glock.

Jessica reared up on one knee, leaned across Murphy's shoulder, and seized his right wrist. "No! No! No! You bastard," she screamed, "not this time."

Snoop burst in the front door, gun drawn, but Jessica blocked a clear shot at Murphy.

She levered her body from behind the table, twisted her legs around, and kicked the Glock across the room.

Murphy rolled his head in her direction. Blood bubbles formed in his mouth when he tried to speak. His head dropped to the floor with a *thunk*.

Snoop rushed over to me while I collapsed onto my back in a spreading pool of my own blood. The last thing I smelled was Snoop's aftershave mixed with the coppery tang of blood. The last thing I heard was sirens.

Chapter 90

I woke to the soft vibration of hospital bed wheels as someone rolled me down the hall. Behind my closed eyes, I detected the mix of hospital sounds and hospital odors. The sound of conversation grew louder, then ceased as I felt the bed slow and turn a corner. I smelled the aromas of overlapping perfumes, aftershaves, and flowers.

I slitted my eyes open, but the eyelids felt heavy. Through blurred vision, the room seemed filled with people. No, only a handful. I blinked and focused. My parents, Grandma, and Grandpa clustered around the bed.

The nurse set up the IV, adjusted the bed, and fluffed my pillow. "He'll be groggy for a while. I'll be back with water for those flowers." She left with a smile.

My mother leaned over and kissed my cheek. "The waiting room is filled with a bunch more people that the hospital wouldn't let in here. They said just immediate family until you were fully awake and responsive."

Grandma kissed my other cheek. "How do you feel?"

I took a mental roll call of my body. "Sleepy... Sore... Stiff... Not as good as I'll feel tomorrow, I hope."

Dad said, "The doctor told us you should rest for an hour of so after you woke up before you take any other visitors."

"Who's waiting to see me?"

Dad smiled. "Practically everyone in Port City, including about a dozen cops." He patted my shoulder. "You just close your eyes, take a nap, and we'll be here when you wake up."

Snoop and Vicky walked in as Grandpa and Grandma left. There were only four chairs for visitors.

Vicky squeezed my hand. "We were so worried about you. How do you feel?"

"As well as can be expected, I suppose."

I tried to lift my other hand but couldn't. My right arm was hidden under a shroud of assorted medical stuff–bandages and such, I guessed. Then I remembered the bullet that hit my right bicep.

I swung my head a fraction of an inch. "Hey, Snoop. How's Jessica Murphy?"

"She was shaken up, but by now I'm sure she's okay. She was waiting with us for several hours until your family arrived from Texas. I finally convinced her to go home and rest. She'll be here tomorrow."

"How long have I been out?"

"Eighteen or twenty hours. I lost count."

"How long have you and Vicky been here?"

Snoop smiled. "Eighteen or twenty hours. I lost count."

"What happened to Dan Murphy?"

"You put three in his chest. He was gone before the ambulance arrived."

"What about me?"

"Murphy shot you in the right thigh and right bicep. He broke a couple of your ribs with a slug that would have hit you in the heart if not for the vest. The right thigh shot nicked an artery. The doc said it was touch and go for a while."

"Only the good die young, Snoop."

"That's bullshit and you know it." He glanced at my mother. "Oops. Sorry, ma'am."

Mom smiled. "I think that's bullshit too, Snoop."

He turned back to me. "You owe me a burger and a beer at the Fat Tummy."

"That's the whole reason I survived. I didn't want to deprive you of a Heart Stopper burger." I smiled. "At least I wasn't unconscious for four days like last time."

Snoop laughed. "You get better at getting shot, the more you practice. You picked a better spot for the bullets this time."

The last time someone shot me, I'd nearly died. Snoop had waited in my hospital room then too. For several days. So had Terry, I remembered. And my family from both Texas and Mexico.

Life goes on, I thought.

Vicky sat on the edge of the bed, careful to avoid my bandaged thigh and arm. She wrapped her arms around me and leaned her head on my chest. She sighed heavily and her body shook as she began to cry.

I stroked her hair. "No need to cry, Vicky. I go home in a couple of days, Doc said. A week or so to heal, then a couple weeks of rehab and I'll be good as new."

Vicky wiped her eyes on my hospital gown before she sat up. Mascara streaked her cheeks. And my gown.

I pointed at the stain on my gown. "You'd better watch it, Vicky, or you'll lose your Macho Certificate."

Vicky and I chortled for several minutes. As the laughter trailed off, one of us would point to the streak on the gown and we would break into giggles again.

Mom and Dad smiled in sympathy, but they probably thought we were both crazy.

I sipped water. "Sorry. This reminds us of the last time that Vicky smeared her mascara when she was with me." We hooted again.

The nurse brought in my cellphone. "I forgot to return this to you."

I thanked her and reviewed my messages.

My parents and my American grandparents had called to say they were on their way. My Mexican grandmother, Uncle Felix, my siblings, about a dozen more aunts, uncles, and cousins had called.

But not Terry. *Well,* I thought, *that's no surprise.*

Renate Crowell's image smiled from my phone's screen when the ring sounded. I left her a message to call back the next day. The hospital was limiting my visitors and I had a waiting room full of friends who had been waiting hours to see me.

By the time I'd seen everyone who had been sitting vigil, it was late afternoon and I was exhausted.

The next morning, Renate called again. I accepted the call. "How did you know yesterday that I was back in my hospital room, Renate? I'd only been there for ten minutes."

"The *Press-Journal* has spies everywhere. How are you, handsome? Ready for an interview?"

"You certainly know how to charm a guy. I'm tired, sore, and weak as hell, but you might as well come on over. When do you expect to be here?"

The door opened and Renate walked in, grinning. She held her phone in one hand with my picture on the screen. In the other hand, she carried a huge flower arrangement.

I lifted my phone to my ear. "I've got to hang up now. I've got a visitor."

Chapter 91

Vicky Ramirez set her mango daiquiri on the end table. We had spent the day on *The Gator Raider Too* and had returned to my condo to watch the sunset over Seeti Bay.

The last time I sat on the balcony at sunset, it had been with Terry. Again today, boats swung at anchor in the bay. Again today, the eastern breeze lined them up for sunset watching.

For an instant, tears welled in my eyes. I blinked them away. *That was then; this is now.*

Vicky broke my reverie. "If I take off my top, do you think my boobs will get any browner?"

"I don't know if it'll make your boobs any browner, but it would sure make my spirits rise. Maybe something else too."

She laughed and untied her top. She swung it in a circle by one string, draped it across the chaise, and took a deep breath.

I watched every movement while she twisted and twirled. She reached for the pitcher and refilled her glass. "What do you hear from Jorge?"

"I talked to Mother Weiner today. He's been reinstated as a police detective with back pay. He needs a new partner. Mother's working on that."

I held out my glass so she could refill it even though it was half full. I just wanted to see her move, and she knew it.

I had spent the last two weeks with Vicky while I recuperated and went to rehab every day. She had taken two weeks of vacation. These weeks had been quite liberating for me. No expectations, no pressure.

I had dated Terry for the better part of a year. I wanted the American dream family so badly that I had seen more in her than was there. The hope for future domestic bliss I saw in Terry had been a reflection of my own desire.

Now she was gone and I understood my self-delusion. Terry never misled me; we simply wanted different things. With Vicky, I had no delusions of domesticity. She was a career woman all the way. *So be it*, I told myself. *Live this one day at a time. The right woman will come along one day.*

I sipped my daiquiri. "Has Karen's divorce been finalized?"

"I'll file the paperwork when I get back from this vacation. She's in no hurry. She and Jessica moved in together. The lack of a divorce hasn't slowed them down."

"Well, it's back to work for me next Monday."

"Let's enjoy the rest of the weekend." She finished the last of her daiquiri and reached over and took my glass. "I think it's time I made you exercise your injured thigh again."

"Slave driver."

She winked. "You get on top this time."

The end

Carlos McCrary
Will Return

As a writer, I love to build relationships with my readers. I occasionally send emails with details on new releases, special offers, and other bits of news relating to my mystery/thriller novels.

If you sign up on my VIP email list, I'll send you advanced notice of my new releases (no spam!). Almost always discounted. Also, I'll send you opportunities to WIN cool prizes in special giveaways. Such as free books written by me or by other mystery/thriller authors I recommend and more!

You can get the advanced notices, and access to the special giveaways FOR FREE by signing up at:

www.DallasGorham.com

Acknowledgement

My thanks to my editor Marsha Butler. She makes me a better writer. Her website is

ButlerInk.com.

Did you enjoy *Double Fake, Double Murder?*
You can make a difference

Reviews are the most powerful tools an independent author like me has to get attention for my books. Much as I'd like to, I don't have the financial muscle of a New York publisher. I can't take out full-page ads in the newspaper or put posters on the subway or bus. (At least not yet, anyway!)

Instead, I have something more powerful and effective than that–something those publishers would kill to get their hands on: I have a committed and loyal bunch of readers.

Honest reviews of my books help bring them to the attention of other readers.

If you enjoyed this story, I would be very grateful if you would spend just two minutes to leave a review (it can be as short as you like) on the book's page at Amazon.com and Goodreads.com.

Your entertainment is the reason I write. I would love to hear from you now that you've finished reading my story. Email me at Dallas@DallasGorham.com. Tell me how you liked my story and what you'd like to see Chuck McCrary do next. Or tell me anything else on your mind.

All the best,

Dallas

Also by Dallas Gorham

I'm No Hero

A suspense thriller short story introducing Carlos McCrary, a U.S. Army Special Forces sergeant serving in Afghanistan. Available on Amazon.com.

Was the Afghan boy asking for help? Or leading them into an ambush?

A hot night in June 2006. Special Forces Operation Detachment Alpha 777, the Triple Seven, gets a call for help. The Taliban have blockaded a village in the Afghan mountains, starving the people. Their crime? Educating girls in the village school.

A village boy escapes through the night to ask the Afghan National Army for help. Or did he?"

Afghan Major Ibrahim Malik says his force is no match for the well-armed Taliban terrorists. Malik and the boy beg the Green Berets of the Triple Seven for help. But which side are the natives on?

The Green Beret soldiers infiltrate the village before dawn to face an ambush…

The soldiers of Team Triple Seven must fight for their lives, or the villagers won't be the only ones the Taliban wipe out.

Novels by Dallas Gorham

Perfect for fans of Jack Reacher and Robert B. Parker's Spenser, these mystery thrillers will draw you in and refuse to let go.

Six Murders Too Many

Book 1 of the Carlos McCrary series, *Six Murders Too Many* is available in electronic and print editions on Amazon.com.

The plan was perfect; all it took was two simple murders...

Then an over-zealous assassin kills an extra victim and things get out of hand.

Private Investigator Carlos McCrary thinks it's a routine paternity case—but $400,000,000 is never routine.

The assignment seems deceptively simple: Discover the identity of the biological father of Gloria Simonetti, the infant alleged to be the heiress to a dead billionaire.

Little by little, the handsome young detective uncovers clues to the truth, and finds himself the target of a powerful enemy determined to stop him and his investigation. *Permanently.* Chuck must stop the killer before he or she claims one final victim—the infant Gloria.

Bodies pile up as the shadowy killer tries to stuff this genie back in the bottle. The scheme seems to be working, but there's one thing the killer didn't count on: Carlos McCrary.

Quarterback Trap

Book 3 of the Carlos Mccrary series, *Quarterback Trap* is available in electronic and print editions on Amazon.com.

Super Bowl Week is supposed to be fun, right? One mafia boss sees a way to make a killing…

The Jets and the Cowboys are playing in the first Super Bowl in Port City's new billion-dollar stadium. My old friend Bob Martinez, is starting quarterback for the Jets.

A week before the game, Bob's supermodel fiancée, Graciela, disappears from the headquarters hotel.

Bob hires me to find her but won't let me involve the cops.

That same day the odds on the Super Bowl game explode when someone bets $100,000,000 on the Cowboys to beat the point spread.

Was Graciela really kidnapped, or did she run away from a twisted secret that threatens her life? And what is Bob struggling so hard to keep me from finding out?

My search leads me from the dangerous streets of a Port City ghetto to the private island mansions of billionaires, movie stars, and crime bosses. When I start to untangle the web of lies and corruption, one crime boss decides to get serious.

As serious as a funeral—mine.

Dangerous Friends

Book 4 of the Carlos Mccrary series, *Dangerous Friends* is available in electronic and print editions on Amazon.com.

There's one born every minute...

College freshman Michelle joins a campus environmental club. Save the planet, right? What could possibly go wrong?

Instead, she's sucked into a gung-ho gang led by her boyfriend, James Ponder, a graduate student obsessed with global warming protests. Ponder has a secret agenda that yields him millions of dollars from government corruption.

Caught in a web of ecoterrorism

Then Michelle wakes me with a 4:30 a.m. phone call, desperate for help. Her enviro-Nazi boyfriend has lured her into an environmental terrorist attack that murdered two people. Now the naïve college freshman faces a lifetime in prison unless I can find her a way out.

Follow the money

I uncover a conspiracy involving arson, murder, and the Chicago mafia. A mysterious millionaire has masterminded a string of mega-million-dollar stock market scams that reach back for five years. The mastermind begins to cut his losses by murdering anyone who can lead the cops back to him. And his targets include an innocent college student and a nosy private investigator.

Day of the Tiger

Book 5 of the Carlos Mccrary series, *Day of the Tiger* is available in electronic and print editions on Amazon.com.

Opposites attract, right?

NFL Hall of Famer Tank Tyler's buddy Al Rice is the polar opposite of Tank. Al is a miserable failure, drowning in drugs and self-pity. That must be why a super-wealthy tiger like Tank keeps bailing out a sheep like Al. Or is there another reason?

Bound by a dark secret

Tank and Al share a secret that ruined Al's life and turned Tank's dreams into nightmares for years, in spite of his outward success. Now Al is targeted by Monster Moffett, a loan shark who threatens Al's mother, Doraleen. Tank hires Private Investigator Chuck McCrary to protect both Doraleen and Al.

Gone without a trace

Al goes missing, and when Chuck searches for him, he uncovers a trail of sex trafficking and forced prostitution. Moffett's organized crime gang kidnaps Doraleen to hold as collateral for her son's debt. Al promises Chuck and Tank to turn his life around, but he's promised that before. Chuck will need more than brawn, balls, and bullets to sort out this mess.

Day of the Tiger is a thrilling ride that will keep you on the edge of your seat!

McCrary's Justice

Book 6 of the Carlos Mccrary series, *McCrary's Justice* is available in electronic and print editions on Amazon.com.

What would you do if your daughter was held by sex traffickers?

Nebraska farmer Wilbur Jenkins learns his missing daughter is a sex slave in Port City, Florida. He grabs the next flight to Port City and begs the cops to find her.

Is an untouchable diplomat behind the abduction?

The only clue is a phone number belonging to Antonio Crucero, a mysterious diplomat from a Caribbean island paradise. The cops can't penetrate Crucero's diplomatic immunity, so Jenkins hires Carlos McCrary, a Private Eye who helps people the cops cannot.

Crucero thumbs his nose at U.S. law, but diplomatic status can't protect him from McCrary

McCrary uncovers a cesspool of sex trafficking and illegal drugs stretching from South Florida to the Caribbean, and the slimy Crucero is the kingpin of the operation.

Crucero fights back and send his thugs after McCrary.

Be prepared for a white-knuckle chase

The final showdown with Crucero circles back to McCrary's own home, where he must confront his worst nightmare. McCrary's Justice slices like a machete through a treacherous jungle of new and fearsome enemies, as Chuck McCrary maneuvers inside the gangs and outside the law.

Yesterday's Trouble

Book 7 of the Carlos Mccrary series, *Yesterday's Trouble* is available in electronic and print editions on Amazon.com.

What is Cleo hiding? Has the yesterday she thought she'd escaped finally found her?

Cleo is a country singer who just wants to make music for her thousands of adoring, newfound fans. NBA superstar "Marvelous" LeMarvis Jones, Cleo's fiancé, bankrolls her first concert tour. Things are upended when an unbalanced cyber-stalker takes issue with the couple's interracial relationship.

Cue the Private Eye, and an onstage murder

Cleo won't take the threats seriously, but LeMarvis hires Private Investigator Carlos McCrary to provide security for Cleo's Summer Fun Concert Tour. At the tour's first stop, a backup singer with a dangerous past is murdered onstage. Was the bullet meant for Cleo?

More murders on tour

Despite Carlos's urging, Cleo refuses to cancel the tour, even as more bodies pile up on the tour's journey across Florida. In Jacksonville, the stakes are raised when the killer tires of Carlos interfering with his quest to do "God's work."

With the killer outsmarting Carlos and the cops at every turn, has Carlos finally met his match?

Will he wind up taking a knife to a gunfight?

Four Years Gone

Book 8 of the Carlos Mccrary series, *Four Years Gone* is available in electronic and print editions on Amazon.com.

When Crazy Aunt Carrie calls...

My morning in my South Florida waterfront condo turns topsy-turvy when Crazy Aunt Carrie calls. Her daughter Emily-my cousin-appeared last night in a vision. "Mom, I'm here," she said. "Come find me. I need you."

My Uncle Frank, Carrie's husband, thinks she's nuts too, but that's the way marriage sometimes goes.

Four year ago, when Emily disappeared, I couldn't find her and the failure still haunts me. Carrie persuades me to drop everything and fly to Austin, Texas. Carrie has nothing new beyond her vision, but, hell, family is family.

The wrong bodies surface

Finding Cousin Emily's body would finally give Aunt Carrie and Uncle Frank closure. But other bodies turn up in the backwoods of the Texas Hill Country. Before I know it, I'm enmeshed in a decade-old cauldron of kidnapping, rape, and serial killings.

As I untangle the web of deception, the killer sets his sights on me.

About the author

I began devouring books in the third grade, when I read every book in the elementary school library on dinosaurs, followed by every book on cavemen, followed by every book featuring horses or dogs. By the time I retired to pursue my own writing career, I must have read over 300 mystery, thriller, and action-adventure books, including every book written by Robert B. Parker and Lee Child. I still read at least two books a month, even while I'm writing.

My Carlos McCrary series combines the Private Investigator and Mystery/Thriller genres-think Spenser meets Jack Reacher. I keep pace rapid, the action exciting, and the plot full of surprises. I write to hit hard, have a good time, and leave as few grammar errors as possible (or is it "grammatical errors"? *Hmm.*)

In my previous life, I worked as a shoe salesman, grocery store sacker, florist deliverer, auditor, management consultant, association executive, accountant, radio announcer, and a paid assassin for the Florida Board of Cosmetology. (I am lying about one of those jobs.) If you ask me about it, I will deny ever having worked as an auditor.

www.DallasGorham.com has more information about my books. If you have too much time on your hands, you can follow me on Twitter at @DallasGorham, or Facebook at https://www.facebook.com/DallasGorham. To get an email whenever I release a new title, sign up for the VIP email list at www.dallasgorham.com.

Internet stuff:

Dallas writes an occasional blog you can read at:

DallasGorham.com/blog/.

It's sometimes funny, but not nearly as funny as he thinks.
His website

DallasGorham.com/welcome

has more information about his books.

If you have too much time on your hands, you can follow him on Twitter at **Twitter.com/DallasGorham** or Facebook. Just go to **Facebook.com** and search for "Dallas Gorham Books.")

His Amazon Author Page is

Amazon.com/Dallas-Gorham/e/B00J4LISCS